ROSES ARE THORNS, VIOLETS ARE TRUE

ROSES ARE THORNS, VIOLETS ARE TRUE

SHELIA M. GOSS

URBAN BOOKS
www.urbanbooks.net

URBAN SOUL is published by

Urban Books LLC
10 Brennan Place
Deer Park, NY 11729

ISBN-13: 978-1-59983-010-0
ISBN-10: 1-59983-010-8

First Printing: February 2007
10 9 8 7 6 5 4 3 2 1

Printed in the United States of America

I

TO EVERYTHING THERE IS A SEASON

PROLOGUE

Two six-year-old girls, who looked identical, fought over a Barbie-sized doll. Rose Purdue, with a head full of ponytails and colorful butterfly hair bows, was dressed in a pink-laced dress. Violet Purdue was dressed exactly as Rose, except she wore a purple dress. Rose managed to get the doll away from Violet and took a pair of scissors and cut off the doll's hair. Violet cried and ran into the connecting bathroom and closed the door.

Rose, with tears flowing down her face, walked into the living room and stood next to a handsome brown-skinned, six-feet-tall man, Louis Purdue. Louis carefully picked her up and wiped the tears from her face and in a soothing voice asked, "What's wrong with daddy's little girl?"

Rose sniffed a few times and batted her eyes at her father. "Violet cut all the hair off my doll." Her father patted her on the back to soothe her.

Louis responded, "Don't cry. We'll just have to get you a new one."

As Louis hugged her, a smirk swept across Rose's face. Violet observed this interaction from the doorway. Rose stuck out her tongue at Violet and continued to bask in the comfort of her father's arms.

Violet turned to walk away and ran smack into their mom, Pearle, who was an older version of the twins with a Creole complexion. She's dressed in a floral housedress and apron.

Pearle shook her head and looked down at Violet. "Violet, remember what Momma told you a few weeks ago. Rose is special. She's not as strong as you are, so we have to overlook some things. Okay?"

Violet, too young to understand, nodded her head in agreement.

Chapter 1
VIOLET

"How much do I love me, let me count the ways?" I love that song. I know it sounds a little vain, but if you had to spend every day competing for your own identity because of your sister, you wouldn't say that. Are you writing all of this down? Well, I hope when she reads this, she's not too upset, but knowing Rose she will swear I only did this interview to embarrass her. Where do you want me to begin?

First, let's start with the name Rose. Rose is such a pretty name representing a beautiful flower. Everyone sees Rose as not only this tall, beige beauty with hypnotizing sparkling eyes, but also as a woman with a heart of gold. Yes, Rose is physically attractive, but if you knew her true character, you would see her thorns. I will share with you several incidents to back up my statement.

Many would be surprised Rose and I have issues with one another, because she makes us seem so perfect. When your magazine called to set up this interview, I was hesitant on doing it, but then it dawned on me; it's about time the public got an inside look at the real Rose.

Anyway, back to what I was saying. Our parents owned a

landscaping company and named us Rose and Violet, after their favorite flowers. They were great parents, but growing up it seemed as if Rose was their favorite. Fortunately before our dad died, he and I were able to make amends concerning the special treatment Rose got.

While growing up, Rose always came across as the good twin, and I was labeled the bad twin. She would do things and made sure I got the blame. I remember when we were around sixteen years old; she stole my mom's pearls, pearls that my grandmother had given her before she passed away. Rose wore the pearls to school and instead of returning them to my mom's jewelry box, she casually brings up the subject of pearls over dinner one night. The next day, my mom realized her pearls were missing; she searched the house and guess where she found the missing pearls? Rose had hidden them under my pillows. I tried to explain to my mom that it was Rose who took them, but she wouldn't hear of it. I was grounded for two weeks. I missed my junior prom because of Rose.

I can't count the times in which I got punished for some of the pranks she pulled. She would cheat on tests by trying to look on my paper; teachers would think we were in cahoots together, and we both would be punished. She would pretend to be me when she wanted to date more than one guy at a time, which caused my boyfriend and I to break up a few times."

The interviewer changed the cassette in her tape recorder when Violet stopped to take a sip of lemonade. A hazy look flashed across Violet's face as she continued to tell her story.

"I was married for seven years. I remember the day I met David. I was on my way up to a potential donor's office. I worked at one of the community centers here in Los Angeles and my job was to raise money for the center's after-school programs. I was so nervous about meeting this client. While on the elevator, I met this friendly guy. He stood over six-feet tall with the sexiest grayest eyes I had ever seen. He had a milk chocolate smooth complexion, which somehow made me keen for a Hershey bar. Even in a suit he had a body like a Nubian knight. His smile brought me comfort as I waited for the elevator to stop on the fifteenth floor. When I exited the elevator, to my surprise he was right behind me. I was even more surprised that he was the man I was scheduled to have my meeting with.

After we both laughed at the coincidence, he gladly signed over a nice check for the community center. As he walked me out, he asked me if it would be okay if he called me and I said yes, of course. At the time, I thought he meant call me at the center for business reasons. When he called me two days later, he asked me out on a date.

We were inseparable. My parents loved him, and even Rose liked him and she normally didn't like any of the guys I dated. She would always find something wrong with them.

We were happily married, up until that ill-fated day I decided to play hooky from work. I had it all planned out. I would go home, take a nice long bubble bath, cook David's favorite dinner, chicken Alfredo, and put on our favorite Nina Simone CD. I had no idea I was going to be the one surprised. When I pulled up into our driveway, David's car was home and he normally worked until seven. I called out his name a few times. When he didn't respond, I ran up the stairs. As I got closer to our bedroom, I heard these strange sounds, sounds that reminded me of a screeching cat. When I opened the door, I got a picture-perfect view of him and Rose together wrapped around my favorite burgundy satin sheets."

The interviewer had a shocked look on her face.

"Don't be shocked. I am used to her antics, because she's always been underhanded. I have to say out of all the things she's done, that one hurt me the most. Yes, how could you deliberately sleep with your sister's husband? She knew exactly what she was doing. She would stop by his office, posing as me, and seduce him.

This went on a couple of times before David realized that it wasn't me, but by then, he had gotten too caught up in it and continued their little affair. When I caught them together, I almost lost it, but something inside of me made me just walk away. I haven't laid eyes on either one of them since my divorce. I found out they were getting married when sweet little Rose sent me an invitation to the wedding. What nerve! She's a bold one, that's for sure!

It took me at least a year before I could hold a conversation with her on the phone. The only reason why I communicate with her at all is because I promised my mom. Otherwise, I wouldn't be talking to her.

I really don't have too many nice things to say about Ms. Thing. I guess this is not what you expected for your "Sisters In Hollywood" issue. I'm sure Rose will be surprised with this interview, but she'll probably find a way to weasel her way out of this story; she always bounces back.

To conclude our interview, I will say that I will probably always love Rose, but I just can't trust her. I don't want her anywhere near me. My friend, Janice, is more of a sister to me than my own twin."

The interviewer for *Noir* magazine turned off the tape recorder and her face showed that she was utterly surprised with what Violet had revealed. Violet could only think that she had opened her eyes to the real Rose Purdue. As the interviewer prepared to leave, she turned around and asked Violet one last question. "Do you think you'll ever be able to forgive your sister?"

As she walked the interviewer to the door, Violet responded, "That's a million dollar question. Maybe one day, but not today."

Chapter 2
ROSE

Where is the mail? The magazine told me I should get my complimentary copy today. I haven't talked to Violet since the magazine called me about doing their "Sisters In Hollywood" interview. I was hoping Violet would have called to let me know how things went on her end. But oh, no, she couldn't do that. I'm glad she decided to do the interview though. Maybe this will help ease the tension between us.

I really do love my sister, but she's just too . . . what's the word, "Ms. Goody Two-shoes." If I admitted it to myself, I might be a little jealous of her. It seems she's so much smarter than I am. She has the nerve to question why I do what I do. If I didn't, I would just disappear into the background. I can't have that. I think I'm good at competing for, and getting, good acting roles, because I had to compete for our parents' attention.

I do regret the last thing that I did to her, but I just couldn't help it. No one told David to be so sexy and wealthy. I always wondered what he saw in my boring sister. I'm the adventurous one, and she is the boring bookworm. I felt like he needed a woman with a little passion. I didn't mean for it to get to the point of marriage; but when she divorced him, I couldn't let another woman get a hold of him. Besides, I also had to show my mom that I really did love him. But, I sort of went about it the wrong way; I faked a pregnancy. When he found out, he was livid. I asked him why he was staying in the marriage, if he didn't love me. He had the nerve to tell me that he felt like our marriage was his sentence for breaking my sister's heart. I probably should divorce him, but I can't come away looking like a failure.

Rose noticed the magazine and threw the rest of the mail on the kitchen counter. She smiled as she admired the cover of her and Violet during happier times. Instead of sitting at the table with David, she was too excited to sit, she stood as she thumbed through the magazine to find the article. Her smile began to fade when she noticed the title to the section about her and Violet—*Roses are Thorns.* Her blood pressure escalated the more and more she read. She took a sip of water and almost choked when she read the part about how she'd slept with David.

Oh, my, I can't believe Violet told them all of this. How could she violate our family secrets? How could she do this to me? I thought she would just keep to the facts, but she didn't have to tell them details. If she didn't have anything nice to say, she should have just declined the interview.

In the past, we have had our issues, but she's always had my back in public. What in the world has gotten into my sister? Doesn't she know the public is fickle and they only need one piece of dirt to turn on you? Now I have to figure out a way to recover from the backlash this is sure to cause. She better hope this doesn't cause me to lose out on this movie deal I'm negotiating or she will have hell to pay.

* * *

She threw the magazine on the counter feeling disgusted. "David! David! Can you believe the trash Violet said about me in this article?"

David's eyes shot up from reading the paper with a look of disbelief on his face. "Rose, what did you expect?"

Rose stood with her hands on her hips and a frown on her face. "You always take up for her. I should have known you wouldn't understand. Your perfect little Violet mentions your name in her interview. Now what do you think of that?"

David's eyes shot back down to the newspaper. He didn't look up as he responded. "Whatever Violet said is more than likely the truth. I accept it, and so should you."

Rose couldn't stand it. "Can you try to show sympathy for me once in your life?"

David put the paper down and stood face to face with Rose. "I have all the sympathy in the world, but for Violet." He walked around Rose and out the door.

Rose yelled, "David! Don't walk away from me. You always do this. Why do you even stay?"

David didn't come back. Rose sat down at the kitchen table feeling empty. She picked up the article again and began to fume over what Violet had revealed. Instead of facing the truth and consequences of her previous actions, she decided to lash out at her sister. She picked up the phone and dialed her number. Violet's answering machine picked up on the third ring. "Violet. I know you're there. Pick up the phone. Okay. Now you want to play the disappearing game. Well, I got the little article you did. If my reputation is ruined because of what you said, you will have hell to pay. How could you do this to me?"

The answering machine clicked off, but Rose called right back. "I don't appreciate your answering machine hanging up on me either. You need to get with the program and get voice mail, like the rest of us. Call me as soon as you get this message." Rose slammed the phone down.

"How in the world could she do this to me! She knows how hard I've worked to maintain my image. She has me over here stressing. I need a massage or something. I feel a migraine coming on."

Chapter 3
VIOLET

Rose had the nerve to call and leave me a nasty message. Now she knows how it feels to be betrayed by someone who supposedly loves you. Do I regret doing the article? No. I probably should have kept some of the information to myself, but I feel so much better. It's like years of frustration were released when I gave that interview.

I can now move on with my life. In her message, she mentioned she would make me pay for what I said. I chuckled when I heard her say that. She must have forgotten about the years of heartache she caused me. I only spoke the truth and I can't say that about her. She's lied on me, to me, and about me, all of our life.

I sat down to read the article after receiving her message. The interviewer was careful with her words, to avoid slander charges. Her chosen title impressed me and now I have a new theme song, "Roses are Thorns, Violets are True."

Violet's phone rang again and as she looked on the caller ID, she saw that it was her mother. "Hi, Mom."

Her mom responded, "I can't get over the fact that you girls have this new caller ID thing."

"Mom, it's not new. Caller ID has been around for a very long time. To what do I owe this call?" Violet sat on the bed, because she knew she was in for a long lecture about keeping family business within the family.

"I was calling to see how one of my favorite girls was doing. If you called me or came down to Louisiana to see me more often, I wouldn't have to wonder."

"Mom, I'm doing fine as usual. Don't worry about me. I will survive."

Violet and her mom continued the conversation until her mom heard a call-waiting tone. "Hold on, dear."

Violet held on and wondered why her mom was taking so long. She stretched out across the bed and waited. If it had been anyone else on the phone, other than her mom, she would have hung up five minutes before. She hated being put on hold for long periods of time. She had few pet peeves, but that was one of them. She started to doze off, when she heard her mom yell in the phone. "Violet! How could you?"

Violet sat up, because now she knew who was on the other end. "Mom. I was told the interview was her idea in the first place." She continued on, playing the dumb role, and said, "I assumed she would want me to tell the truth."

Her mom scolded her to a point where she now felt a little regretful for doing the interview. "Violet, I expect that from Rose, but never from you. You have always been the sensible one. You were wrong dear and you should apologize to your sister."

Violet began to feel numb. "Whatever you say, Mom."

"Violet, don't get smart with me. When will you girls start acting like sisters?"

Violet, not wanting to tell her mom off, tried to end the conversation. "I think I hear someone at my front door. Mom, love you. Got to go." She hung the phone up and continued to lie across her bed.

* * *

My mom knows how to make me feel like a little girl. She has me feeling bad for what I said. She's probably right, but I don't feel like being the sensible twin right now. Let me get up and go to the center. People need me, even if my sister doesn't.

Chapter 4
ROSE

Shortly after the "Sisters In Hollywood" issue hit the stands, Rose's phone rang off the hook. David was tired of the phone calls and decided to check into a hotel so he could get some peace and quiet while he worked on his latest project. Rose let her voice mail receive her calls, and her personal assistant, Tina, spent many hours clearing out the messages.

Tina heard an important call from Rose's agent and delivered the message. "Rose, I think you need to call your agent. Carmen has left at least ten messages."

Rose, carrying a raspberry frozen margarita in one hand and her cell phone in the other, went out on her patio and looked out toward the ocean. This was the one place she felt relaxed. She purchased the house because of its location and the ocean with its clear, blue-green water, rushing up to the sandy shore provided a breath-taking view. There was something calming about the tranquil waters. Being in the limelight was beginning to stress her out more and more. She took a sip from her margarita, sat in her lawn chair, leaned back and made her dreaded phone call.

Her agent, Carmen, had been very supportive and took a chance on her when no one else would. Carmen picked up on the first ring. "Rose, dear, why are you just now returning my calls? I've been calling you all week."

Rose knew she was in for a lecture, so she continued to sip on her drink and listened. "Are you through, Carmen?"

Carmen, sounding displeased with Rose's attitude, asked, "Rose, how am I supposed to beat off the press hounds, when my own client won't return my calls?"

"Okay. You're right. I'm sorry. I thought if I didn't do anything, this thing would blow over soon."

"I have all of the major television stations and print magazines calling me; and let's not forget about all the tabloids. I am bombarded. This thing is not going away." Without giving Rose a chance to respond, Carmen continued. "I got a phone call about the part you wanted."

Hearing those words sent a feeling of excitement through Rose. "Really? So when do we start filming?"

"Hold on. I said I got a phone call. It's not good news. Your squeaky clean image is being questioned now and the producer wants someone with a little less drama going on in her life."

Sitting up straight, anger grew in Rose. "What does my personal life have to do with portraying a character in a movie? Not one thing. That's bull."

Carmen, in her calming voice, said, "I know. You know how they can be. It's not fair, but it's their choice."

Rose was never one to show weakness. "So what's next? Am I supposed to just sit here and not do anything?"

"I have a couple of things in the works for you. Right now, we need to do some damage control. I've set up an interview with one of *Noir* magazine's competitors."

"Who?"

"*Channel* magazine. One of the editors and I have known

each other for years. She's setting up an interview with one of her best writers."

She took the last sip of her margarita. "Carmen, whatever you feel is best. I trust your judgment. Just let me know when. And Carmen?"

"Yes."

"Thanks for everything."

"That's what I'm here for."

Rose, not usually sentimental, said, "You know sometimes I feel like you're more like a friend. You know more about me and spend more time talking to me than anyone."

"Well, you're not so bad yourself. Rose, dear, I got to go. Turn your cell phone on. I'll call you when I hear something. Stay strong."

"Okay. Bye."

When the call ended, Rose decided to go for a stroll along the beach. The water was calling her, with its gentle blue color and soothing hypnotizing waves.

The ocean water is exactly what I needed to clear my head. My phone keeps ringing off the hook. Everybody has called me, except the one who started all of this. I might need to pay my sister a visit. I really wanted the role in the movie The Future Mrs. Wallingford. *I've always loved the story and it was a dream come true to be considered for the part and now because of her, I didn't get it.*

Rose went back to the house and pulled out one of her designer outfits. Today she decided to wear a short black denim skirt and matching silk blouse with a frilly collar that accented the outfit. Instead of her signature pumps, she wore a pair of flat black sandals with a golden buckle across the toe. Her closet was full of outfits by a new designer who wanted to name his collection after her. As an actress, she made sure she always looked her best. She sometimes received complimentary clothes from designers; that was one of her favorite perks.

Okay. Where is my purse? I swear somebody must be moving my stuff. There it is. Violet, you can avoid me, but you can't hide forever.

Chapter 5
VIOLET

Violet got home just in time to catch her favorite game show. She loved to answer the questions along with the contestants. If it weren't for the fact she and her sister looked exactly alike, she would have gone on one of them a long time ago. As soon as the last commercial played, she heard a knock at her door.

She wasn't expecting anyone, so when she looked through the peephole, she was surprised to see her own reflection staring back. In a hurry, she fixed her clothes and smoothed stray hairs along her ponytail, because being around Rose always made her feel less beautiful.

"Hi, Rose. What brings you out this way?" she asked.

Rose sashayed right past Violet into her living room. "My, my. I see you have developed some good taste over the years."

Violet, riled that Rose was violating her space, responded, "We both know this is no social visit. So please get straight to the point."

"Yes, I missed you too and yes, I think I will have a glass of wine."

Violet stood there with her hands on her hips. "You'll never change. How are you going to come into my house and demand I serve you? B—, I mean Rose." She held one of her hands up in the air as she said, "See you almost made me call you out of your name."

Rose looked at Violet over the rim of her shades. "I am a guest, so why don't you be the gracious hostess that I know you can be."

Violet tried not to lose her temper and smiled. "Rose darling, have a seat and I'll be right back."

Violet stormed into the kitchen. She took two clear glasses out of the cabinet, one trimmed with gold, the other plain. She put the glasses and the wine on a tray and poured some wine in each glass. A thought crossed her mind and she thought about Rose's attitude since entering her home, so she bent down and spit in the gold trimmed glass that she would give Rose. She got a spoon and stirred it up, so it wouldn't be noticeable and with a plastered smile on her face, she went back to the living room.

Let me take these drinks out there. Because the sooner I see what she wants, the sooner I can get the heifer out of my house.

Chapter 6
ROSE

My dear sweet sister has a backbone. I was wondering when she was going to start using it. If I weren't reaping the repercussions of her tongue, I would applaud her. She must be making more money than I thought. I didn't know working at a community center would provide the type of income to support such lavish things. Hmm. Impressive, these are nice Oriental and Egyptian artifacts. I better stop picking up her stuff; the last thing I want to do is break one of her precious pieces. Now, where is she with my wine?

"It's about time."

Violet looked upside her head. "You're lucky I'm giving you a drink."

Rose took the gold-trimmed glass and sipped it. "I see you've acquired a taste for some of the finer things in life. I was admiring your collection."

Violet, not taking her eyes off of her, sat down on the loveseat and smiled. "Rose, there are some things we do have in common."

Rose continued to drink the wine. "Yes, we may have some things in common; but for the life of me, I can't figure out why you won't do something with your hair. Look at you."

"Please don't start. Some of us are not as superficial as you are. My ponytail works for me."

"Violet, you're a beautiful lady and I'm not just saying that because you're my twin. I know you may not make much on your salary volunteering at those centers, but you should be able to afford to get your hair done every once in a while."

Violet remained quiet for a moment, cleared her throat, and said, "For the last time, I love what I do. I love helping people. It's more rewarding than anything else that I can think of."

Rose, tired and bored of Violet's innocent nature, asked, "Whatever the case, how can you afford to live so lavishly on your salary? I've offered to give you money on a regular basis, but you keep turning me down."

"Although it is none of your business, I am paid quite nicely to do the things I do, and I do not need your money."

Rose reached for the bottle of white wine and poured herself another glass. "Anyway, I didn't come over here to talk about your financial situation, because it looks like you're doing just fine there."

"What did you come over here for, Rose?"

Rose stood and walked around the room as if she was admiring the room's spaciousness. "As you well know, in my field, image is everything."

"I was wondering when you were going to get around to that," Violet said with a smirk on her face. "What's the problem now, Rose?"

Rose walked to the loveseat and sat down next to Violet. She batted her eyes, looked straight at her, and placed her right hand over Violet's. "You know what you did. How could you? No matter what goes on between us, we keep it between us. This interview was very important and now everybody is calling me the Evil Twin. Did you see the headline? 'Roses Are Thorns.' "

Violet moved her hand. "I spoke the truth. Did it ever dawn on you that I was tired of lying for you?"

"Violet, we had an agreement that no matter what happens, in the public, we would put on a united front."

Violet looked at Rose as if she were from Mars. "That agreement became null and void the moment I caught you sleeping with my husband," Violet said before jumping off the couch. She was tempted to reach over and punch Rose.

Rose stood up as well. "I see coming over here hasn't done any good."

"And you thought that it would? Do I need to rehash the last year for you? Starting with sleeping with—and then turning around and marrying—my husband. If it wasn't for Mom, I wouldn't talk to your crazy behind." Violet put some distance between them, because she was about to reach out and touch Rose in the worst way.

Rose was surprised that Violet was still holding onto the pain, because Violet usually forgave her no matter what she did. She knew she could always depend on Violet to back her up; that was one of the reasons why she was shocked to read the article. Although she knew she shouldn't have slept with David, she could not resist the temptation. He was her perfect leading man, with his tall physique and exceptionally good looks. When Violet introduced David to the family, she could not see why he would want her boring sister over her. David was a successful business developer. He was a challenge and she had meant to sample the forbidden fruit before her sister married him.

"Violet. How many times do I have to tell you I never meant to hurt you?"

"Not enough, because your acting may have helped ease the strain between you and Mother, but I can see right through you. Rose gets what she wants, no matter who gets hurt in the process. Frankly, I'm tired of being the target. Now I think you've worn out your welcome here, so please see yourself out."

Violet walked up the stairway, as Rose stood there looking at her back. The next sound Rose heard was Violet slamming her bedroom door.

I can't believe she dismissed me like that. I see now I won't be able to depend on her to smooth things out with the media. Now, where are my keys?

Chapter 7
VIOLET

After she watched Rose leave from her bedroom window, she wiped streams of tears from her eyes. No matter how much she pretended her relationship or lack of a relationship with Rose didn't hurt, it did.

As if Rose could hear her, Violet cried out, "How did we get like this? Even when you did those crazy things as kids, we were still friends. I find myself hating the fact that we're sisters sometimes."

Violet walked over to the mirror and looked at her reflection. She and her sister had the same smooth beige complexion. If you looked closely, you could tell Violet had a distinctive mole on her face. While growing up, the mole was how people were able to tell one from the other. They both had long flowing hair. The original color was jet black, but Rose currently sported a honey blond hairdo with long flowing curls. Violet still had her original jet-black color, but added some auburn highlights. She normally wore hers pinned up with a few strands coming down in her face or she would wear a ponytail.

She wiped her face with a warm, damp towel, hoping to

wipe the sadness away. Her phone rang and broke her solemn trance.

She didn't bother to look at the caller ID. "Hello."

"Hi. Violet?"

It sounded like David, so she paused before saying anything. "Yes, it is. Who is this?"

"It's David. I wanted to make sure you were okay after Rose's visit."

"I'm fine, but I'm no longer your concern." She hung up without giving David the opportunity to finish his statement.

It must be a full moon tonight. First Rose and now David. Between the two of them, they are going to drive me crazy. The way I feel, I might finish the whole bottle of wine.

Chapter 8
ROSE

My phone will not stop ringing off the hook and Violet is being unbearable right now. I've tried calling David, but his phone went straight to voice mail. Now, what hotel did he tell me he was staying at? I remember now.

David picked up on the second ring. "Hello."

"Hi, David. It's me."

David sounded disappointed. "Oh, hey."

Rose, perturbed with the way he sounded, yelled, "Well, you don't have to sound like that!"

David, with anger in his voice, said, "Look, Rose. I don't have time to play your games tonight. I was on my way to sleep and like always, your timing is off."

"David, I do not like your attitude."

"Ask me if I care."

"I only called to say good night and the only thing you do is talk to me any kind of way. I am tired of this. I can't take this much longer. If you don't want me, why are you here?"

"Rose," David said, as he cleared his throat. "It's late and I don't feel like getting into this with you."

"You are going to answer me, damn it!" Rose demanded.

David hung up the phone without waiting to hear what else Rose had to say.

Rose cursed him.

If I can't depend on my husband to comfort me, then what is he here for? David pushes me away all of the time. I don't know how much more of his crap I can take. I should take Lance King up on his offer. He's a little flashy for me, but at least he listens and has no problem letting me know what he would do for me—if I were his woman. I don't feel like going back home to an empty house.

Rose found Lance's number and decided to give him a call. She was surprised when he answered. "Lance?"

"This is he," Lance said, sounding sleepy.

"It's Rose. I was driving around and you crossed my mind. Do you mind company?"

"No. Come right over. Let me know when you're ready for the directions."

Rose wrote down the information and headed in the opposite direction of her home. Although her marriage to David was not the best, she had remained faithful. She knew tonight would change everything and it would only be a matter of time before David got tired of the loveless marriage. If the truth were told, they never had a real marriage; it was doomed by deception from the beginning. She lied about being pregnant. Since he didn't want his child to be a bastard child, he married her. She knew he still loved her sister. But it didn't matter, because she had her leading man. She thought she could make him forget all about the dutiful Violet. She didn't realize David worshipped the ground her sister walked on. If she had known, she wouldn't have bothered seducing him.

David you pushed me to this; so whatever the consequences, it's your fault. A woman like me needs plenty of attention. Sometimes I just need to be held. Lance, Lance, Lance. I haven't had sex since my wedding night a year ago, so you're in for a treat.

Chapter 9
VIOLET

After drinking the entire bottle of chardonnay, Violet reclined on the couch with the television remote control. While she flipped through the channels, something caught her attention. *Entertainment Source News* was talking about her and Rose. She shook her head. People were so concerned with what she considered trivial things, instead of worrying about the things in life that really mattered. She dozed off and kept having the same dream that she had been having for over a month.

The dream took her to a mysterious place, filled with beautiful landscaping. The colors of the flowers were vibrant. She could smell the freshness of the ocean air as she was hypnotized by the sounds of its waves. She walked along the beach and in the distance there was a tall darkskinned man. She wanted to turn around and go the other way; however, there was a magnetic force bringing her and the mystery man closer and closer toward each other. She continued walking and the closer she got to him, the more heated her body felt. They both stopped within inches of each other and he took his hand and placed it on her face.

She looked up into the deepest, grayest eyes she'd ever seen and from that moment on, his eyes held her captive.

The sound of the television station going off the air woke her. Looking at the time, she turned the television off and headed upstairs to bed. She was so exhausted, that she didn't bother to put on her nightgown. She soon dozed off to sleep again and began dreaming shortly thereafter.

She visited the same dream, sounds of birds sang in the distance, as she relaxed across a nice long white blanket. She thought she was there by herself, until a strong hand caressed her calf. Looking down and back into those hypnotizing gray eyes, her mystery lover licked her toes, and then traced his mouth on her legs with small circular kisses. Her body reacted to each touch.

He reached the center of her forest and taking both hands, moved her legs apart in one calculated move. She attempted to protest, but her legs failed to cooperate and they automatically flung wide open. Her lover dipped his tongue into the depths of her desire, as to the beat of the ocean, causing a tidal wave to explode deep within her.

The mystery man kissed her navel and worked his way up toward her face; stopping to tease her silver-dollar nipples with his tongue. Her womanhood was as wet as the ocean.

The more she moaned, the more he kissed and licked. He made his way up toward her neck, driving her wild with pleasure. She could not imagine feeling like this ever again.

He took her mouth and kissed her with so much intensity that she had an orgasm from his kiss. He gazed into her eyes, as the trance was broken. As she examined his fine masculine features, she woke up.

David. All of this time, I've been dreaming about David. This can't be. I thought I was over him. Why did he have to call me? I was doing so well. I really loved that man and I thought he loved me too. I can still hear him begging me for forgiveness. My heart broke when I saw him with Rose. For weeks he attempted to get me to forgive him and give him another chance. My heart could not take another heartbreak, so I walked away. I can still see the hurt and regret in his eyes. He offered me the world to make up for what he did, but if I couldn't have his fidelity, then I didn't want anything. Now, here he is, him and his gray eyes invading my dreams. They say dreams are sometimes thoughts of the true subconscious.

Does that mean I still want David? Am I capable of forgiving David and not my sister? How can that be? Blood is supposed to be thicker.

Chapter 10
ROSE

Upon awakening, Rose realized that she was not in her bed, nor was she alone. For a moment, she forgot where she was. She looked into the face of one of the sexiest men in the music industry. Lance stood six-two, with a Hershey-chocolate complexion. The ice in the North Pole could melt from the glow of his radiant pearly white teeth. Besides his refined good looks and killer smile, he had a way of making a woman feel special.

Rose should have been overjoyed; however, she felt like she was trapped. Yes, she enjoyed their night of passion, but what was she going to do about David? She had to figure out a way to juggle both David and Lance. If Lance and she were to continue their liaison, it would have to be kept on the down low.

She was getting up to put her clothes on when Lance woke up. "Honey, come back to bed. I can't seem to get enough of you."

"Lance, darling," Rose said as she found her underwear. "I can't. I overstayed as it is. You know I'm a married woman."

"I know, but I couldn't tell from your response last night," he said, as he got up and went to where she was standing. He wrapped his arms around her waist.

"Lance, you know the situation. If you can't handle it, let me know now and we can stop this from going any further."

Lance placed small kisses on the nape of her neck. "Rose, I couldn't stop now even if I wanted to. Did anyone ever tell you that you smell like roses? Your skin, it's so . . . mmm . . . so silky smooth."

"Lance, answer this question," she said while getting aroused. "Can you deal with me being married and keeping our relationship a secret?"

"Yes, baby. This will be our little secret. I don't know how long I can stand by and watch you go home to another man every night; but for you, I'll try."

As she turned around to face him, she responded, "Thank you, Lance, for understanding."

"I would be more understanding if you would let me taste you one more time before leaving."

Rose, turned on by his bluntness, allowed him to prop her up on the chair near his bed, while he dove into her headfirst.

They continued to make love throughout the morning, until Rose's cell phone broke their stride. After taking the call, she made excuses to leave. Rose wanted desperately to stay in his arms, but instead knew she had to return to her loveless marriage.

Once she was back in her car, she returned David's call. "David, it's me. I'm back. Now what were you saying?"

David, clearly annoyed, said, "We need to talk. Where were you last night? I decided to check out of the hotel and came home early. You were nowhere to be found."

"I don't need you checking up on me. But if you must know, after you hung up on me, I was so upset with the confrontation I had with you and my sister that I rode around. I ended up falling asleep in my car by the side of the road."

"I'd appreciate it if you would call and let someone know these things."

"Why? Do you care?" Rose said with a hint of sarcasm in her voice.

"We might not have the ideal marriage, but you are still my wife."

Rose was shocked that he showed that much respect. "Whatever you say, dear. I have to go now. Bye."

She hung the phone up and headed home.

Chapter 11
VIOLET

Violet spent the first couple of hours at work going through her e-mail and voicemail. She was grateful that she was appointed Director of Community Affairs, but she missed her fieldwork. She thrived on helping people and the only thing she didn't like about her job was the bureaucracy and having to play the numbers game with so many different committees. One of her duties included finding ways to generate funds, without having to depend on the city for its contributions. On this particular day, by the time lunch came around, she was mentally exhausted. As she prepared to leave her office, the assistant director, Janice King, walked through the door.

"Hi, Missy. How are you holding up with the media blitz?"

Violet didn't like discussing her private affairs with people at the center, but then again, Janice was more than just a coworker. Janice had become a good friend over the years. They had worked on many community action programs together and when the assistant director for community affairs position became available, she recommended Janice to the board. To her delight, the board was impressed with Janice's resume and she got the necessary approval and hired her. Whenever either one of them had an issue with anything, regardless if it was personal or business, they were always there for each other.

Violet hugged Janice and then walked back to her desk. "I'm doing okay. I'm thankful they don't have access to my numbers at home. I noticed the calls haven't stopped coming to the center, though. Some of the tabloids are offering a whole bunch of money to hear my story."

Janice chuckled, because she liked to read the tabloids. "You know, you could sell them your story and who knows what may come out of it. You might even be offered a role in a movie."

Violet laughed along with her. "Now you know Rose would have a cow. Both of us can't be in the limelight."

"You're right about that. I could see it now. Violet takes Hollywood by storm." Janice held her side laughing.

"Well, I'm not calling them or any of the other entertainment papers. You already know how I hate the tabloids."

"Girl, you don't know what you're missing. That's how I get all of my gossip."

"I thought you only read them for, how did you put it: entertainment purposes only."

"I do. But you have to admit, some of the stuff is probably true."

Violet shook her head. "Whatever you say. So what's for lunch today?"

"Since you're not going to come around to my way of thinking, why don't you choose and pay today."

"Ha. Ha. Only because it's my turn to treat anyway."

They headed over to the local Souper and Salads. After eating a hearty, healthy lunch, they drove back to the office in silence. Violet thought about how she wished that she and Rose could spend time like this. She would love to call her up one day and say, meet me here or there; but they could not be in the same place at the same time without some type of drama.

"Earth to Violet. You just missed our turn."

Violet shook out of her trance and at that moment realized she had not been fully concentrating on her driving. "Sorry. I don't know where my head is today. I really need to get it together, because I need to make sure I'm ready for the meeting with the deputy mayor."

Janice moved her head to the beat of the music playing on the radio. "You'll do fine. I'll be there. If I notice you getting stuck in a certain area, I'll be able to move the conversation along. Girl, I got your back. Don't worry."

They were pulling up at the center by then. "I know. Thank you for being patient with me these past few weeks."

Janice turned around and looked at her. "Violet, you are like a sister to me and there is nothing I wouldn't do to erase the things that you are going through. But honey, unfortunately I can't. If you can, please try to work things out with Rose. I know she is the reason for a lot of your pain. If you can't work it out with her, think about just forgiving her."

"Janice, you know it's not that easy."

As Janice got out of the car, she said, "Never said it would be."

Chapter 12
ROSE

Rose turned over and pulled the comforter over her head, so she could avoid seeing the bright sunlight. In between yawns, she blurted out, "When will I ever get some peace? Why did he leave the blinds open? I told him to keep the blinds closed. He knows I like to sleep late. I don't know why I even bother to tell him anything. It goes in one ear and out the other."

Rose wiped the sleep from her eyes, got up, and took a long hot bubble bath. While she was drying off, she glimpsed a view of herself through the steam on the mirror. A queasy feeling rushed over her that almost knocked her off her feet.

What is wrong with me? I have been feeling nauseated for the past week now. I haven't had breakfast yet, so I know it's nothing that I ate. Where are my pills? I don't know why I can never find anything.

* * *

She got dressed and headed over to her agent's office. When she walked in the building, people stopped and stared. Some were even bold enough to ask her for an autograph. She was used to the attention and she loved it. She adored the public and always stopped to take pictures with her fans and sign autographs. She glanced at her watch and realized that she was running late with her meeting with Carmen.

She smiled her sunshine smile to the mail clerk, who rushed to hold the elevator for her. "Thank you, Calvin."

"No problem, ma'am."

When she walked into the office, the receptionist shook her head and pointed to the clock.

"Cindy, I know. I'm late. But you have to admit, I'm on time by my clock."

Cindy laughed and led her to Carmen's office. "Come on in, Rose, and have a seat."

Rose sat down in the plush leather chair. She took her sunglasses off and laid them on the desk. "Hi. Sorry I am late."

"Lucky for you, I was on a conference call that ran over. So are you ready for your interview?"

"Yes and no. I'm just ready to get this over with."

"Just be yourself and also realize that they will be asking some personal questions."

"I'm prepared. Have you heard anything else about my role in *The Future Mrs. Wallingford?*"

Carmen avoided looking Rose straight in the eye. "It's a done deal. The powers that be have decided to use someone else. Right now, they aren't saying who it is—I just know it isn't you. I'm sorry, dear."

"It isn't your fault," Rose said, feeling a little disappointed. "If it were not for the article, we would be celebrating right now. I still can't believe my sister would do something like this."

"Rose, don't you think it's time you made up with your sister?"

"Carmen, I have bent over backwards to make amends with her. She is the one that can't forgive or forget."

Carmen looked upside Rose's head before commenting. "Do you think she could forget the fact that you are married to her husband? This is the real world, not a movie. Now I didn't say you guys would be the best of friends, but you do need to work on having some type of relationship."

Rose rolled her eyes. "If she wasn't so selfish, we wouldn't be having this problem."

Carmen stared at Rose in amazement. "I must say; I'm shocked you would even say that. You need to take some responsibility for your part in all of this. If you don't, you'll be the one to suffer."

"Enough about my sister. I am not paying you to talk about her."

"Last time I checked, this was a free world, where I have freedom of speech and I'm going to say what I need to say."

Rose continued to sit in silence and listened.

Carmen continued to talk and spoke of her own past. "My sister Angelica was my best friend and I would give up everything I have, if I could just spend one more minute with my sister. She was two years older than I, but she never treated me bad or made me feel inferior to her." Tears started to flow down Carmen's face. "Rose, you have a sister and you don't even know how lucky you are."

Rose walked around the desk and gave her a hug. "Carmen, I'm sorry. I didn't mean to make you cry. Why don't I treat you to a Rocky Road at the ice cream parlor downstairs?"

"I'm okay. No Rocky Road for me, because I'm still trying to lose the ten pounds I gained from the holidays," Carmen said as she wiped the tears away with a tissue.

"Well, I've been craving Rocky Road ever since I walked into this building. Besides, I haven't eaten all day. Was there anything else? If not, I'm about to go get me something to eat."

"Yes, there is. Hold on and I'll have Cindy go pick up something for you." Carmen repeated to Cindy the order.

Rose looked out the window at the Los Angeles skyline. She was admiring the view. Even among the smog, the skyline was beautiful. From this height, she felt like she was on top of the world. The only other time she felt like she was on top of the world was when she was in front of the camera. "Do you have any more scripts for me to read?"

"Yes, I do. The interview was not as bad as we thought it would be. By the way, you are interviewing at the end of the week. Would you rather her come to your place or do you want to go by their office?"

"I would rather go by their office. I don't like too many reporters in my house. If you would have asked me that a couple of months ago, it wouldn't have mattered, but I've watched them say nasty things about me and some even joke about me."

Carmen tried to sound reassuring. "Don't let it get to you. Look at it like this. Now more people know about you and will be curious to see if what they say is true. Told you, you need to work the publicity. Whether it's bad or good. This interview is the first step. Tell your side of the story and things will work themselves out."

Cindy knocked on the door before walking in with Rose's ice cream. Rose ate a spoonful of ice cream. "Now this was well worth the wait. You sure you don't want any?"

"No, and I'm really surprised you do. It looks like you've picked up a couple of extra pounds."

Rose stood up and pressed her hand against her belly and butt at the same time. "You think so? I knew this skirt fit a little tight. I thought it was the dry cleaners messing up my clothes again."

"Yes, but it looks becoming on you. You still look good."

"I guess I need to spend more time on the treadmill," Rose said as she sat back down and ate the rest of her ice cream.

Chapter 13
VIOLET

Violet was ecstatic that the deputy mayor had good news. Although, he did let her go through an entire hour's presentation, she was still thrilled that she got the money she needed to start up the new recreational center. When she got home, she felt a bout of loneliness and decided to go tend to her garden of flowers. She inherited her love of flowers from her parents. She had one of the prettiest gardens in her neighborhood. People assumed she had it done professionally, and were surprised when she told them that she did most of the landscaping herself.

She spent the last few daylight hours in her garden. She got up and wiped the sweat from her brow with her right arm. She looked around and admired her garden. It brought a smile to her face and a sense of comfort to her, a comfort that she had not been able to find anywhere else, a comfort she longed for.

Instead of treading the dirt throughout the house, she decided to take a long hot shower in her downstairs bathroom. While she was showering, her mind wandered over the events of the past few weeks. Although a part of her regretted giving the interview, because of the backlash she got from her mom, another part of her felt rejuvenated. It felt like a load had been lifted off of her shoulders and she no longer had to play the role of the dutiful sister.

When she got out of the shower, a wave of nausea swept over her. She knew she probably needed to drink some water and eat something. She had not eaten anything since the salad she had earlier.

I wonder what's going on with my body. I've been feeling funny all week long, it must be my nerves. I have to get ready for this charity ball and I need all of my energy. I'm so thankful that Janice is handling the entertainment part. At least I don't have to worry about that. I just have to make sure the invitations go out to the right people. So many things to do and so little time to do them in. Those kids better be glad I love them so much.

A smile came across her face as she thought about some of the kids she'd mentored over the past few years. She noticed positive changes in the majority of the young men and women she'd come in contact with. Every now and then, she would run into one who was too far gone to reach, but even then, it didn't stop her from trying. She felt like kids only needed to have hope, and with hope, everything else was possible.

She wasn't in a sorority, but she worked closely with all of the fraternity and sorority chapters in the area. They were always looking to contribute time or money to some worthy cause. She made sure they were kept informed of anything that was needed in the community. One of the biggest fundraisers in the area was the Sickle Cell Anemia Drive. She hoped the celebrity charity ball would also raise a lot of money.

After she ate dinner and relaxed on the sofa, she decided to go through her mail. Most of it was bills, but she came across one piece that was a card. It didn't have a return address and it wasn't her birthday, so she wondered who sent it.

She took her letter opener and carefully opened the card. It was beautiful. The outside of the card was covered in purple violets. Whoever sent the card must have known those were her favorite flowers. She opened it to see who it was from and it was simply signed, *Your Forever Love.* She read the card and had a feeling she knew who the sender was. She closed it and gathered the other mail and placed them in her desk drawer reserved for bills.

She got in bed and as she leaned over to turn off the lamp, her phone rang. She saw a cellular number on the caller ID, but didn't recognize it. She decided to answer. "Hello."

"Hi."

Violet's heart skipped a beat, because this time there was no mistake who was on the other end. She was trying to decide if she should cuss him out, hang up on him, or see why he sent the card and was now calling. "Yes?"

"I was calling to see how you were doing."

"David. I told you before. My well being is no longer your concern. You have a wife. Worry about her."

"Sweetness, I know you're still upset and I know I have no right to call, but there is not a day that goes by that I don't think about you."

Violet grunted. "David, if you're calling me to see if I got your card, yes I did, but please stop contacting me. What is the purpose? We are over. Do we have an understanding?"

David sighed. "Violet, just meet me once. I need to talk to you and apologize to you in person. You never gave me that opportunity."

Violet tried to control her temper because she was determined not to let him know he still got under her skin. "David. The last time I saw you, it wasn't a pleasant experience, so I do not feel like reliving it."

David sounded reluctant to end the conversation. "Sweetness, I will let you go for now, but I will be contacting you."

"Please stop calling me sweetness. Do us both a favor and please stop calling me period!" With her last statement, she heard him hang up the phone. She placed the phone back on the charger and lay down for another restless night.

Chapter 14
ROSE

Rose pulled up at *Channel* magazine's headquarters located on Centura Boulevard. She was not in the mood for her convertible candy-apple red Porsche today, so she opted for the sports utility vehicle. She valet parked her emerald-green Cadillac Escalade. The valet gave her a green stub and she waltzed into the lobby. Carmen had impressed on her the importance of being on time and to not show up fashionably late, so Rose made it a point to get there early. She glanced down at her watch and saw that she had fifteen minutes to spare. She checked out her surroundings before heading to the fifth floor.

She was greeted by a friendly receptionist, who then walked with her to an office located at the end of a long hallway. The receptionist knocked on the door and the woman on the other side motioned for them to come in.

The woman behind the desk got up and walked around to greet Rose. She reached out to shake her hand. "Hi, I'm Lisa and thank you for coming. We really do appreciate you taking the time to interview with us."

Rose tried to size up the interviewer. She returned her handshake. "I am happy to oblige."

Lisa led Rose toward an area in the office with a couch and ottoman chair with a glass coffee table in the center. "Would you like something to drink or snack on before we get started?"

"A cola would be nice."

Lisa got a cup of ice, a cola off the bar, and a straw. "Here you go. You sure we can't get you anything else?"

Rose took the items and poured the cola in her cup. "Thank you. This will suffice."

Lisa took a seat across from Rose and gathered her notepad and a tape recorder. "I usually record my interviews, but if you're uncomfortable, I don't have to."

Rose tried not to show her nervousness. "Oh, no, I'm comfortable. I have no problem with you taping."

Lisa looked at her watch and then cleared her throat. "Okay. Let's get started. The article in *Noir* showed us a different side to the Rose we normally see. Our magazine wanted to give you an opportunity to respond to what your twin sister shared with the world. Is it true that you and your twin do not get along?"

Rose put the drink down and faced Lisa. "Violet and I have a special type of relationship."

"Special? Define special."

"We talk. I guess we're not as close as two sisters could be."

Lisa looked as if she was taking notes. "Most twins are closer to one another than regular siblings."

"Maybe. Like I said we have a special relationship."

Lisa put her pen down and looked Rose straight in the eyes. "According to her, you guys don't have a relationship at all. In your past interviews, you came across as if family was very important to you. You would mention the closeness between you and your sister and how much you love your husband. Why put up the front?"

Rose stared directly back at her and exclaimed, "Excuse me, if this entire interview is going to be about my sister, we can end it now."

Lisa attempted to sound apologetic. "I'm sorry, but I was told that your publicist knew this would be a very personal interview. I'm not being judgmental. I'm just trying to get your side of the story."

"Yes, my sister and I are going through something right now. Tell me what family doesn't. We will make up and be back to our normal selves."

"What about your marriage? Is it true that David was your sister's husband first?"

"I should have known you were going to bring that up."

Lisa, not one to be easily intimidated by Hollywood's elite, responded, "Rose, no need to get an attitude. I'm asking you what the readers all want to know."

At that moment, Rose decided to approach the interview differently. "My marriage is perfect. David and I are very happy. We are even planning on expanding our family. As far as the way we met, it was unfortunate that my sister got caught up in a love game that David and I had been playing, long before he met my sister."

"Are you saying that David married your sister to get to you?"

Rose attempted to act like she was bothered by her question. "Yes, because he knew I would be jealous."

By now Lisa had put her pen and pad down. She made sure the tape recorder was still recording and leaned in closer, as if the closer she leaned in, the more she'd understand what Rose was trying to tell her. "Did you ever mention this to your sister?"

"No, because I didn't want to hurt her and she seemed to be so in love with him."

"Correct me if I'm wrong. You let your twin sister marry

a man you were in love with and whom you say was in love with me. Where was the sisterly love?"

Rose got upset and started to cry. "Sisterly love. I love my sister. This had nothing to do with Violet. She just got caught in the middle. I tried to explain it to her after she found out, but by then, she didn't want to hear what I had to say."

Lisa got up and found a box of tissue and handed the box to Rose. "I didn't mean to upset you. Maybe we should continue this interview another time."

Rose wiped her face and began to sniffle. "No. I'll be okay."

"Are you sure? We can put the interview off to another time; when you're not so emotional."

Rose took another tissue and blew her nose. "I'm okay. It's just that I love my sister and I didn't mean to hurt her. It's like the love for this man has torn my sister and I apart. I cry myself to sleep every night, because she and I are no longer close. I blame myself, but I can't leave my husband, because I love him so much."

"That's some dilemma. Why don't we take a five minute break?"

Rose handed her back the box of tissue and then took a sip of her drink. "Only if you feel like one is needed."

Lisa looked down at her watch. "Let's continue. Do you think you and your sister will ever be close again?"

Rose did not look up at Lisa this time, but held her head down as if masking tears. "It's really up to her. I have apologized for my mistake. I even admitted to her that I was a little jealous because she has always been so much smarter. I'll go on record saying that whenever she wants to talk, I'm here. I want her to know that I love her and she means more to me than she'll ever know."

"That's touching. I'm sure our readers hope she finds it in her heart to forgive you. Keep us posted."

Rose looked up with watery eyes. "I hope she can too, because I can't see going through life without her."

Lisa sat in silence for a moment, to give Rose time to get herself together. "It has been rumored that the scandal with your sister caused the director to recast the role of Mrs. Wallingford in the movie *The Future Mrs. Wallingford*."

"We were only in negotiations and they never could meet my asking price."

"So if they would have met your asking price, you would be playing Mrs. Wallingford instead of Holly?"

Rose tried to sound convincing. "Yes."

"What about the role in King's new movie?"

"We're still in negotiations, so I would rather not discuss it right now."

"So, any other projects on your plate?"

Rose remembered one of her conversations with her agent and Lance. "Yes. I'll be going into the studio to record my first CD. I have some of the hottest producers lined up."

Lisa took the tape out of the recorder and flipped it over. "Why are you venturing off into music, when you have a very solid movie career?"

"My first love will always be acting, but I've wanted to record a CD for some time now. Since I'm in between films, this is the perfect time."

"Before you go, do you have anything else you would like to share with our readers?"

Rose took the last sip of her drink. "Yes. Learn how to look beyond a person's faults and try to love one another unconditionally."

Lisa stood up and shook Rose's hand. "Thank you again for your interview and we'll be in contact with your publicist. We hope you'll be satisfied with the article and I do wish you and your sister much success in your reconciliation efforts."

"Thank you. You're good at what you do, and I hope your boss recognizes that."

Lisa smiled. "I hope so too. I'll know when it's time for me to get my next raise."

* * *

After Rose picked up her SUV from the valet, she decided to call Lance. "Lance, baby. Can you meet me at your house?"

"I'm in the middle of a recording session; however, you could stop by the studio. There are a couple of people I want you to meet anyway."

"I don't know if that's a good idea. Too many people shouldn't see us together."

"Rose. I don't have time to argue with you. We are supposed to work together on your CD anyway, so no one would be the wiser. Your choice, but hey, I have to go."

Rose hung up and headed toward the studio.

Chapter 15
VIOLET

Violet invited Janice to spend the weekend at her place, so that they could finalize the celebrity charity ball events. She stopped at the grocery store to buy a couple of items. All of the lines at the cash registers were long. She finally decided on a line near the door. While she waited to be checked out, the guy behind her tried to strike up a conversation. She turned around and was immediately captivated by his gorgeous features. He looked to be about six-six, bald, dark chocolate complexion, with a beaming smile.

It had been a while since she felt like flirting, and his smile was enough reason to start anew. "Hi. I'm doing just lovely. Wish I didn't have to stand in this long line, though."

He agreed and introduced himself. "I'm Marcus."

"I'm Violet. Nice to meet you."

He extended his hand. "No, the pleasure is all mine. You look familiar."

"I get that all of the time." Violet felt the electricity that sparked between them after they shook hands.

The line continued to move up. Violet enjoyed their conversation and then it was her turn to check out.

"Ms. Violet, thank you for making the time in line an enjoyable one."

She smiled as she responded, "No problem mon, as they say in Jamaica."

He laughed and said, "Jamaica. I've been there a few times."

She looked for her wallet so she could pay for her items. She normally was more prepared, but she had gotten distracted this time. She turned to the cashier and said, "Give me one second and I'll give you my card."

As she was digging through her purse, he reached out and passed her a card. "While you're in your purse, why don't you drop that in there, that way I'll know you have it."

She looked up and he had a big mischievous grin on his face. "I'll be sure to find it later."

By then the people behind them were getting aggravated and Violet could hear a couple of people with fake coughs. "I hope it's sooner than later. Guess we better move you along, before we get ambushed."

She laughed, but agreed, and paid for her groceries. While she walked out, she could feel a set of eyes on her back. She put a little twitch in her walk just for him. She headed home.

I can't believe that I have been shamelessly flirting. I can't wait to see the expression on Janice's face when I tell her.

She and Janice pulled up in the driveway at the same time. She rolled down her window and shouted, "You're just in time to help me take in the groceries."

Janice moaned. "Something told me to wait thirty more minutes."

As they unpacked the groceries, Violet told her about the

guy she met while standing in line. "He is so tall, he makes your brother look like a dwarf." Violet noticed that Janice got quiet for a moment when she mentioned her brother.

"Hmmm. So what's his name again?"

"Marcus."

"Marcus what? Girl, where is that card?"

"It's in my purse. I haven't even looked at it since he handed it to me. I just dropped it in. I'll look at it later."

Janice found her purse and handed it to her. "Oh, no you don't. You won't get any work out of me, until you find that card and tell me exactly who this Marcus person is."

Violet attempted to find it in her purse. She ended up pouring the contents of her purse on the kitchen counter, before she could find the card. "Here it is."

Before she could read it, Janice snatched it out of her hand. "Girl. Do you know who he is? He is the one and only Marcus Jameson. He's one of the best forwards in the professional basketball league."

"You're kidding me, right?"

"No, look for yourself. That's his business card and he has included his home number and personal e-mail address." Janice snapped her finger in the air twice. "You go girl."

Violet smiled. "Hmm. I might have to give Mr. Sexy Chocolate a call, but not because he plays basketball either. He was a gentleman and he has a great sense of humor."

Janice acted as if she didn't believe a word of what Violet said. "Yeah. Right. You were too busy being captivated by his radiant smile."

"I want to call him, but I'm not sure I'm ready to get back in the dating scene."

"Girl, you better forget David. It has been long enough and it's about time you get back in the dating scene."

"I guess you're right." Violet didn't inform Janice that David had been calling and sending her cards.

"There's no guessing to it. I know I'm right. We need to

hurry up and work on the stuff for the ball, because Saturday we are going shopping."

"I have enough things in my closet already."

"The stuff you have in your closet is for old women. You're still in your twenties and should dress like it. You know I don't agree with Rose on anything else, but this is one area we both agree on. I will have you looking like you walked off a Paris runway."

"I shouldn't have told you. Now you're going to have me looking like a grand diva."

"You are a diva. Well, you're a sister to one anyway."

They both laughed. They spent the rest of the night going over things for the ball. The next morning they headed to the Galleria. Violet couldn't remember having so much fun shopping. "Janice, are you sure I need this outfit? I've bought six already."

"Yes, I'm sure. Try it on. I bet red looks good on you."

"Well, I think we are being premature about all of this. What if he doesn't ask me out?"

"What if he does? I want you to be prepared. Have you ever thought about asking him out?"

"No. Never. I'm old fashioned. I think the man should still be the one to ask the woman out. That is—if he's interested."

Janice nodded her head and agreed. "If he doesn't ask you, then somebody will."

Violet tried the dress on and was amazed at what she saw in the mirror. She felt a confidence she didn't know she had. She strutted out to the waiting area, so Janice could give her opinion. She twirled around a couple of times and asked, "So what do you think?"

Janice whistled. "Watch out now. I told you I was going to have you looking like a model before it was all over with."

"You really think I look good?"

Janice got up and turned Violet around toward the mirror.

"Look at you. You are gorgeous. I don't know how you can look at yourself and not see that."

Violet posed in front of the mirror. "I think I look okay, but Rose has always been the glamorous one."

"You both look alike. If she's glamorous, so are you. I swear, sometimes I don't know what I'm going to do with you."

"Compared to Rose, I just feel so plain."

"Face it. You are drop-dead gorgeous. If you don't believe me, just watch the reaction you get next week when you start wearing some of your new outfits to work. We do need to do something to your hair, though."

Violet rubbed her hands through her ponytail. "What's wrong with my hair?"

"Let's just say, give me two hours and you'll feel like a new woman."

"Sounds like you have your work cut out for you."

Violet continued to try on more outfits. She decided on two evening dresses and three pantsuits. After shopping for shoes, they both agreed on an early dinner at a national seafood restaurant located around the corner from the Galleria.

Chapter 16
ROSE

Rose watched Lance as he put the final touches on a track he was working on. It was still early, but he had been in the studio for over twenty hours and hadn't had any sleep. Everyone else had been there just as long and they were all leaving for the night. "Bye, Rose. Thanks for singing backup; if you need us for your album, let Lance know," said one of the guys in the popular group, Jaded, as he and the rest of the group were leaving.

Rose locked the door behind them before walking over to massage Lance's shoulders. He moaned and moved his head from side to side. "Don't stop. That feels good."

"I know you're tired. Why don't I go out and get us something to eat, while you finish up here?"

Lance turned around in his chair and put his hands on each side of her hips and pulled her toward him. "I have a better idea. Why don't you sit on my lap?"

"Lance. Anybody can walk in."

"Everyone is gone for at least the next couple of hours."

Rose pulled up her skirt and sat on his lap. "Well in that case, what are we waiting for?"

They made beautiful music of their own. By the time everyone else returned to the studio, they had cleaned themselves up and were about to leave. "You guys lock up when you finish. A copy of the track is on the CD rack."

Lance walked Rose to her car. "Are you sure you don't want to come over to the house? I only need a couple of hours of sleep and then I'll have all the time you need."

Rose hugged him and gave him a kiss on the mouth. In between kisses she said, "Baby, I'm sure. I need to go take care of some things anyway."

Lance showed a surprised look on his face after she kissed him. "Not that I'm complaining, but I'm surprised you kissed me out in public."

"I couldn't resist." She squeezed his butt before getting in her car. "You're just so irresistible."

"You are something else. Call me later."

"I will." She blew him a kiss and headed down the freeway toward her beachfront house.

Her phone rang and she picked up thinking it was Lance calling her from his cell phone. "Hi, dear."

"Dear. This is your mother."

Rose, startled, blurted out, "Hi, Mom. I'm sorry, I thought you were somebody else."

"Somebody else, like your dear husband?"

"Yes, Mom. Who else?"

"Just checking. You don't think I know anything, but I know you guys don't have a real marriage."

Rose was stuck behind a slow moving car, and couldn't get over because of the cars speeding by her. "Do we have to get into this right now? By the way, I'm doing lovely and how are you, Mom?"

"Don't get smart with me young lady. I might be old, but I can still bring you down a peg or two. I'm not one of your adoring fans."

"I'm sorry."

"Have you talked to your sister?"

Rose started to curse because the traffic suddenly stopped. "Damn."

"What did you say?"

"Nothing. Uh. No. I haven't. I went to see her a couple of weeks ago, but we haven't talked since. Why?"

"Why? She's your sister for God's sake. I don't know what I'm going to do with you girls. Lord knows I taught you better than this."

"I tried talking to her, even after she lied on me to the press."

"I read the article and your sister didn't lie. It doesn't make it right for her to air the family business like she did, but the article is truthful."

Rose, shocked that her mom said that, asked, "How could you take her side? She told them about David and everything."

Her mom got silent. For a moment, Rose thought they had lost their connection. "That's what I wanted to talk to you about. I feel like all of this is all my fault."

"What do you mean?"

"I shouldn't have made you girls so competitive growing up. I tried to shower you both with lots of love and attention. I tried to teach you the importance of family."

Rose decided to take a side road. To avoid missing her exit, she had to cut someone off. The angry motorist blew his horn at her. "We're just going through some things right now. We'll work them out."

Rose heard her mom sniffle. "I don't know about that. You really hurt Violet this time. You shouldn't have done what you did."

"I didn't mean to hurt her. It just happened."

"Dear, I don't blame you. I blame myself, because I should have stopped you from doing things to your sister when I first noticed it."

"Mom. What are you saying?"

"You have always taken your sister for granted and treated

her any kind of way and she's taken the fall for you so many times. Your father and I didn't put our foot down with you young lady, and now look at what's happened."

Rose didn't know if she should be angry or sad that her mom was defending Violet. She was used to her husband taking up for her, but her Mom had always been on Rose's side. "Maybe we should talk later, because I don't want you to run your blood pressure up."

"I'm fine. I should have said something years ago. You need to stop being self-centered and thinking that the world revolves around you."

"It's not my fault. You guys gave me everything I ever wanted. As a star, I'm so used to getting practically anything I want. What's wrong with wanting things to go my way?"

Her mom let out a sad moan. "Lord help me. My child is lost."

"Momma. Momma. Calm down. Why are you saying all of this to me? Why now?"

"Because child. If I don't tell you, you will continue on the path you're headed. I see how this rift between you two is hurting your sister. She loves you very much you know."

"I love her too, but she makes me feel so . . . so stupid."

"You need to make amends. Don't look back over your life and wish you could have or should have done something."

"I know, but she won't talk to me. I tried to apologize."

"Try harder. You have a lot of making up to do. You slept with her husband for God's sake. I would have beaten you down for that one, if I were Violet. She's a better woman than me in that aspect."

Rose was appalled at her mom's comments. "I can't believe you just said that."

"It's true. You stole the girl's husband and you really don't want him."

"I do want him. I love him."

"I'm your Mom. I'm not on the panel handing out Oscars, so stop the acting."

Rose pouted, as if her mom could really see her. "I love David."

"No. You wanted David. I bet you right now, you wish you weren't married to him. I also know about the fake pregnancy."

"Who told you that?"

"David told me. Right after you told me about your miscarriage. I called your house and you were out, and I asked David why would you be out so soon after losing your baby. He then informed me that there never was a baby."

"How could he? It wasn't his right to tell you."

"That is where you are wrong. He is your husband and he had every right."

"So you're telling me all of this time, you knew I was lying."

"Yes. I'm your mother. I know a lot of things."

Rose pulled up in her driveway. She was exhausted. "I will think about everything you said. I've made it home now, and I need to take care of some things."

"I'll let you go. Don't wait too much longer. You hear me?"

"Yes. I hear you." Rose turned off her cell phone and leaned her head on the steering wheel.

My life is such a mess. My sister hates me. My mom has turned against me. My husband despises me. The only comfort I get, is the time I spend with Lance. He'll get tired of sharing my time, so I'm sure this little love affair won't last too much longer. I need to be in front of the camera. That's the only time I feel exuberant. When I'm in front of the camera, I can release and be whoever I want to be.

* * *

Rose got out of her car and went to the house. She dreaded what she knew was waiting for her on the inside. She hoped David was in his study, so she could slip into her room unnoticed. He was, so she slipped upstairs and locked her door. She took a shower instead of a bath. Afterward, she threw herself across her bed and made a phone call. No one answered, so she hung up. She lay there until she fell asleep.

Chapter 17
VIOLET

"Janice, who was that on the phone?"

"I don't know. By the time I answered it, they had already hung up."

Violet got up from under the dryer. "It was probably a wrong number. You and my mom are the only two people who call me. I guess I better check to make sure it wasn't her."

She walked over to her caller ID and did a double take as she saw Rose's number displayed on the caller ID. "She must have dialed the wrong number."

"Who?"

"Rose's number is showing up on the caller ID box."

"Call her back. It might be important."

"Everything is important to Rose. I'll call her on Monday. Besides, you need to take these rollers out of my head."

"Oh, I didn't tell you. You have to keep those in your head until tomorrow."

Violet frowned. "Sleep on these? How am I supposed to sleep?"

Janice rolled over laughing. "You'll be all right. You won't even know they are there."

"Yeah, right."

Violet tossed and turned throughout the night. Although she had a full night's sleep, the next morning she woke up feeling as if she'd run a marathon.

I need to stop drinking cola so late at night. I know I'm going to need some make-up today, to cover up these bags under my eyes. What time is it? I better hurry up before we're late for church.

After the church service, Violet and Janice were walking back to Janice's car, when Violet heard someone call out her name. They stopped and turned around.

"Marcus?" Violet was the first to speak.

"In the flesh. You're still looking as lovely as when I first met you."

He caught up to where Violet and Janice were standing. They hugged and in the background you could hear Janice clearing her throat. "Sorry. Marcus, this is my best friend Janice."

Marcus reached out to shake Janice's hand. He then turned his attention back to Violet. "I don't normally come to this church, but a friend invited me, and now I'm so glad I took him up on his offer. What are you ladies about to get into?"

Violet tried to remain calm, because of the butterflies in her stomach. "We were about to go to Roscoe's."

Janice used her elbow to hint to Violet to invite him, but Marcus invited himself. "Really? Do you ladies mind if we meet you there?"

Janice spoke up before Violet could say anything. "If your friend is as cute as you are, then no, we don't."

He laughed. "I guess he's all right for a man."

Violet jumped into the conversation. "We'll see you there."

When they got in the car, Violet turned to Janice and said, "Janice, how could you do that? Now he's going to think I'm one of those hoochies."

Janice started up the car and drove to Roscoe's. "I doubt it. He knows you're a good girl. That's probably what attracted him to you. That bad suit you're wearing, didn't hurt either. My hat goes off to your fashion coordinator."

They both laughed. Violet had to agree that with her hair down and curled, she looked different, and the sun was setting off her auburn highlights. She was wearing a violet designer suit accented by small gold buttons and a floral scarf. The violet snakeskin three-inch heels showed off her shapely legs. Some of the men, who normally just looked and then went back to reading or doing whatever, took several looks at her today. She didn't expect such a reaction.

"I'm nervous," Violet admitted.

"Just be yourself. After meeting him briefly, he seems down to earth. I'm glad, because some of those ballplayers can be arrogant."

"Yes. He seems to be. We'll see."

When they first got to the restaurant, they didn't see Marcus. Since he wasn't there yet, they got a table for four and waited for him and his friend to show up. It appeared to be taking Marcus a long time, so when the waiter came back over to the table, they decided to order. At that moment, Marcus and a shorter man, who actually stood six-feet-two inches, but standing next to Marcus seemed short, showed up. "Sorry we're late, ladies. Terrence needed to get gas along with the whole east side."

The waiter moved out of their way as they took their seats. "Do you guys need extra time to order?"

They both responded in unison. "No, I know what I want."

The waiter took all of their orders. Marcus made the introductions. "Ladies, we thank you both for allowing us to be with the prettiest women in the City of Angels."

Violet and Marcus flirted with one another throughout dinner. Terrence looked as if he was interested in Janice, but Janice didn't seem too moved by his tactics. "Violet. I don't mean to rush you, girl, but I have to run by Nana's house before it gets too late."

Violet looked at Marcus and said, "I guess I better be going. It was nice seeing you again."

"You're not getting away that quick. May I have your number please? You had me rushing to the phone all weekend, hoping it was you."

Violet laughed. "Sure."

Marcus, with an innocent look on his face, said, "I did. Scout's honor."

After they exchanged numbers, both sets of friends went their separate ways.

"What did you think of Marcus?"

"I thought he was cool. I don't particularly care for his friend, though."

"Really. I thought Terrence was nice enough. What is it about him you don't like?"

"I can't put my finger on it right now, but when I figure it out, you'll be the first to know."

"Looks like we're going back toward my house and not your Nana's."

"We are. I used that as an excuse to get away. Two hours with his friend was as much as I could stand."

Violet laughed. "Thou protest too much. You don't like him just a little bit?"

Janice shook her head no.

Janice dropped Violet off at her house and decided to head on home. "Ms. Violet, remember what I said about wrapping your hair, and wear the emerald-green suit tomorrow. Good thing you know how to put on your own make-up, or else I would have to move in."

Violet put one hand on her hip and leaned her head to the side. "Whatever. I'll see you tomorrow."

Violet watched her as she pulled out of the driveway. After she entered her home and felt comfortable that everything was secure, she decided to take a nap. After her nap, Violet couldn't wait to start her Sunday evening ritual. She normally took Sunday afternoons to catch up on her reading and she had just purchased several books by her favorite authors the week before. She reached into her book bag and picked up the first book her hand touched. She looked at the cover and smiled at her choice. As she lounged on her sofa, she relaxed as she read Deidre Savoy's latest romance novel. She was almost at the end of the second chapter when her phone rang. Violet marked her spot in the book and placed it on the coffee table before she answered the phone.

"This better be important."

Chapter 18
ROSE

"Hi, Violet."

"Rose?"

"How are you? I tried calling you Friday."

"I'm doing fine. Why didn't you leave a message?"

"Your answering machine didn't pick up."

"Oh, it may have been unplugged. Okay, so what's on your mind?"

"Nothing really. I was calling to see how you were doing. We didn't leave on such good terms the last time I saw you."

"When do we ever?"

"I swear you and David are so alike."

"Excuse me. Thought I told you I never wanted to hear you say his name. That was my condition on talking to you."

"Violet, I'm sorry. I won't mention his name again."

"I know you won't because I'm about to end this conversation."

Rose, tired of the bitterness she heard in Violet's voice, asked, "Why are you being so difficult? I'm trying to make up and you won't give our relationship a chance."

"I've given our relationship plenty of chances. You are the

one who keeps messing it up. Look, I had a pleasant day and I want to end it on a pleasant note. This conversation is over. Bye."

Rose was left holding the phone, as she heard the loud sound of a click from Violet's end.

Why do I even try? I can't make her talk to me. If she wants to talk, she'll have to call me. I have better things to do. Such as, figure out why I keep gaining weight, because I've been working out every day. I'm too young for my body to be going through these many changes.

She was in the process of turning off her lamp, when she heard a knock at her door. "Come in."

"I wanted to see if you had a minute," David said as he entered the room.

"What is it? I'm tired and I really don't feel like any more arguing."

David sat on the edge of the bed. "What do you think we should do about our situation? This marriage has been hell on us both."

Rose fluffed a couple of pillows but didn't look up. "Hell on me, because you take out your frustrations on me. You did not have to marry me."

David looked her directly in the eyes and said, "Come on, now. You know you tricked me into marrying you."

"I didn't put a gun up to your head. I thought you enjoyed our time together."

"It was purely sexual. Which we haven't had since our wedding night and even that was a mistake."

Rose was feeling emotional. "It's not my fault. I've tried to make this marriage work, but you keep talking about Violet this, Violet that. I love my sister, but she has no place in our bedroom."

David faced her. "She's never left my heart, and so she'll be where I am."

Rose beat one of her pillows and yelled back, "You make me so sick. Why don't you go back with your precious Violet? You should have never married me if you loved her that much! I hope she never forgives you!"

David stood and headed for the door. "At least she has a heart," he mumbled.

Rose took her pillows and threw them, hitting him on the back of his head. David turned around. "What's your problem?"

At that moment, Rose doubled over in pain. She yelled out, "Help me. The pain, it won't stop. David, help me!"

David assumed she was acting to get his sympathy, but the look on her face erased the doubt and he could tell she was not acting this time. He located the phone and called for an ambulance. "We need an ambulance at 9000 Riverfront Drive. My wife is doubled over in pain and I don't know what's wrong with her."

It took the ambulance twenty minutes to get to the house. By that time, David had dressed Rose as best as he could under the circumstances. Rose's voice sounded weak from being in so much pain. She whimpered. "Help me, please."

David gave her hand a reassuring tug as they placed her on the stretcher. "Rose, I'll be right behind you in our car."

Lord, what is wrong with me? I know I've done wrong. I promise, I'll do better. Lord, take this pain away. It hurts so bad. Somebody help me. Somebody hit me upside the head and put me out of my misery.

When they arrived at Doctor's General, she was rushed into a private room because of her celebrity status. Normally, they would see the patients in the busy emergency room. David went into the room and tried to find out how she was. "I'm here for you, Rose."

The doctor entered the room. "Sir, I know this is your wife, but we are going have to ask you to leave now. She's been sedated, but there's been a lot of bleeding. We need to do some further testing."

David got up to leave. "Okay."

The doctor began to examine Rose and saw a pool of blood. He called for assistance. "Let's get her into surgery now."

David saw them rush Rose to surgery. Rose looked back and for a brief moment, she thought she saw a look of concern on his face. She relaxed while the medication in the IV took its toll.

Rose was groggy when they wheeled her in from the recovery room. She remembered hearing the doctors and nurses talk. The doctor walked in with David. He took a seat by the head of the bed. The doctor had a serious look on his face. "I'm glad I have both of you here. Rose, you are one lucky woman. If your husband hadn't gotten you here as soon as he did, you could have bled to death."

Rose still felt a little shaky. "What's wrong? Why was I bleeding?"

The doctor had a solemn look on his face. "I hate to be the one to inform you, but we did everything we could."

"I'm still not understanding."

"The baby. We weren't able to save the baby."

David sat there and stared at the doctor as if he were talking in a foreign language.

Rose's mouth hung wide open as she spoke. "Baby, I wasn't pregnant. That's impossible."

The doctor rubbed her shoulder. "You were, and we're sorry we couldn't save the baby. It will take your body a little while to recover. I would suggest you refrain from having sex for at least six weeks. Follow up with your normal gynecologist afterward and he or she should be able to give you the okay from there." The doctor looked at both of the shocked faces before continuing, "We want to keep you here overnight for observation. Otherwise, you should be able to go home tomorrow. I'll leave you two alone. Looks like you have a lot to talk about."

When the door closed, David stood up. He remained silent and that scared Rose.

"David. The doctor doesn't know what he's talking about. It's impossible."

"You slut. I should have known better. To think for a moment I was feeling sorry for you being in all of that pain."

Rose started to whine. "David, the doctor is lying."

"Rose, for once in your life. Tell the truth. You've been sleeping around and now you've gotten caught. Well, this was the final straw. You will be hearing from my attorney."

Rose felt like her world was coming to an end. "We can work this out. Let me explain. You weren't touching me and a woman has her needs. He didn't mean anything to me. He was an occasional screw. We used protection, so I don't know how this happened."

David hung his head and shook it. "You're pathetic. You always have an excuse. This last little number you pulled was a wake up call. I can't take this anymore. My stuff will be gone by the time you get home from the hospital."

Rose tried to get up out of the bed, but the IV in her arm reminded her that she shouldn't. "David. Please don't leave. Can't we talk about this when I get out?"

David walked to the door. "I'm all talked out."

"How am I supposed to get home? I have nobody."

"I'll call your sister."

Rose stiffened up and said, "Don't. I'll find somebody. I can ask Carmen."

"Whatever. It's your choice. I can't say it was nice knowing you, but I will say this; I hope you get everything you deserve."

David walked out the door. Rose closed her eyes, leaned back in the bed and allowed the medicine to put her to sleep. When she woke up, she was disoriented. Then it dawned on her that she was alone in a hospital room.

Why do these things keep happening to me? Who can I call? I don't trust too many people. The last thing I need is for this to get out to the media. Hmm. I guess I should call the baby's daddy, but then the nurses will be curious why he's picking me up instead of my husband. I have no choice. I have to call Carmen.

Carmen picked up the phone on the third ring. "Hello."

"Carmen, it's me."

"Hi. I was going to call you on Monday. The magazine will be on the stands tomorrow."

Rose held the phone in silence. She had forgotten about her interview. Now when news got out about the end of her marriage, she was going to be the laughing stock of Hollywood.

"Rose, are you still there?"

"Yes. I have a lot on my mind. I need a huge favor."

"You name it."

"I need you to come pick me up from Doctor's General sometime in the morning." .

With concern in her voice, Carmen asked, "What's wrong? What happened?"

Rose, not wanting to discuss it on the phone, just in case the lines were monitored, said, "Just know that David can't pick me up and I need a ride home."

"You still didn't answer my question. Why are you in the hospital?"

"I had a miscarriage."

"You what? Why didn't you tell me you were pregnant? That explains why you've put on those extra pounds. Why didn't you tell me? I should have been the first to know, well, after David of course."

Rose tried not to sound frustrated when she said, "Carmen, calm down. I just found out myself and by then I had already lost the baby. Just promise me you'll be here."

"I'll be there bright and early. Get some rest and I'll see you in the morning."

"Thanks. Bye."

The medication took its toll again and Rose fell into a deep sleep. The next morning, the doctor said she could go home.

Carmen arrived just as they were about to release her. Carmen walked over and gave her a hug and Rose felt a little relief having her there. "How you holding up, kid?"

"I'm okay. The doctor said I could be released, so I'm ready to go."

As Carmen gathered her stuff, she turned and said, "I need to prepare you. Apparently someone has leaked it to the press that you're here, so we'll have to go out the back way."

"Can't I get some privacy?"

Carmen looked at her before stating the obvious. "Now, you know better. I'll try to protect you as much as I can, but they will want a statement." Carmen saw the empty look in Rose's eyes. "Well, let's not worry about that now. First thing's first; we need to get you home."

They managed to get past the reporters. Carmen made sure Rose was settled in.

"Thank you, Carmen, for everything. I don't know how I would get through this without you."

"I'm more than your agent, you know."

"I know. You're the only friend I have."

Carmen gave Rose a sisterly hug. "Do you feel like talking about it now?"

Rose recanted the events of the past twenty-four hours, plus told her about her relationship with Lance. Carmen's face was expressionless, so Rose couldn't figure out what was going through her mind. She didn't know if she had lost respect from the only friend she had. She cleared her throat for emphasis. "That sums it all up."

"Rose, I must admit. I didn't expect all of this. So that's why David couldn't pick you up this morning. I now see why you didn't want Lance to come."

"What should I do?"

"Have you told Lance about the loss?"

"No. You and David are the only ones who know."

"Good. I will take care of the media. Just make sure you keep quiet. Don't discuss this with anybody. I will also refer you to a good divorce attorney."

"Divorce attorney? I don't need one."

"Yes, you do. David will have his lawyer eat you alive."

"I don't want to contest it. I was tired of being ignored and treated like a second-class citizen, anyway."

"Trust me. You still need an attorney. The attorney can make sure David never discloses the reason why you guys are divorcing."

"I see what you're saying now. What would I do without you?"

Carmen gave her a reassuring smile. "Let's hope we'll never have to find out. Now you get some rest. I have sent for my cook to come over so you'll have meals for the next few days. Stay in bed. Don't answer the phone. You gave me your spare key, so if you need to talk, I'll just come by. Understood?"

"Yes."

Carmen left the room.

* * *

I feel so empty. I should care if I'm married or not, but I don't. It's as if David's leaving me is lifting a huge boulder off my shoulders.

She lifted up her glass of orange juice and made a declaration. "Here's to new beginnings."

Chapter 19
VIOLET

Violet looked around the ballroom. She admired the past six-months' hard work and hoped that the ticket sales for the night's event indicated how successful the Charity Ball would be. She would not have been able to accomplish the event without the help of Janice and several other volunteers. The time was ticking for the event to start. While she made sure everything was in place, she spotted her date, Marcus.

"Hi, sexy."

Violet turned around. "Marcus. Hi, baby."

He embraced her and planted a small kiss on her lips. "Now that's how I like to be greeted."

"I didn't think you were going to be able to make it."

"I couldn't let your big night go by without me sharing it with you."

She gave him a tight hug before releasing her embrace. She was about to take his hand and guide him to the other side of the room, when she noticed something in one of his hands. "What do you have there?"

Marcus took the box and placed it in her hand. "Why don't you open it and see?"

She took the box and unwrapped it. When she opened it, she was greeted by a set of sparkling diamond earrings and necklace. "These are beautiful. Thank you."

"You're quite welcome."

"I want to wear them now. Help me switch these out."

"My pleasure."

Over the past few months, Violet and Marcus had spent as much time together as his schedule allowed. He was on the road with the team, but made sure he kept in constant contact with her. At this moment, she was glad that she allowed herself to get involved with Marcus. He was fun to be around and he was also understanding of her idea to not rush things. As he placed the necklace around her neck, the feel of his hand sent a chill down her spine. If she could survive the night, she knew that tonight was the night their relationship would go to a whole new level.

She turned around and placed one of her hands over the necklace. "These are beautiful. Thank you again. You're going to make me cry all of my make-up off."

"Now we can't have that."

"Our table is over there. I'll be back as soon as I can."

"Violet, this is your night. I understand, darling. I know how to keep myself busy in the meantime."

She blew him a kiss. "Thank you."

Violet excused herself and continued to oversee the event. Janice showed up in the kitchen, while Violet was making sure the food was being prepared to their specifications. "I was told I would find you back here," Janice said.

"Janice, you look absolutely wonderful. That lavender suits you well."

Janice pretended to be shy. "Thank you. You are wearing the silver well yourself. I swear since we went on that shopping spree, you have transformed into a new woman. Or is it because of that tall, fine, hunk of a man out there?"

Violet giggled. "Might be a combination."

"Whatever it is. I like it."

"I've gone over everything and things are looking well. Now all we have to do is wait for the people to show up and the party to begin."

They walked back out toward the ballroom. "Violet, I have something to tell you."

Before Janice could tell her anything, someone came up to Violet with an issue.

"Janice, I'll get back to you in a minute. Let me take care of this." Janice stood there and watched as Violet left for the other room.

After the small mix-up was resolved, Violet noticed the time and knew that people would be showing up soon. She walked back through the lobby and was happy to see some people walking toward the ballroom. As she walked in the direction of the ballroom, she dropped the program she had in her right hand. She leaned down to pick it up and when she stood back up, she was looking David straight in the face. "Violet. You look beautiful."

"David."

David tried to take her hand, and because she didn't want to make a scene in front of anyone, she gently snatched it out of his grip. "I'm sorry. I was just trying to help."

"I'll manage." She tried not to snap back at him, but failed. "Now if you'll move, I have people I need to greet."

At that moment, a petite, dark complexioned woman with short, crepe hair came and wrapped her arm through David's. "There you are. I was wondering where you had slipped to so quickly."

David looked as if he wanted to be anywhere else but in between the two women. "Dena, I want you to meet some-body. She's the reason why we're here tonight. Dena, this is Violet."

Violet showed some grace and reached out to shake her

hand. "Hi. Thanks for coming. Now if you guys will excuse me, I have to find someone."

As she was walking away, she heard Dena say, "I thought you told me she was the nice one. She acted like she had an attitude toward me."

After Violet heard Dena's comment she decided to put extra twists in her walk.

Oh, I have an attitude. I swear. What she doesn't know is I don't want him. She can have him and his issues. Speaking of men. I better find my friend, before he thinks I've abandoned him.

As the night got under way, items were auctioned off. From the way things looked, the community center was going to be in the red for at least another year. Before the dancing was to begin, it was Violet's duty to make a toast to announce the opening of the dance floor. "Hello everybody. Once again, I would like to thank you all for coming and we at Community Affairs appreciate everything that you have done. Thanks to those who gave their money and to those who have signed up to donate their time. This was the most successful charity ball yet, so you all give yourselves a hand and let the party begin."

As she walked from the podium, she felt someone's eyes on her. She ignored the feeling and took the hand Marcus had extended. He leaned down and whispered in her ear, "May I have the first dance?"

They danced to the next couple of songs. They were leaving the dance floor, when the DJ played the newest version of the electric slide. "I don't know where you're going, mister, but let me show you how it's really done."

They continued to dance and laugh. When the song

ended, Violet excused herself to the ladies' room. She was feeling bubbly from the champagne and from having fun with Marcus. She was applying some more lipstick, when she became startled to see not one, but two exact faces staring at her in the reflection of the mirror. She turned around and instead of her normal reaction of tensing up she gave her a hug.

The woman in the reflection was stunned and didn't immediately react to the hug. The woman hugged Violet back. "You look so gorgeous."

"Rose, I didn't expect you here."

"I came with Lance and I didn't expect such a warm greeting."

"Lance. Lance King, the music mogul?"

"One and the same. His sister works with you."

"Yes, his sister and I are good friends."

They continued to talk as if they were friends catching up. Violet looked at her watch again as other women started to pile into the bathroom. "I guess I better get out of here, before they send a search party out looking for me. I'm glad you came."

"See you later."

Violet didn't respond to Rose's last comment. She continued to walk out of the door. She surprised herself when she became openly affectionate toward Rose. "Maybe there's hope for us after all."

The rest of the night went by well, and even though they didn't hold another conversation, they occasionally caught each other looking in the other's direction. Marcus tried to be attentive and noticed a change in Violet. Violet tried to reassure him she was okay. "I'm tired from preparing for the ball. It's stress from trying to make sure everything ran smoothly."

"Baby, we could leave now if you're ready."

"No, I can't leave until the last person does."

Janice overheard them. "Go ahead. You've done more than enough of your share of work. Terrence and I can make sure everything closes down properly."

"Terrence, are you okay with this?"

"Yes. You guys go ahead. We got this. Now go."

Violet and Janice hugged and as they walked away, she turned around and mouthed the words "Thank you" to Janice.

As they were waiting for the valet to bring their cars around, David walked out with his date and Rose was walking behind him with Lance. Violet saw the scene and felt as if the walls were closing in on her. "Oh, no."

Marcus leaned over and whispered, "What's wrong, baby?"

"Look."

"There's your car. You don't have to acknowledge them. Come on, let's just get you in your car."

No one had noticed her until the petite woman David was with pointed and made a statement, "Both of your women are here. I never would have believed it, if I didn't see it for myself."

Rose was standing behind David by now and questioned his date. "Excuse me, and you are?"

Marcus touched Violet's arm and motioned for her to move. "Come on, baby. You don't have to stay if you don't want to."

"I know, but I can't leave like this."

"Yes you can. There's my car and I'll follow you."

Violet got in her car and while she waited on Marcus to get into his, she looked over and saw that Rose's height overshadowed David's date's. She couldn't hear what they were saying, but it looked as if they were arguing. A horn blew and broke her concentration. The valet attendant knocked on her window and motioned for her to move her car.

When she reached her house, she tried to give Marcus her undivided attention. She had to take a few minutes to gather

her thoughts, so she left him waiting for her in the living room.

Marcus has been so patient with me. I had planned on a nice romantic rendezvous after the party, but this night has been full of surprises. I don't know if I'm up for it.

Before she could change her mind, she undressed and put on her bronze colored satin lingerie that stopped a little above the knee. She grabbed the matching short robe and headed back downstairs. She heard the sounds of soothing jazz as she descended the stairway. "Sorry for taking so long."

Marcus stared at her and desire flamed from his eyes. "It was well worth the wait. Watching you come down the stairs was like watching an angel come from on high."

She let out a schoolgirl laugh. "I wouldn't go that far."

"Dance with me."

They danced and were enthralled with one another. She leaned on him and inhaled a mixture of his natural scent and cologne. His scent was like an aphrodisiac to her. He bent down and placed a short passionate kiss on her lips before ravenously taking her mouth with his. She felt as if she were floating on a cloud. As they kissed, she could feel the rise of his manhood. He picked her up and carried her upstairs to her bedroom. He placed her on the bed and looked deep into her sparkling brown eyes. "If you're not ready, we can wait. I'm satisfied with holding you."

She had years of frustration built up and she was so in tune with her body that at this point, she couldn't think of a legitimate reason to turn back. "I am ready."

She reached up and pulled him on top of her. While they kissed, she undressed him. She ran into a snag with his belt buckle, but he stepped in to assist her. His moans got deeper.

"Oh, Violet. I've dreamed of this moment while on the road."

He helped her take off the rest of his clothes, while he used the other hand to find a condom tucked in his wallet. He handed the condom to her and she placed it on his stiff outer member. He leaned her back as he continued to place small kisses all over her body. She begged him to mount her, but he declined. "No baby. It's not time yet. Lie back and let me take care of you."

He continued to please her in ways she hadn't experienced with David, in ways that she only dreamed about. He turned her over, took his tongue and licked down the center of her back. Before she could get over the excitement of his tongue on her back, he placed more kisses in spots on her body that she wasn't aware were sensitive. With each move, she could feel the water falling. He turned her around facing him and buried his face deep within her garden. The moans that came from her sounded foreign to her, but she allowed him to take her on a much overdue journey. She enjoyed each stroke as he entered and pushed her over the edge. She was brought to her sexual peak so many times, that she felt as if her head would explode from the excitement. She enjoyed every minute of it. After being completely fulfilled, they lay in each other's arms and fell asleep.

Chapter 20

ROSE

"Can you believe the tramp that David was with?" Rose said while getting in the bed with Lance. "If you wouldn't have pulled me away when you did, I was going to cold pop her in the mouth."

Lance laughed. "You are something else. Forget about her and come give daddy what he's been wanting all night."

Annoyed, Rose yelled, "I swear Lance! You're like a dog in heat."

"You shouldn't be so desirable. I'm thankful your husband divorced you."

She leaned down and kissed him. "Oh, Lance."

After they made love, Lance fell asleep immediately. Rose stayed awake and thought back to the encounter she had with her sister. For a few minutes, they talked as if they were old high school friends who lost contact and were running into each other at a reunion. Rose saw Violet when she was getting ready to leave and before Rose could speak to her, Violet had already gotten into her car. The man Violet was with was tall and one of LA's most eligible bachelors. She was surprised her sister was interested in a basketball player.

* * *

Violet, you're full of surprises girl. First I notice that your escort is Marcus Jameson, the finest man in basketball and then you hug me as if you were glad to see me. I don't know if I should call you or wait for you to call me. I know one thing, Momma will sure be glad. I'm so tired of not having someone to share things with. Oh well, let me go to sleep, staying up all night won't change anything.

The next few days she was kept busy by auditioning for several different movie roles. She was finally able to bounce back from the negative publicity of Violet's interview and her much-talked-about divorce. The media had a field day with the divorce. Fortunately, David agreed to file for divorce under the reason of irreconcilable differences, instead of adultery. She agreed to not ask for any type of alimony or any other type of monetary award. She spent months in the studio with Lance recording her music CD. She was scheduled to do a photo shoot for the cover and the first single would be released the following week.

As she drove to her destination, her mind was on her music. She barely heard the cell phone ringing over the loud music. She scrambled to find it. She tumbled through her purse, to realize only that it fell between the seats in her car. She caught the caller on the last ring. "Hello."

"Hello, stranger."

"Momma, I was going to call you."

"Sure you were. That's the same thing your sister told me when I called her yesterday."

"You talked to Violet?"

Her mom sounded joyful. "She told me she saw you a couple of weeks ago."

"Yes. Did she tell you we talked and she hugged me out

of the blue? I was surprised, but it felt good. I do miss not having someone to talk to and hang out with."

"See. I told you if you worked at it, things would work out."

"Hold on. I didn't say we were the best of friends. It's the first time we've been in the same room and not argued. It was decent."

"That's good. I know my girls can work it out. I'm getting sleepy, so I'll talk to you later, okay dear?"

"Love you."

"Love you too."

After the phone call with her mom, she decided to call Violet. "Hi, Violet. Sorry I missed you. Give me a call when you get a chance; maybe we can do lunch this weekend."

The photo shoot went well. Lance decided to take her to LeMeridian, a French restaurant, to celebrate. "Rose, you are about to be the next Whitney."

Rose loved to hear him sing her praises. "You really think so? There are a few songs I feel will do well."

"A few? You have a hit CD."

Rose raised her champagne glass and cheered. "Thanks to the best producer."

After dinner, he dropped her off at home. "I wish I didn't have to go back to the studio, but I have an artist flying in from Dallas tonight and this is the only time we'll be able to get together."

She kissed him and pushed him out the door. "I understand. Call me tomorrow."

This has been a long week. I can't wait to sit down and relax. I know what I need, a vacation. It's been a long time since I've gone somewhere for fun.

* * *

   She went to her computer and accessed the Internet. She typed in the words "vacation packages" in the search browser. She looked at her calendar to confirm some dates and paid for a four-day weekend to Puerto Vallarta, Mexico. She spent the rest of the night surfing the net until she was too tired to see the screen and eventually went to bed.

Chapter 21

VIOLET

Janice waltzed into Violet's office. "How's it going, Ms. Lady?"

Violet ended her conversation on the phone, before addressing Janice. "It's going. I just got off the phone with Rose. We're supposed to meet for lunch tomorrow."

"Say what? Cool. It's about time."

"Don't read more into it. It's only lunch."

"Lunch today, shopping tomorrow."

Violet laughed. "Whatever. I still have a bone to pick with you anyway. I've been meaning to ask you something. How long have you known that Rose was dating your brother?"

Janice stopped laughing. "I've known for quite a while, but I was sworn to secrecy, because she was still married to your ex at the time."

Violet's mouth dropped. "Say what?"

Janice walked to the door and closed it before pulling up a seat. "Well, since it's all out in the open now, I guess I can tell you everything that I do know."

"Yes. Do tell."

Janice brushed back her bangs from her forehead and continued. "Well, apparently Lance and Rose met when her agent started shopping for a producer to work on her CD. Lance said he had always had the hots for her, so he thought it was the perfect opportunity to make his moves."

"Didn't he know she was married?"

Janice sneered. "Like that's going to stop a dog from sniffing. Anyway. She ignored his advances and one night out of the blue she called him and they have been messing around ever since."

"Man, I wonder if David found out. Is that why they divorced?"

"You know it. You know the time you heard from your mom that Rose had been in the hospital for exhaustion. It was around that same time. Her publicist had to pick her up."

"Interesting. Are they serious?"

"Now, that I don't know. This week she's his flavor, but she's stayed around longer than some of the others. He might have a love jones for her."

"Momma told me about the divorce, but I didn't know all of that was going on."

"Well, if you talked to your sister more, maybe you would know what was going on in her life."

Violet looked down at her calendar. "Well I do have lunch tomorrow with the drama queen. I'm sure it will be full of surprises. I doubt if I'll get a chance to talk. You know how she likes to dominate a conversation."

"What time is it? I was supposed to meet Terrence at the gym and I'm tired of him complaining about me being late."

Violet chuckled.

"What are you laughing at?"

"You. Remember when you couldn't stand Terrence? Now it's Terrence this, Terrence that. Now I can't stand to hear his name, because you say it so much."

Janice snapped her fingers in the air. "Don't hate."

"I don't have to hate, because I have a man."
They both laughed and Janice left to meet Terrence.

I guess I should wrap things up here and head home. My bed is calling me. I will need all of my energy to deal with my sister tomorrow.

Violet slept well. The next morning, instead of going shopping, she decided to lounge around the house. She needed to mentally prepare herself for her meeting with Rose at Café Max. She dressed in a short purple skirt and matching silk shirt. On the weekends, she normally threw on a pair of sweats or old pair of jeans, but she wanted to show Rose that she wasn't the only one who could get all dolled up.

After she pulled up in the parking lot at the restaurant, she looked in the driver's mirror and added some lip gloss over her lipstick for the final touches. She blew herself a kiss in the mirror and exited her car. She strode into the restaurant.

When she entered, the maitre'd recognized her right away and showed her to her table. As she walked toward the table, she was surprised that Rose had beaten her there.

Hmm. Normally, Rose is late for everything. Maybe she has changed. I guess I should keep an open mind.

Rose stood up and pushed her chair back. They hugged each other, and then sat.

After sipping her water, Violet commented, "Rose, you're looking good. I was concerned about your health for a while there."

"Thanks. I'm fine."

Violet took her napkin and placed it across her lap as the waiter poured them both water and asked, "Would you ladies like any wine today?"

Rose, sounding jovial, responded to the waiter. "Yes. Bring out your best white wine."

Violet picked up her menu. "It has been a while since I've been here. What do you recommend?"

"The Chicken Fettuccine Alfredo is excellent."

The waiter came back and poured the wine. "Would you ladies like an appetizer with your meals today?"

"Yes. I would like an order of mozzarella squares."

Rose added, "And I would like the chicken fingers."

"I see you haven't given up your love for chicken fingers," Violet laughed.

Rose also laughed. "Never. Don't you see my wings? Lord knows I feel like flying away."

Rose's phone rang. "Sorry. This is Carmen, so I must take this. Excuse me a minute."

I have to say, Rose seems a little different. I still don't know about her though. This almost feels right.

Rose ended her phone call and they continued their lunch. The conversation remained light, neither wanting to irritate the other. After lunch, Rose insisted she pay for the meal, so Violet let her. As they left the restaurant, they discovered they were parked by one another. Not much was said at this point, so they hugged and promised to meet again in the following week for lunch.

Before she started her car, Violet checked her voice mail on her cell phone and heard a message from Marcus. "Sweetie, my flight was delayed. It'll be so late when I get in, that all

I'll want to do is hit the sack. I'll call you in the morning. Love you."

Looks like I'll be home alone tonight. Sometimes I think I'm falling for Marcus, but it doesn't feel like it did when I fell for David. It's probably more lust than love. We might as well be living together, because when he's in town, I can never get him to go home. Lately though he's been extremely busy, more than usual.

Violet decided to take a detour and instead of going home to watch movies on her television, she stopped off at the neighborhood movie theater. She knew she was overdressed for the movies, but she didn't want to go home to change. People started staring at her, as she paid for her ticket. Someone stopped and asked her for an autograph. "Sorry. I'm not Rose, I'm her sister." The fan seemed disappointed as she walked away.

After the movie was over, Violet drove the long way home. It was still early enough for her to go out in her garden when she got home. She changed into some old sweats and spent the rest of the evening in her garden.

Chapter 22
ROSE

Rose enjoyed lunch with Violet. She was looking forward to the next one. This time, she was going to ask her about going on a four-day vacation with her. She knew it was a long shot, but she would try.

I could invite her to my CD release party. It might be best if I try lunch again first and see what happens. No. I'm going to ask her. This makes the second time, we've been together and it's actually been civil. I tried to explain our relationship to Lance, but he says I'm being childish. Men, what do they know? Well, my body is sure craving some Lance right now, so I guess men are good for something.

It was late and she hadn't heard anything else from Lance confirming that she was supposed to come over. Lately both of their schedules had been hectic and they took advantage of each moment they could find to be alone.

She decided to surprise him, so when she got there, instead of ringing the doorbell, she used her key to access the house. The alarm didn't go off, but she double-checked to make sure it was deactivated.

She went toward his bedroom and the closer she got, the louder the noises she heard coming from his bedroom. She walked in and found Lance in a compromising position. A brunette woman had her head between his legs. She stood there with her mouth wide open before she responded, "You dog. Who's this ho?"

The brunette tried to get up to gather her clothes. Rose grabbed her by her hair and threw her on the bed. "Oh, no heifer. You're not going anywhere."

Lance tried to pull Rose off of the woman. "Rose, baby, calm down. It's not what you think."

"You bastard. This tramp is sucking on you and you got the nerve to say it's not what I think."

The brunette then opened her mouth and said, "Who you calling a tramp, b—?"

Rose hauled off and slapped her. "That's Queen B to you."

The woman rubbed her face from where Rose slapped her and didn't say anything else.

Lance tried to calm Rose down. Rose punched him in the chest. "Baby. I don't think you want to keep hitting me."

Rose jumped in his face. "Why? What? Are you going to hit me?" She pointed her finger back and forth in his face. "Hit me. Come on. You're man enough to do it. Hit me and you'll be six feet under."

Lance yelled at the brunette to get her things and leave. She responded, "But I got dropped off, I don't have a car."

Lance yelled, "Well, that's not my problem! Trick, get out."

The brunette grabbed her stuff and ran out of the house.

Rose gave out a wicked laugh and said, "Oh, now she a ho trick tramp. But you wasn't saying that when she went down on you."

"Calm down, baby."

"Baby. I got your baby. Move. I'm out of here."

"No. You're too upset to drive."

"Now you want to be concerned. You are dismissed. I'll send my assistant over to get my things tomorrow."

Lance blocked the doorway, attempting to stop her from leaving the room.

Rose gave him a look that could bring the strongest man to his knees before stating, "I suggest you move out of the way or else they will be surgically removing my foot from your behind."

Lance moved, but continued to beg. "Baby, I'm sorry. What can I do to make it up to you?"

Rose opened the door and jumped into her Porsche. As she drove out of his subdivision, she saw the brunette walking. She pulled over and yelled, "Get in!"

The brunette kept walking as if she was afraid that Rose was going to do something else to her.

"Get in. I'm not going to hurt you anymore. I hate trifling men. He should have at least dropped you off somewhere."

The brunette got in and gave Rose an address. Rose dropped the top down on her convertible and let the wind blow through her hair and she drove through the valley. She dropped the brunette off at a place that looked like a shack. When the brunette got out, she said, "Thanks. What do I owe you?"

"You don't owe me anything. Just stay out of trouble. Just because a man has money doesn't mean he's going to treat you like a lady. Stay away from flashy men."

Rose drove off with no particular destination in mind.

Chapter 23

VIOLET

"How much longer do I have, before getting out from under this dryer?"

The stylist shouted so she could hear, "You only have fifteen more minutes."

"Okay."

While under the dryer, Violet thought about the events of the past few months. Her relationship with Rose was better. Not perfect, but better. She remembered the album release party she'd attended. The cameras wouldn't stop flashing. She didn't see how her sister could stand to be in the limelight all of the time. She wanted to leave the party early, but since she promised her she would be there, she stayed and bore the flashing cameras. She had to hand it to Rose; she played her role well with the media and with Lance. Although Rose didn't talk about it, she knew from talking with Janice that Lance was caught cheating a week before the party. A part of her felt as if it was justice or payback, but she did feel sorry for her sister. She and Janice laughed at some of the things Lance would try to do. Lance was still suckering up to Rose, even now, months later. Rose treated him like trash, but he kept going back for more abuse.

There's no pain deeper, than the pain of a woman scorned.

Violet looked down at her hand. Marcus was always buying her something, whether it was the matching wrist and ankle tennis bracelet she was now wearing or clothes. He had bought her five watches. She was currently wearing the black Movado that matched her black pantsuit. She admired her birthstone ring he had specially made. It was a diamond-cut gemstone with two-karat diamonds surrounding it; the design was unique and no matter which way her hand moved, the sparkle from the diamonds were brilliant.

She was not materialistic, but it felt good to be spoiled. She started to trust men again. The only problem she had with dating Marcus was the groupies that seemed to be everywhere. Sometimes they would be out, and some bold groupie would literally push her out of the way to get to him. She'd informed Marcus the first time it happened that she was not going to fight for his attention. She also told him that he needed to handle those types of situations, because she was not going to be disrespected.

"Okay. Ms. Violet, you can come out now."

Violet was still day dreaming when her hairdresser tapped her on the shoulder. "I'm sorry. My mind was a thousand miles away."

"I'm sure it was with that fine boyfriend of yours."

Violet laughed. As she paid her hairdresser, she turned around to walk away and ran right into the petite woman she had seen with David at the center's last charity function. "Excuse me."

She looked Violet up and down before responding. "You're excused. Just watch yourself next time."

Violet, not one for confrontation, walked away. She knew if she stayed, she would have slapped the wench. Violet heard her tell her hairdresser, "I didn't know you did her hair. She's my man's ex. I can't stand her, because she's all he talks about."

Her hairdresser responded, "Really, now? Well that's between you two. I'm here to do your hair." Hearing that, Violet placed a smile on her face and continued on out of the door. The sun was shining bright and she could tell it was going to be a beautiful day. She had taken an extended lunch, so she headed back to the community center.

She passed Janice on the way in. "Slow down."

Janice slowed her pace. "Oh, sorry. I'm running late for a meeting with the Realtor."

"Well, the Realtor will wait, trust me. They want their commission."

Janice laughed and continued on to her destination.

Violet checked her messages and the first call she made was to Rose.

"Hi. I was returning your call."

Rose's phone sounded as if she was inside of a tunnel. "Have you changed your mind about going with me to Mexico?"

"I can barely make out what you're saying. Can you repeat that?"

Rose repeated what she said. "Is that better?"

"Yes. I heard you that time. No. I have tried to clear my schedule, but I forgot I had given several people the time off on both of those days and Janice is one of them; otherwise I would be able to go."

Rose sounded disappointed. "Maybe next time then. Do you want to meet me later? I need to buy a couple of bathing suits, so if you're not busy, I can just swing by there and pick you up."

Violet thought about it, but she didn't like Rose coming up to the center too much, because it always caused a commotion. The teenagers would hound her for weeks after her visit, hoping for autographs or pictures. She had to threaten some of the over-active teens with clean-up duty, in order for them to stop bothering her about Rose. "I have a better idea. I'll meet you at your house and we can leave from there."

"Cool. See you later."

Violet pulled up to Rose's house a quarter past six. Instead of going in, she called her from her cell phone and Rose met her outside. "I can drive if you like."

"That's okay. I still remember when you first learned how to drive."

"Now, Rose, I know you don't want to go there. You're the one who hit the parked car."

They got in the Escalade, both cracking jokes on the other's driving. "At least I didn't park my car on a hill and hit the police car coming up the hill."

"Oh, I almost forgot about that one."

The radio was blasting and one of Rose's songs came on. Violet sat there and listened to the words. It was a beautiful ballad and she was amazed that the voice of the songbird was her own sister. "That is one of my favorite songs on your CD."

"Really? Mine too. When we were in the studio, I got so into the song, they just left me alone and let me ad-lib. The original words were fine, but the part you hear in the end, that's all me."

Violet reached over and squeezed her hand. "You are very talented and I'm proud of you."

Rose smiled as if overjoyed. "Thanks. That means a lot to me."

They went from store to store, because Rose couldn't find

everything in one store. They shopped until the Galleria closed.

After helping Rose carry in her bags, Violet hugged her. As Violet pulled out of Rose's driveway, she yelled out the window, "Have fun."

Rose waved and Violet headed home.

Chapter 24
ROSE

Rose went out on her balcony and held both hands up in the air, leaned her head back, and yelled, "The world is mine."

Look at this view. It's even more beautiful than my ocean-front view back in Cali. I'm so glad to get away. No media, no telephones; just the ocean and me. I wish I could have talked Violet into coming along anyway, but oh, well. I have a couple of novels with me and I plan on reading every single one of them while lounging on the beach. Now, where did I put my shades?

She was staying in an exclusive resort hotel that catered to the rich and famous. The staff was at her beck and call. The hotel had a private beach area, and Rose was determined to take full advantage of it all. She lounged on the beach while she enjoyed the sounds that came from the ocean waves. While she sipped on her third margarita, she saw a couple walking in the sand holding hands and from a distance, the man looked familiar. She couldn't pinpoint who the man was, because she didn't have a close enough view. She pulled her shades back down over her eyes and leaned back in her chair. She returned her attention back to her novel *The Family Curse* written by New Orleans native Magdalene Breaux. Feeling relaxed, she dozed off and when she woke up, she was unaware of how long she had been sleeping. It didn't matter to her, because she was at peace.

Rose took a bubble bath in the hot tub that was located in her huge luxury bathroom. The hotel staff even provided her with a couple of mood music CDs. After changing into a short white skirt and red halter top, she left her room and went to the hotel's restaurant for dinner. While she waited on her dinner, she decided she would spend a night out on the town dancing.

At dinner she noticed quite a few familiar faces among the crowd. When eye contact was made, each person would nod his or her head slightly in acknowledgment of knowing the other. The popular African-American award-winning actor Fabian and his wife stopped by her table for a few minutes before they exited the restaurant.

My, my, that's some lucky woman. I ain't mad at her though. Not only is he fine, but he's also a good family man. Oh, well. I remember when we did a movie together. I begged the producers for a love scene with him, but oh, no. The director said that it was not necessary to move the scenes along. That was probably best, because my heart probably couldn't handle it.

Now who do we have here? Everybody in Hollywood must have decided to take a trip to Mexico this week. I hope he doesn't see me and just walks on by. He's the producer with octopus hands. I've had to fight him off of me on many occasions. It got so bad; I finally told Carmen that if he was the producer on the film, then I wouldn't do the film. I see he has his showpiece of the week. I need to warn her that no matter how much she puts out, he will only do the bare minimum. She'll be lucky if she gets to be an extra in his movie. Rumor mill also has it that he's really not a good lay anyway. Oh, no. Here he comes.

"Rose darling, you're looking exquisite as usual."

"Thank you and you're looking . . . well you're you."

"Oh, this is Tiffany. Tiffany, Rose Purdue."

Tiffany held her hand out and Rose stared at her and spoke without once lifting her hand. "Hi, Tiffany."

Tiffany pulled her hand back embarrassed. "Hi. Nice to meet you."

Rose, with her nose turned up in the air said, "Likewise. Well if you two don't mind. I would like to finish eating my dinner before it gets cold."

She went back to eating her food and they moved on to their table.

Rose signaled for the waiter because she wanted a refill on her drink. She needed a little liquor before she left to go get her groove on. She had lost count of the amount of margaritas she had drunk in one day. After she left the restaurant, she took a cab to the club located on the other side of the strip. When they got to the club, the driver asked for American dollars, but Rose ignored him and reached into her purse for some pesos.

He then said, "Ésa es 250 pesos" or "That will be 250 pesos."

She paid the cab driver the correct amount in pesos. He tried to cheat her and he was shocked that she spoke fluent Spanish, as she yelled out at him in his native tongue and in English the correct amount of pesos, "Aquí están 150 pesos. Here is 150 pesos."

He decided not to argue with her, took the money, and sped off.

When she walked up to the door, all eyes were on her. Noticing that she was the center of attention, she strutted through the door in her five-inch, red high-heel shoes that accented her long shapely legs. She didn't have the legs of Tina, but she sure could give her a run for her money. She paid the entry fee and started walking and dancing to the beat. She walked around the club to get a feel for which floor she wanted to spend the majority of her time on. She loved all types of music. She chose the rhythm and blues room. Right now, no one noticed that she was the actual singer of the fast song that the DJ was spinning. She got herself a drink and stood at the bar. She tapped her feet to the beat of the music. Across the bar, she locked eyes with a handsome olive complexioned Spanish gentleman.

He walked over to her side of the bar and asked her to dance.

"La Srta, puede yo tener esta danza? Señorita, may I have this dance?"

"Si. Yes, Señor."

The handsome Spanish gentleman was a very good dancer. Rose started having a great time. She danced; she drank, and then danced some more. He offered to take her to her room, but she declined. Instead she asked him to get her a cab. "Por favor consígame un taxi. Please get me a cab."

He hailed the cab and opened the door. "Su taxi la espera. Your cab awaits you."

She thanked him. "Gracias."

He took her right hand and kissed the outside of it. As the cab pulled off, he told her good-bye. "Adiós Señorita."

She waved good-bye and went back to her hotel. She didn't have problems out of this cab driver when it came time to pay.

* * *

The next morning, the sun that shined through the window blinded her; she tried to hide under the covers. She was thankful she remembered to take an aspirin before going to bed, because otherwise, her head would be hurting along with her eyes.

After taking a shower, she decided to eat a light breakfast on her balcony so she could enjoy the ocean view. She looked up from reading the American paper and looked out across the beach. She saw the same couple that she had seen the day before a few doors down on their balcony. This time, she knew she recognized the man. She did a double take, because she didn't recognize the woman. She made it a point to count how many rooms down, so she could confirm that it was indeed the man she thought it was.

She finished her meal. She made sure she had her sunblock, her sunglasses, and the rest of her beach gear. While she walked down the hall, she counted the doors and knocked on the one she thought belonged to the couple. A maid opened up the door. Rose had a clear view of the room but couldn't think of a legitimate reason to be there, so she apologized to the maid as if she had the wrong room. "I'm sorry. Wrong room."

Maybe he just has a look alike. I hope I'm wrong. I guess I'll lounge around all day and just enjoy this good tropical weather.

Rose headed to the beach and spent the entire day there.

Chapter 25
VIOLET

These numbers are not adding up. I've got to have this report to the board in less than a week and I can't figure out where some of the funds have gone. There are only two people that I know of that should have access and I'm one of them. I know I haven't used them. I need to get Janice in here to help me with this, because right now all of the numbers are running together. Looks like I'll be putting in some overtime this weekend. Fortunately for me, Marcus is out of town visiting his parents. He can be just like a child sometimes, because he requires a lot of attention. This weekend I won't have enough time for myself, let alone him.

Violet dialed Janice's extension. "Janice, can you come to my office for a minute?"

"Sure. Be right over," Janice kindly responded.

She heard Janice as she walked up. "No. Don't sit down there. Let's go over to the table. We're going to need some elbow room. I need you to help me figure out something. The auditor the city uses has brought back a report that

shows some funds are missing from the community center. I
need to have a counter report in the Board's hands by next
week. I've looked at it over and over, and honestly I can't see
where the money went."

Janice scanned over the report. "We keep our own records
and we've been very thorough."

Violet tapped the head of the pen on the table. "I know.
Our numbers don't match their numbers at all. It's as if the
money went into a black hole."

"What do you need me to do?"

"I hate to do this to you, because I know you're supposed
to have a long four-day-weekend. But, can you come over
Saturday and help me go through the files?"

"Now you know I will. It's entirely too much stuff for one
person to go through. In fact, why don't I just cancel my day
off and we'll work on it tomorrow."

"You don't have to do that. There is no sense in both of us
stressing."

"I won't be able to enjoy my day off anyway if I'm worried about you."

"Okay. Let's come in a little earlier. The children's party
is Friday afternoon and I don't want to miss it."

"Cool. I'll see you tomorrow."

Violet locked her office and went home.

*This is a Calgon night. I don't want to see anything with a
number on it. Dang it, there's the phone. I can be home all
night and my phone won't ring, but as soon as I get in the
tub, it wants to ring. Maybe whoever it is, will get tired and
just hang up. Why isn't my answering machine picking up?*

Violet exited the tub, wrapping a towel around her as she
rushed to the phone. The caller ID box said unavailable, so
she picked up. "Hello."

"Hi, baby. You sound like you've been running."

"I was in the tub. How are you and your parents?"

"Everything is fine. I needed this time with my family. Sometimes I hate being on the road. I'm enjoying this down period. I miss you."

"Marcus, I miss you too."

Marcus's end sounded muffled. "I can't wait to see you. I've been having some wild dreams about you."

"Oh, really now?"

"Yes. So when I get back, just have the strawberries and champagne waiting."

"Slow your roll. By the time you get back, I'll be having a visitor."

Marcus sighed as if disappointed. "Can it visit early, because I'm in heat?"

Violet laughed. "No, silly. You know it don't work like that."

The phone crackled and Marcus said, "This phone keeps messing up."

"It's a bad connection. Do you want me to call you right back?"

"No, I'm getting off anyway. I just wanted to tell you I miss you and to let you know that you've been on my mind constantly."

"I miss you too. Now hurry home, so momma will have something to play with."

"You naughty girl. I'm going to tell your momma."

"If you do, then the honey is off limits."

He laughed. "Okay. I'll be quiet, as long as there is an endless supply of honey."

"Whatever. Bye."

Violet thought she heard someone in the background as she hung up the phone. She thought about calling him back, but one glance at the file on her bed dissuaded her from doing so.

* * *

I need to put this file up and get me at least one good night's rest. I will be knee deep in it the entire weekend anyway. Now this is the time I wish Marcus were here because I need my shoulders massaged. Let me put this eye mask on. That will help eliminate some of the bags under my eyes from exhaustion.

The next morning, she arrived at the center early. She set everything up, so that when Janice got there, she could start outlining their strategy. They needed a plan to figure out the problem or they wouldn't accomplish anything. She would use her desk and she set up a laptop and an adding machine on the table in her office for Janice to use.

"Good morning. I thought you would be here. I know you haven't eaten, so I bought us both some bagels and juice."

Violet took the bagel and used the plastic knife to spread strawberry cream cheese over it. "Thanks. I was starving, but I just couldn't leave."

"I know you girl. So where do I begin?"

For the next fifteen minutes, she went over what she needed Janice to do and how she wanted her to arrange things, so that they both would be using the same method.

They spent the next eight hours going through all of the files and formatting the information. They took a break to enjoy the children's party and each went home to get some rest. They spent the next day, which was Saturday, comparing the data with that of the auditors.

Violet wiped the sweat off of her forehead as she continued to go through the papers. "We've spent two days and still things are not adding up."

"Hold up, Violet."

"What?"

"I think I found it." Janice jumped up and started doing the Cabbage Patch and sang, "I found it. I found it."

Violet took the paper she was holding out of her hand. "Where? Now, show me."

"See, we've been looking in this area, when all along it was in the miscellaneous funds area."

"How did the funds get moved over to miscellaneous, when they were originally broken down by each project?"

"Looks like somebody has been playing monopoly with the center's money."

"Yes, but who is that someone?"

"I don't know."

Violet closed and opened her eyes, then shook her head. "I wish I did, because now there's another problem. All evidence points toward me."

Chapter 26
ROSE

I'm so glad I extended my stay for a week. I thought I would be bored, but not having to rehearse or be at a shoot, has been so relaxing. I've been spoiled. I must bring the family down here for a vacation. Even Momma would have fun here. The tours have been well put together. I really loved the snorkeling. I don't know why I don't have an aquarium at home as much as I love the ocean. That's the first thing on my agenda when I get back to the States.

I will need an extra suitcase to fit all of the things I just bought. Tonight I'm going to the fiesta in the hotel. I don't know what to wear. I like this light blue floral wrap. I wonder if I have some shoes that will go with it, or I can just wear my sandals.

Rose took a quick shower to freshen up. She coordinated her outfit with some jewelry she had purchased and found a pair of black sandals that matched the outline of the floral wrap. She took a final look in the mirror. "This will have to do." She touched her ears. "I love these big colorful earrings." She grabbed her hotel key and placed it in her bra and walked out the door.

The party was in full swing when she got downstairs. Everybody was drinking and laughing and dancing wherever they stood. While she danced, somebody came behind her singing. "Hey, pretty lady."

She turned around to the familiar voice. "John. What are you doing here?"

She gave him a tight hug. "We're filming in a town up the road there. I heard about the fiesta, so I decided to stop by and get my party on. What are you doing here?"

"I came down for a week vacation and I have seen so many people from LA here. But everybody has pretty much kept to themselves."

"Cool. So you want to hang out with me and my crew or are you enjoying your solo act?"

She danced around him. "I guess you can hang with me."

John laughed and they continued dancing off the song. John made introductions to the rest of the production staff; although they knew who Rose was, she hadn't worked with this crew before. Her drink was never low and she danced to almost every song.

Rose got out breath. "Whew. I think I'm going to sit out on the next couple of songs."

She found her a chair and flopped down. She bent over to put her sandal strap back around her ankle, and when she sat up she was looking directly at the man who had been on the balcony. A slow song was on and he was all over the woman she had seen him with earlier. She rushed over to where John was standing and grabbed his hand and led him to the dance floor. "John, I need you to do me a favor. Dance with me. I see somebody I know, but I have to make sure it's him, before I say something to him."

"Oh, you're trying to make one of your old boyfriends jealous? Well, use me."

She wrapped her arm around his neck and they danced

and slowly moved toward the man. "No. It's not even like that. I think I see someone's man."

"What? Don't tell me there's going to be some drama tonight."

"Let's hope not," she said as they danced and swirled until they got right near the couple.

She purposely bumped into them, so he would have to look her way. "Excuse me."

Marcus's face showed a shocked expression. "Violet, what are you doing here?"

"I could ask you the same thing, and who is this woman?"

Marcus stuttered. "You're not Violet. Rose?"

Rose stepped in between him and the woman he was dancing with. "Who else would it be? How dare you cheat on my sister!"

The woman walked from behind Rose and looped her arm through Marcus's arm. "Marcus, who is this and what is she yelling about?"

Still stuttering, Marcus responded, "This is Rose. You know—the actress."

Rose interrupted him. "I am his girlfriend's sister and who are you?"

The woman looked at Rose as if she was ready to fight. "Look Rose, I don't care how many movies or CDs you have out. Marcus is my man and for you to go through all these dramatics is not even necessary."

"Look here, wench. This is between Marcus and me."

John stepped between them both because he could tell that blows were not far behind. "Rose, maybe we should leave now. He knows he's been busted."

Marcus tried to pacify both women. "Yes. Let's table it for now and we can talk about this later."

Rose turned around. "Marcus, I have John's phone right here. All I have to do is dial a number. I want you to explain to her what you are doing here with another woman. You told her you were going to your parents'. Now she might look old, but she ain't quite old enough to be your momma."

The woman took her shoes off and was about to haul off and hit Rose, when Marcus intervened. "Rose, please don't tell Violet."

The woman then took one of the shoes and hit him with it and turned to walk away. "What do you mean don't tell Violet, Violet or whatever you said? You sorry son of a . . ." She continued out the door.

Marcus tried to go after her, but Rose grabbed his arm. "No, mister. You're not going anywhere. I should have known you were trifling and I could have saved my sister much grief."

"You're not going to tell her about this, are you?"

"What do you think?"

"She never has to know. I promise, I will stop seeing Marie. You know I really care about your sister."

Rose started singing, "Heard it all before."

He interrupted her. "I'm serious. Promise me you won't tell her."

"I'm not promising you anything. If it wasn't so late, I would go call her right now."

Rose was about to walk away, when she heard him say, "If you do, I'll tell her you made a pass at me."

She spun around and headed back in his direction. "Come again?"

Marcus had a smug look on his face. "I think you heard me. Now we wouldn't want that, since you guys have made some progress."

Although she was five-feet-ten inches, he still towered over her, but it didn't stop her from getting as close to his face as she could. "I don't take to threats too kindly."

"It's not a threat. It's a promise. If you say anything, I will tell her how you got drunk and tried to seduce me. Simple as that."

John could tell Rose was getting in deeper and deeper. "Come on, girl. Maybe we should just leave."

Marcus agreed. "Yes. Remember, Violet never has to know and we'll all walk away happy."

Rose stormed off the dance floor, with John close behind her. "John, I could kill him. He's cheating on my sister and now I can't say anything because if I do, he's going to lie on me and claim I made a pass."

John placed his arms around her shoulders. "If you like, I can be there with you when you tell her. I normally wouldn't get involved in other people's drama, but if you care about your sister, you must tell her."

Rose leaned on John and cried. "We're getting close again and what if she doesn't believe me?"

John wrapped his arm around her and offered her some advice. "I really don't know what all is going on with you and your sister, but I'm sure it'll all work out. Just ask yourself one question. If she eventually finds out you knew about this, what do you think she's going to say or feel?"

As John walked her to the elevator, she responded, "I don't know. I honestly don't know."

"Sleep on it. Don't make a decision tonight. Do you need me to come up to your room with you?"

"As fine as you are John, I think I'll pass this time."

John chuckled. "All right, now that's the Rose I know." They hugged and as the elevator door closed, she waved good-bye and blew John a kiss.

Although she had plenty to drink, she ordered another margarita and a hamburger from room service. After she ate, she sat on the couch in her suite and flipped through the channels on the television.

No luck in finding anything that caught her attention, she turned it off, grabbed a blanket and went and sat in the long patio chair on her balcony.

*   *   *

Just when things were looking good for Violet and me, this happens. I could kill that lying bastard for what he's doing to my sister, to me. I know he's not going to stop seeing that woman. They never do. She'll believe whatever wild story he comes up with and then he'll still be juggling my sister and her. There has got to be a way.

She continued going back and forth in her mind with the pros and cons of telling Violet. She came to the conclusion that she would have to let Violet find out what type of man she was dealing with on her own. It didn't feel right, but she couldn't think of any alternatives.

Chapter 27
VIOLET

Yawning, Violet got out of her car and tried to shake the feeling that her Monday wasn't going to be good. The first thing she encountered when she got to her office were messages from several board members concerned about the center's activities. After she returned the first call, she was informed of an emergency meeting being held that night and she was asked to be in attendance. The previous night, she stayed up trying to figure out who could have stolen the funds and why.

What am I going to do? I have no clue where that money is. At this point, I don't know who I can trust. I know it wasn't Janice. At least I hope not. Look at me; I even doubt my best friend. It must be the stress. Okay. It's not me. It's not Janice, so it only leaves one other person. It's going to be hard to show I didn't take it, but if I can find out how to prove he did it, then and only then, can I clear my name.

* * *

She leaned back in her chair and rubbed her temple. She sat up when she heard the sound of Janice entering. Janice closed the door. "I guess you've heard about the emergency board meeting tonight."

"Yes. I was coming to check on you. You know we're in this together." Janice took a seat as she responded.

"Yes. I was sitting here thinking about it. We both will be under the firing squad, me more so than you, but you're the assistant director, so they'll be looking at us both."

Janice balled up her fist. "I'm pissed. All of the time and effort we've both invested and these snotty nose folks are going to accuse us of embezzlement."

Violet reached over the desk and squeezed Janice's hand. "What we need to do is prove that Carlton took the funds and our minds need to be clear, so try to control the anger."

"I don't know how you do it. You're going to be officially accused tonight of doing something with the funds, but yet you sit here asking me not to be angry." Janice shook her head.

Violet leaned back with a solemn look on her face. "Trust me. I'm livid right now. It's just that I can't let what he's done ruin what I've tried to do for the kids, for the community. These people have trusted me and I will do whatever I have to, to clear my name. I can't be consumed with anger. It'll only deter me from finding out how to prove I'm not guilty."

"I hear you, but I'm not as good at hiding my emotions as you are, and don't forget we're both in the hot seat, not just you."

"I thought about that last night and we need to have a strategy going into this meeting."

While they were brainstorming, Violet's cell phone rang. "Hello."

She heard what sounded like planes in the background. "Hi. I'm back in town and I wanted to see what you were doing tonight, so I could drop off the gifts I bought you and tell you about my trip."

"Rose. Welcome back. I'll have to call you later. I have a lot of things going on right now, so I don't know when that'll be."

Rose sounded disappointed. "What's going on? Is there anything I can do to help?"

"No. Unfortunately I have to take care of this myself, but thanks for asking."

"I'll send my assistant to your office or to your home later on tonight. I have some things I need to catch up on anyway from being gone for a week."

Violet tried to rush her off the phone, so she could deal with her problem. "Sure. Either one works for me. We'll talk later. I have to go now. Talk to you soon."

Violet took a sip from her cold coffee. "Eww. That's nasty."

"So the drama queen is back in town?"

Violet chuckled. "Now Janice. Be nice. That is my sister you're talking about."

"Okay, I will. I'm glad you guys are working through your differences."

Violet smiled for the first time in days. "I am too. It's been a big relief."

They finished going over their plans for that night's meeting. They worked way past lunch and weren't aware of the time, until Rose's assistant showed up. Janice left to go get them something to eat. While waiting on Janice to return, Violet opened up her gifts.

She placed a call to Rose. "Hi. I wanted to let you know I got the gifts. Thank you."

"You're quite welcome. I was hoping you would like them."

"These figurines will go perfectly in my collection and I love those bracelets. My favorite one is the silver one."

"You're talking about the one that has a heart-shaped face with the turquoise stone surrounded by little diamonds?"

"Exactly. I have the perfect outfit to wear it with."

"I'm glad you like your gifts and I hope we can get together later on this week to catch up."

Janice walked back in with their lunch, so Violet ended their call. "I'll call you later and we'll set something up."

On full stomachs they were able to concentrate more and devised a strategy for exposing Carlton, the real culprit in the entire mess. The first phase of their plan would be made at that night's board meeting.

Chapter 28
ROSE

I'm glad to be back in the States. I enjoyed my trip up until that run in with Marcus. I still can't believe he's such a snake in the grass and had the nerve to threaten me—Queen Rose. A part of me is glad Violet was too busy to see me. I don't know how I'll be able to face her knowing what I do. She deserves a whole lot better than trash like him.

Her phone rang. "Hello."

"Rose. This is Carmen. I'm glad to hear you're back. Are you ready to start going on tour?"

"No. I mean yes."

Carmen gritted her teeth. "Now, we talked about this before you left to go on vacation. People want to see you perform and I have the perfect concert tour lined up. You won't be the headliner, but it will satisfy your fans' need to see you."

"What do you mean, I won't be the headliner?"

"Rose, dear. You only have one CD out and you're good, but promoters want to see a profit, so they have to have a good headliner. An artist that's more established, you understand me now?"

"I guess. I'll only do it because you've put up with me for so long."

Carmen let out a sigh of relief. "Good. I will fax over the papers in a few minutes. Call me if you have any questions."

Rose hung up with Carmen and turned the fax machine on. After reviewing the papers, she signed them and faxed them back to her.

She unpacked everything and was now ready to relax. It was hard for her to relax, because she kept playing the whole scene with Marcus over and over in her head. She decided to make herself an apple martini to ease her mind. Nothing she did would erase the fact that she was caught in the middle and didn't know which way to go.

The last few months of having Violet back in her life as not only a sister, but as a friend, brought joy to her heart. She wouldn't admit it to anyone, but she had led a lonely adult life. Her attempts at making friends always resulted in one of two things. Some of the women would be too competitive or accuse her of trying to steal their men's attention. If it was a man she was trying to befriend, he would make a pass, so she basically became a loner. She made sure she kept good working relationships with the other actors and crew members on the movie sets she worked on. She would socialize with everyone, but didn't let anyone too close to her. Her agent, Carmen, was the only other friend she had besides Violet.

I can't let this man ruin our relationship. I have to think of something to do. I'll set it up so that she finds out, but not from me. I'll teach him not to mess with the Purdue sisters.

* * *

Rose was heavy in thought trying to think of a way to expose Marcus, when her doorbell rang. Since her assistant was given the afternoon off, she got up to answer. She could see the imprint of the man through her stained side-glass window. She swung the door open. "What the hell are you doing here?"

"You can either let me in or we can discuss this out here."

Rose moved out of the way and motioned for him to enter. "You're not welcome here. So please tell me what this visit is all about."

He leaned down and attempted to kiss her on the forehead, but she put her hand up, which blocked the kiss. "Dear, you don't have to be rude. I wanted to make sure we were on the same page. You slipped away before I could confirm."

Rose didn't move. She lifted her hand and shook her finger in the air. "Marcus. It's like this. We both know your little game. I have to admit you're good, but there is no way I'm going to allow you or anyone else to come in between me and my sister again."

He smiled. "So that means you're going to keep your mouth shut, right?"

"What that means is, you need to break it off with my sister."

The smile left his face. "I can't and won't do that, because I care for your sister."

Rose leaned her head back and let out a strange laugh. "You what? Let's break this down once more. You lie to her and tell her you're spending time with your parents. You take another woman on a rendezvous to another country. You then threaten to ruin her relationship with her sister and you want to call that caring. Please!"

Marcus leaned in closer to her as if to make sure she understood where he stood on the subject. "Look here. I care about your sister and if you don't interfere, I will be marrying your sister."

Rose got as close to his face as she could, since he towered over her by eight inches. "I can't believe what I'm hearing. You are full of crap. I'm not going to allow you to ruin her life."

"I have no plans to ruin her life. What she doesn't know won't hurt her. You just keep your mouth shut and things will work themselves out."

Rose got silent, because she was on the brink of losing her composure and she had to bide her time before exposing Marcus. She didn't want to take the chance of him following through on his threat of lying about her making a pass at him.

"This is what I can do for you, Marcus, and after this I can't make any promises. I won't say anything about what I saw in Mexico for now; however, if I even hear a rumor that you are messing with another woman, all bets are off. I will tell Violet everything that I know. Understood?"

Marcus turned to walk toward the door, with a look of satisfaction on his face. "Understood. Like I said. I just wanted to make sure we were on the same page."

He walked out the door and Rose let off steam by slamming the door behind him. She slammed the door so hard, one of her pictures fell from the wall. She got the broom and cleaned up the glass. She went and sat on the bottom step of her stairway. She was mentally exhausted, so she put her head on her lap hoping that her migraine would disappear.

Chapter 29
VIOLET

Violet and Janice sat at the end of the table and listened to all of the accusations brought forth by the board. Violet was determined to hold her head up high, because she knew she didn't do anything wrong, but she was surprised that even some of her diehard supporters were saying disgusting things about how she had run the community center.

Janice looked over and gave her a reassuring look. They both scanned the room for abnormal behavior from Carlton. Violet saw that Carlton had a smug look on his face and thus far, he was one of the few members who hadn't said anything negative about the whole situation. After everyone spoke, Violet was given the floor.

Violet stood up, so she could see everyone's expressions. The chairman stated, "Violet, you can sit if you like."

"No, I would rather stand."

"As you wish."

She surveyed their faces one last time and began to go over what she and Janice rehearsed earlier. As she ended her speech, she felt better. "In conclusion, I would like to think that the board is fair and will look at my recommendation for hiring an investigator. Yes, after carefully going over all of the records, including that of the auditors, it is true that some funds are missing; however, neither Janice nor I know where the funds are or who has taken them. We haven't done anything to abuse the trust you or the community has placed in us. We will do our best to work with any investigator of your choice to ensure whoever is responsible will be discovered and dealt with accordingly. Thank you all for giving me the floor."

Janice gave her a look that confirmed she did okay. She walked back and took her seat and the chairman took over from there. "Thank you both for coming. You can be excused for now. Either the cochairman or I will call you some time tonight, to let you know what we have decided. The rest of us will take a fifteen minute break before concluding the meeting."

As they got ready to leave the meeting, Carlton ran up behind them. "Ladies. You've done an excellent job of running the center. You can be assured that I will do whatever I can to make sure the board is fair."

Violet reached over to shake his hand. "Thank you, Carlton. We know we can count on you."

They continued walking to Janice's car. They didn't say a word until they were on the road back toward Violet's house. "Can you believe the nerve of that man?"

Janice tried to suppress from cussing because of the heavy traffic. "After finding out what we know, nothing surprises me anymore."

"As soon as I get home, I'm taking me a long hot bath. I refuse to pace the floor waiting on the board to call me."

"I know. It was intense in there for a moment. You were very impressive with your speech. It sounded impromptu, yet convincing."

"Thanks. I couldn't have done it without your help."

Janice pulled up in front of her house. "I feel they will agree to the investigator."

"I hope so."

Janice gave her friend a reassuring hand tug and stayed in the driveway until she entered her house.

Violet heard Janice pull off and headed directly to her dresser drawer to find something relaxing to put on after her bath.

This has been a very long day. I didn't think it would ever end. I have never had to go through anything remotely like this. I have to clear my name, because I don't know how this is going to affect the kids or other center participants. I have worked too hard to get funding for various programs and I can see the positive results. I don't want to lose their trust or respect and I don't want donors feeling vulnerable either.

Violet sat in the bathtub and relaxed to the smooth sounds of jazz. Her phone rang, bringing her out of a sedated state. She reached for the phone that she had placed on the towel next to the tub. "Hello."

"Violet. How I've wished to hear the sound of your voice."

She sat straight up in the tub. "Who is this?"

"It's me."

"David. I've told you to stop calling me. There is nothing we have to say to one another. Why can't you get it through your thick skull? We've been divorced for how long now?"

David responded in a calm voice. "I know how you feel, but I can't give up on us."

Violet let out all of the built-up anger from the past seventy-two hours. "Us? There is no us! There has not been an us in a very long time."

David got silent.

Violet continued, "I have to go. I'm expecting a very important phone call."

"I won't give up."

Violet slammed the phone down and at that point, she was no longer relaxed. She decided to go ahead and get out of the tub. After dressing in her satin pajamas, she went and ate some leftovers she had from lunch.

She took the last bite of her meal. This time when the phone rang, she looked at the caller ID and picked up the phone when she saw it was the chairman. "Hello."

"Violet, I'm glad we caught you still up. Sorry it has taken us this long to get back to you."

"No problem. I was sitting here eating a late dinner."

He cleared his throat. "I guess I should get straight to the point. We have decided to go with your recommendation and hire an investigator."

Violet remained silent, because she felt a "but" coming on.

"We also have decided it is probably best that you take a leave of absence while this investigation is being conducted."

"But sir, how will things get done? Janice and I both can't be out; no one else knows how to run the center."

"We've thought of that, too. Janice can stay on and take over things until the investigation is over. We're sure you understand why we made our decision, right?"

Violet held back tears of frustration. "Sure. I understand. Let me know when I can return to work."

She was about to end the call, when she heard him say, "The investigator will be in touch. We ask for your full co-operation and I'm sure this will be resolved soon and you can get back to work. Look at this as a mini-vacation."

"Thanks."

She hung up and screamed. "Vacation. The nerve of them."

She got up and went to her den and found a comedy movie and placed it in the DVD player. She needed a good laugh, just to keep from crying. As she placed the movie in the player, her doorbell rang.

She looked at the time and knew she wasn't expecting

anyone. She got up and looked out of the peephole, and to her surprise it was Marcus.

She unlocked the door and welcomed him into open arms. He kissed her passionately. "Oh my precious Violet. I've missed you so much."

She led him into the den. "I've missed you too. I didn't expect you back. Why didn't you tell me you were coming back today?"

He swooped her in his arms again. "I wanted to surprise you."

"A nice surprise it is."

They made up for being separated for the past two weeks. Violet took his hand and he followed her to the bedroom and they made love throughout the entire night.

Chapter 30
ROSE

Rose woke up with a nerve-racking headache she couldn't get rid of. She didn't realize until the previous night that she had run out of her medicine. She called her assistant and told her to stop by the pharmacist on her way over that morning.

While Rose waited on her assistant to come with her medicine, she decided to call Violet so they could make plans to get together for lunch or dinner soon. Violet answered after the fifth ring. "Violet, I was trying to catch you before you left for the office."

Violet sounded as if she was just waking up. "I'm not going into the office today."

"Really? So you've decided to do what I suggested?"

"I wish it were that simple. I'll have to tell you about it later."

Rose, trying not to be impatient, said, "I have time. You can tell me now or do you want to meet for lunch later on today?"

"Let's just say that now is not a good time." Violet sounded distracted. "I'm a little preoccupied, but lunch sounds good. Why don't you come over, say, around one? I'll cook us up something really nice."

Rose heard what sounded like someone kissing Violet. "One will be fine. I'll bring the dessert. Bye."

As Violet was hanging up, Rose heard her giggle and then the phone disconnected.

That scoundrel is over there in bed with my sister. I have to come up with a way to expose him without incriminating myself and from the way things are looking, I need to do it as soon as possible.

Rose spent the rest of the morning going over her itinerary for the upcoming weeks. She worked with her assistant to get her wardrobe together. She also talked to Carmen and confirmed flights and hotel accommodations. Although she was paying them both well to help keep her on schedule, she tried to make sure she knew what was supposed to happen and when.

Rose pulled into Violet's driveway at exactly one o'clock. She was relieved to see that Marcus was not there. She gathered up the dessert and rang the doorbell. Violet met her at the door with a tight sisterly hug. "Welcome back."

"Thank you," Rose said as she held out the bag in her hand. "Look. I brought your favorite."

Violet took the bag and placed the contents on her dining room table. They each took a seat and Violet said the grace. "Thank you Father for bringing my sister safely back to us. Thank you for showing us mercy and grace. Thank you for allowing us to fellowship with one another once again. God Bless this food that we are about to eat. Let it nourish us, as we allow you to nourish our souls. Amen."

Rose looked up teary eyed. "Amen."

They had light conversation while they enjoyed the turkey-ham sandwiches that Violet prepared. She also made some seafood pasta salad that was scrumptious. By the time it came to dessert they were both full, but each decided to indulge in a slice of the lemon meringue pie anyway.

Violet was the first to get up. She grabbed some of the dishes to take to the kitchen. Rose got up to assist her. "Violet, why don't you let me help you with that?"

"No. Sit. It'll only take a minute for me to put these in the dishwasher."

Rose didn't hesitate to say, "Okay."

While she was putting the dishes away, Rose wandered into her living room and admired the figurines she had purchased for her. She noticed Violet had placed them on her mantel and for some reason that brought a smile to her face.

Violet walked in the room. "What are you smiling at?"

Rose placed the figurine back down on the mantel and went and sat on the couch. "Just thinking about the past few months and how I've enjoyed getting to know you as a friend. You are a remarkable woman."

Violet followed and sat on the opposite end of the couch and crossed her legs up under her. "Thank you. I really needed to hear that."

Rose turned to face her. "What's going on? I didn't want to bring it up over lunch, but you seemed a little preoccupied. Is it Marcus?"

"Oh, no. What would give you that idea?"

"I was just checking. I know how some men are. If it's not him, then what?"

"It's the job. I guess I should tell you, just in case you get a distorted version."

Rose sat with a curious look on her face. "Is that why you're not at the office today?"

"Yes. I guess I should start at the beginning." Violet told her everything she knew up until that point.

"Are you sure you can trust their investigator? I can hire another investigator if you like."

"I don't think that'll be necessary, but thanks for the offer."

The conversation shifted as Rose told her everything about what happened in Mexico, with one exception; she left out the encounter with Marcus. Rose's cell phone rang. "Excuse me, Violet, I have to get this. Hello."

Carmen sounded antsy. "Rose, we need to talk. Do you have a minute?"

"I will call you back in a few minutes." She hung the phone up and made her excuses to Violet. She gathered her things and said her good-byes. "Now don't let me have to track you down for that seafood pasta salad recipe."

Violet laughed. "I won't. Just promise me, you'll make me another pie."

"For you sister, I will do anything." Rose hugged her and rushed to her car.

As soon as Rose pulled out of the driveway, she returned Carmen's call. "I'm back."

"Are you sitting down or driving?"

"I'm driving, why?"

"Just say that I warned you. Someone let it slip to me, that they have some photographs of you while you were in Mexico."

Rose weaved in and out of traffic while continuing to talk. "So what? They caught me in a skimpy bikini; what's the big deal?"

"I haven't seen the pictures, so I don't know what the big deal is. I do know they were sold to one of the tabloids and apparently there is a juicy story going right along with it. I'm telling you because the source wanted me to be on the lookout for the next issue."

Rose pressed the OFF button on her phone and said out loud, "What now?"

Chapter 31
VIOLET

This past week has been a week from hell. The only good thing about all of this mess is that the media has stuck with the facts and didn't add any unnecessary opinions. Marcus has been there for me to lean on and it's been comforting to have him by my side. Rose has been my sounding board and hasn't complained once. I guess something good has come out of all of this mess.

"Violet. Are you in the back?"

Violet heard Janice call out her name. She was in her backyard, pulling up weeds. She yelled for her to come around. "I'm back here. The gate is open."

Janice pushed the gate open and walked over to where Violet was kneeling. "I tell you. You and your plants. You ain't going to worry me. I hired me a landscaping company to take care of all my needs."

Violet was sweating and before the sweat could drip in her eyes, she wiped her brow with the back of her arm. "I told you, I could teach you what you needed to know."

"I'll pass on that lesson. When you finish up, why don't we go in, so I can give you the latest and greatest."

"Just give me a minute. You can go through the patio door if you like and make yourself at home. I have some chicken salad I made earlier in the refrigerator."

Janice rubbed her stomach. "Now that sounds tasty, because I haven't eaten all day. Take your time. You know where to find me."

Violet finished pulling up the weeds in her flowerbed. She slipped upstairs so she could take a quick shower. She found Janice lounging in the den. Janice blurted out as she walked in the room, "I didn't know you were into the ol' school like this."

"Thought you knew. I'm an ol' school junkie. I have everybody's collection down there." Violet started to do some old dances like the prep. They both laughed.

Janice stopped laughing. "Well, Ms. Thang. I know you probably have things to do with your boy, so let me tell you what's been going on."

"Girl, Marcus and I are taking a break today. He told me one of his buddies was flying in tonight, so I gave him the okay to hang with his friends."

Janice took a seat on the ottoman. "I love this. I could fall asleep right here."

"You better wake your behind up and tell me what's going on."

With a fake yawn, she proceeded to tell Violet about what the investigator had discovered. "You and I will both be cleared of any wrongdoing very soon. The investigator gave his report to the chairman and right now the chairman is not sharing the information with the rest of the board. Some of the board members are mad, because they feel like they should have the information as soon as he got it. The chairman, on the other hand, says when he gets the final report he will then let the investigator present everything to the board."

Violet looked up in disbelief with all of the information

she was getting. "Okay. One question. Inspector Gadget, how did you find all of this out?"

Janice swayed to an old Lakeside tune. "Let's just say me and the investigator have something in common."

"And what's that?"

"We both like the way I work it."

Violet laughed. "Girl, you don't have any sense. Don't tell me you're doing it with the detective?"

"No, girl. I wouldn't jeopardize the investigation. I just do a little flirting and he volunteers information."

"Okay. That's what your mouth says."

"I'm serious. Our birthdays are both on the same day and the same year. You know kindred spirits."

Violet shook her head. "You are something else. I'll buy that."

"Speaking of birthdays, are you prepared for your birthday bash?"

"To be honest, I had forgotten all about it. I thought you and Rose were taking care of all of that."

"We are, and I have to admit the drama queen has been accommodating to some of my suggestions."

"One day you'll be talking to her and let her private nickname slip out."

Janice rolled her eyes at her. "Whatever. Just make sure you and Marcus are there on time."

"We will be, because I'm really looking forward to this party at Rose's."

They continued to talk for another hour and then Janice left for home. Violet decided to call Marcus, although she thought he would have called her by now. "Hi, baby."

Marcus sounded preoccupied. "Hey, you."

Violet thought she was just tired and she didn't hear agitation in his voice, so she responded, "Are you guys busy?"

"We went straight from the airport to dinner and we're getting situated now."

"I'm not going to hold you. Just wanted to tell you good night and to let you know I was thinking about you."

"Me too. Good night."

That's strange. I could have sworn he was acting funny. It's as if he was rushing me off the phone. I know what it is. I'm just stressed and tired. I haven't been able to get a good night's rest since this investigation started and now I'm trying to make problems elsewhere. Where are those sleeping pills that Rose gave me? I need to get at least one full night of rest.

Chapter 32

ROSE

"Happy birthday, sleepyhead."

"Mom. I wasn't asleep. I was resting my eyes."

"Sure. Tell me anything. Hold on, while I call your sister."

"Yes, Mom." Rose got out of the bed and pushed the speaker button on her phone. She ran to the bathroom to wash her face and while there she also ran some water in the tub.

"Rose, you there? Violet, you there?"

"I'm here. Happy Birthday, Rose."

Rose sang, "Happy Birthday back at you."

"I wanted to tell you both how much I love you and although I can't be there for your birthday celebration, you will both be in my thoughts."

While she listened to her Mom and Violet talk, she soaked in the tub.

Their mom stopped talking to Violet and said, "Baby girl, you're awfully quiet."

Violet chimed in and said, "Yes, Rose, I haven't heard you this quiet in years."

Rose laughed. "Don't even start. I was just thinking how

great it is to have you both in my life. You both mean the world to me and I care about you guys very much."

Her mom sniffled. "I love you, baby."

Violet also sniffled. "I care about you too."

Violet's phone clicked and she placed them on hold.

Rose continued talking to her Mom and as they were getting ready to end their call, Violet clicked back over. Rose commented, "We were beginning to wonder what happened to you."

"Since I have you both on the phone, I got some good news from Janice about the investigation."

Rose, at this point, was drying off from her long bath. "What gives? Don't keep us in suspense."

Violet recanted what she had found out from Janice. "It looks like I'll be back to work soon, but because they are now trying to gather enough evidence on Carlton, they have to make it look like I'm still a suspect."

Their mom sounded joyful. "Thank you, Jesus. I told you, there's nothing the Lord won't do, if you ask and believe."

"Yes, Momma, you did."

Rose's other line clicked. "Ladies, I hate to end our lovely conversation, but my other line is beeping for the tenth time, so I guess I better get it."

They ended their conversation and Rose clicked over to the other line. "Hello."

She heard a husky voice on the other end, singing the birthday song. "And many moreeee."

"Thank you, John. When did you get back to the States?"

"We rolled in on the midnight flight and I was about to crash. I couldn't forget your birthday, kid."

"I take it you got my invitation in the mail."

John tapped on the phone. "What? I think we have a bad connection."

Rose laughed. "You heard me. I see you'll never change."

"If I did, you wouldn't know what to do with me, would you?"

"Do I have a choice?" Rose asked as she pulled her shirt over her head.

"You always have a choice. By the way, did you get your problem resolved?"

Rose stuttered, "Well, uhh . . . Not exactly, but, oh well. I decided not to say anything."

"Okay. I still think you should have told her and let her deal with it."

"Whose birthday is it again?"

"I can catch a hint. I'll lighten up. See you tonight." John jokingly said, "Wear something sexy for me, now."

"Bye!"

After she hung up with John, she called her personal assistant to come upstairs. When she got upstairs, she asked her a couple of questions. "Are you sure everybody will be here at the times specified?"

"Yes, Rose. I've called and confirmed with everyone again this morning. Calm down. I got everything covered."

Rose was getting annoyed. "I am calm. Just make sure everything is set up. This is a special night for me and my sister and I want everything to be perfect."

"It will be." Her assistant turned around to walk out the door and mumbled under her breath, "If you only knew how perfect."

"Excuse me. Did you say something?"

"I was just saying that it would be perfect."

Rose didn't look up. She was too busy reading her birthday cards. "Just make sure it is. When the masseur comes, send him upstairs."

"Yes, ma'am." Her assistant then closed the door.

Shortly thereafter, someone knocked on the door. "Who is it?"

"It's Ramone."

"Come in."

"Happy Birthday, Mademoiselle."

"Thank you. I want the works."

After her massage, she had someone come in to give her a manicure, pedicure, and facial. She also had Nina, her hairdresser, and Trish, her make-up artist, over to do her hair and make-up. This was a day of pampering and she had also paid for the same services for Violet. She hoped Violet enjoyed her birthday present.

Chapter 33
VIOLET

My mom sounded so happy on the phone this morning and that started my day off right. This has been one of the best birthdays ever. First Rose surprised me with a morning of pampering, and now I'm waiting on Marcus to pick me up for a late lunch. He's been such a sweetheart and our relationship has been drama-free. I'm actually looking forward to our birthday bash over at Rose's tonight.

Violet buttoned her blouse and stopped in front of the mirror to confirm her overall appearance looked okay. She did a double take in the mirror because she looked more like Rose than herself. The long flowing curls looked elegant and the make-up applied was flawless. She was given some make-up samples to touch up with later on that night.

She heard the doorbell and knew from the clock chime that it was Marcus, so she grabbed her purse and headed toward the door.

When she opened the door, she was faced with a big bouquet of red roses. Marcus leaned down and kissed her. "These are for you, my beautiful Violet."

Violet took the roses and placed them in a vase she had on her table located by the stairway. "These will go perfect right here. Thanks, baby."

"Only the best for you. Our chariot awaits."

Marcus led her outside and she was greeted with the sight of a long, stretch, white limousine, instead of one of Marcus's cars. "Marcus, you didn't?"

As the limousine driver pulled away from her house, Violet reached up and placed her hand behind Marcus's head and gave him a big juicy wet kiss. He responded, "Mmm. What was that for?"

She took her fingers and wiped the lipstick from his mouth. "That's for being there for me throughout this whole ordeal at the center and for treating me like a queen."

He took her hand, touched her chin, tilted her face up, and looked down into her eyes. "You are my queen and don't you ever forget it."

Their lips locked and they spent the rest of the ride enjoying each other's kisses.

When they arrived at their destination, Violet was surprised to see that her favorite Italian restaurant had closed its doors to other patrons for two hours just for her. "You are full of surprises today."

As they dined on her favorite Italian cuisine, and drank a bottle of her favorite wine, her favorite singing group, Jaded, serenaded her. They sang one of their famous ballads. *"This is just the beginning of what to expect from me. As long as we are together, you will get the best of me."*

Violet's eyes had a glazed look as she glanced over at Marcus. "You don't have to worry about me going anywhere."

Marcus took her hand and although there wasn't an official dance floor, they danced to the smooth ballads being sung. Afterward, Jaded all wished Violet a happy birthday.

Marcus walked them to the door and handed their manager a white envelope. He returned to the table and although he had already paid for the meal and the romantic setup, he left a generous tip. "Baby, I think we should be going. I don't want to tire you out before tonight's party."

"I'm far from being tired. I can't remember a time where I was more relaxed. First this morning's pampering and now this lovely lunch. I feel like I'm on cloud nine. Could this day get any better?"

They sat in silence on the limousine ride back to her place. Violet rested her head on his chest as he played with the curls in her hair. "You know, I like your hair like this. It's fun to play in."

She smiled. "You would say something like that."

"It's true. I love playing in your hair. I better stop, before I have the driver take the long way home."

"Oh, no mister. Maybe later on tonight, but I can't do anything to mess up my hair. If I had to spend over an hour under the dryer, you are not going to mess it up."

He leaned over and kissed her on the forehead. "Ten hours from now, you're not going to care about your hair being messed up. All you'll be saying is 'big daddy, don't stop'."

She playfully tapped him. "Whatever."

They spent the rest of the time enjoying each other's presence.

He walked her to the door and decided to end their date for now. "I hope I was able to make your day a special one."

"Yes, you have. Thank you. I've really enjoyed everything."

"I'm glad. Let me go before I change my mind. I'll pick you up around eight tonight."

"I can meet you over there if you like."

He looked at her. "Now, you know I'm not going to have my woman driving herself anywhere on her birthday. Actually, the limousine driver will be at your disposal for the entire weekend."

He reached into his pocket and gave her a card.

"Marcus, you don't have to do this. Thanks."

He interrupted her. "You're welcome. No, you can't give the gift back. Bye, love."

She gave him a tight hug and watched him walk back toward the limousine. She waved as he turned around to blow her a kiss.

Chapter 34
ROSE

Rose held her stomach in, while her assistant attempted to zip up her short, tight, silver sequin dress. "I know I should have had him adjust the dress, but no, he said, it's supposed to fit this way."

Her assistant had a skeptical look on her face. "You look great. It's as if the dress was made perfectly for your figure."

Rose looked in the mirror sideways and then turned around and tried to see how it looked from the rear view. "Yes. I guess you're right. The fabric does allow me breathing room." She attempted to bend her legs. "I can even sit down, without busting a seam."

"If there is nothing else, I'll let you finish getting ready."

"No. There's nothing else. Just make sure the guests are taken care of, in case they start coming before I can make it down."

Rose touched up her make-up and put on her signature spiked heels. She took a final look in the mirror and admired her total ensemble. "Looking good, girl. I love these curls. Nina, outdid herself today."

She received a phone call from Janice. "Rose. Just wanted

to let you know that we're stuck in a traffic jam on I-110. The driver still has to go pick up Violet. Marcus is supposed to be waiting for us there. We'll be at the party as soon as we can. I told you I was going to make sure she got there and that's a promise."

"Cool. I'm glad you called. I'll look for you guys in about an hour."

"See you later. We'll be there."

Rose stayed in her room as long as she could and after an hour passed, she decided it was time for her to make her entrance. If she weren't hosting the party at her house, she would have shown up later. When she made it downstairs, she was bombarded with birthday wishes from her guests. She was enjoying the attention and thanked everyone for coming. She noticed that the other guest of honor hadn't made it there yet.

The party was growing and it looked like it was going to be a success. She had invited a small group of people, but didn't mind the big turnout. She periodically watched the door for signs of Violet. While her attention was diverted at the door, someone walked up to her from behind and scooped her in his arms.

"Happy birthday, birthday girl."

She recognized the voice and eventually was able to get out of his grip and turned around. "Lance. What are you doing here?"

With his playboy smile, Lance said, "You know I wasn't going to let your birthday go by without acknowledging it."

She frowned. "A simple phone call would have worked."

"Well maybe you'll change your mind when you open up your present."

"I doubt it. Now, excuse me. I have other guests to attend to."

He bowed and watched her as she left to greet other guests.

She continued to have small talk and when someone

placed two hands around her eyes, she knew immediately who it was. "Violet, you made it." They hugged as onlookers watched.

"Yes. Sorry we're late, but you know how LA traffic is."

"I know, sweetie. Now that you're here, we can serve dinner. Most of the guests are probably full on the hors d'oeuvres from the look of their plates."

Violet laughed. "Let's eat before there's nothing left; even though I ate lunch, I'm starved."

Rose looked Violet up and down. "You look marvelous. That violet looks great on you. I could swear I'm looking at a reflection of myself."

"Thank you. The dress was a gift from Marcus."

Rose faked enthusiasm. "Where is Marcus by the way?"

"Marcus is here somewhere. I left all of them over near the front talking to what's his name. You know—the one in the new comedy action flick."

"George T."

"Yes, that's him."

"Oh, they'll be there a while. He is so funny, and you hate to leave while he's telling one of his jokes. Let's go eat."

They looped their arms around each other and headed toward the dining room. Rose's personal assistant came out to inform everyone that dinner was being served. The people who had reserved seating sat in the official dining room and everyone else was seated at the additional tables that were set up in the backyard.

Rose watched Marcus and her stomach almost churned at the sight of him wrapping his arms around Violet's chair. Marcus looked up and caught her staring at him. He showed all of his pearly white teeth as he flashed her a smile. When it didn't appear that anyone else was looking, he winked at her. Rose looked away suddenly before her emotions caused her to react. The last thing she wanted to do was cause a scene.

She took a quick gulp of her champagne.

Violet whispered, "Are you all right?"

Rose reassured her that she was fine. As the caterers started serving the guests, Rose had her champagne glass refilled. Everyone around her looked to be enjoying the meal. The menu consisted of a choice of beef Angus sirloin steak or baked Cornish hen, and baked potatoes with any topping or rice pilaf. There was also a choice of French bread, rolls, or sesame bread. Rose decided on getting the steak and rice. She only ate enough to put something in her stomach to counteract the drinks she had already consumed, and she wanted to make sure her stomach could withstand any more drinking she was sure to do throughout the night.

"Violet dear, we need to plan a weekend getaway." Rose took another bite of her food before she continued to say, "I'll be in New York in a few weeks. Why don't you meet me there and we can hang out and do some major shopping?"

"That sounds like fun, but I don't know about the shopping part. I can't think of anything I really need."

Rose didn't want to argue about her favorite pasttime. "Well meet me there anyway and we'll paint the town red."

Marcus interrupted. "Only if I can be there."

Rose made a snide remark. "I don't think so."

Violet looked at them both. "Hey you guys, there is enough of me to go around. Rose, I'll meet you there and we can do the shopping or whatever else you want to do, but on one condition."

"And what's that?" Rose asked as she sipped the rest of her drink.

"It's your treat," Violet said to ease the tension.

Rose gave her fake smile. "Of course dear, I'll have my assistant make the plans." She then looked over at Marcus and commented, "This trip is for ladies only."

Marcus raised his glass in the air. Violet had a clueless expression on her face and Rose continued to eat the rest of her food.

While everyone was busy with small talk, her assistant announced the cutting of the cake, and those who were through eating followed as they all walked out to the patio. A table had been set up for the cake and punch. There was also a pretty dolphin ice sculpture and a champagne water fountain sitting on the same table. The cake was a three-tier yellow cake with white creamy icing trimmed in gold. Each section was covered with a bouquet of yellow roses and purple violets.

As everyone sang "Happy Birthday," Rose and Violet blew out the candles and gave each other a tight sisterly hug. They each took turns cutting the cake. They cut a few pieces and then the caterer took over.

While they stuffed themselves with cake, someone announced that an area had been cleared as a dance floor. John asked Rose to dance and she excused herself from the others.

"Thank you, John. The sight of Marcus just makes me sick."

"I figured you needed rescuing."

Rose danced closer to him, so no one could overhear the conversation. "If you keep rescuing me like this, I might have to wrap a cape around you."

He twirled her around. "It's long enough for you to wrap whatever you want to around it."

"John. You need to stop."

They continued to dance and the dance area soon filled up. The new electric slide was played and the floor got even more crowded. She ended up dancing by Marcus and Violet. Marcus accidentally bumped into her. "Sorry."

She rolled her eyes at him. Violet didn't appear to notice the little exchange between the two of them. After the song ended, Rose escaped into her house and made her way to one of the downstairs bathrooms. She turned the water on to mask the scream she had built up. She checked her make-up and turned the water off. She was in the process of leaving the bathroom when, as she opened the door, Marcus stood in front of her and pushed her back in.

"What are you doing?"

Marcus took her by the arm. "I wanted to check on you and make sure you were all right. You've been acting funny with me all night. Violet is worried that you're not having a good time."

Rose yanked her arm from his hand. "As long as you're not in my view, I'm having a great time."

"Rose, a flower by any other name, is just not a flower."

"Move out of my way please."

Marcus bent down as if he wanted to kiss her. "Thou detest me too much. Is it that you really do have the hots for me?"

"You bastard. My sister is only a few feet away and you're making a pass at me. You're walking a thin line."

"No. You're on a thin line, and I know you won't break our agreement."

She swung the bathroom door open and walked madly out of the room. She almost knocked over one of the servers. She grabbed a glass off one of the trays and swished down some champagne. She then returned to the party as if nothing happened.

Chapter 35
VIOLET

"Violet, do you want a refill on your drink?"

Violet looked startled. "Marcus, where did you come from? I thought you were with Terrence?"

"I went to use the rest room."

"Oh, okay. I think I have had enough to drink tonight. You have been downing a lot of those."

Marcus took his drink and sat it on a tray as someone walked by. "In that case, I won't drink any more either."

"Don't stop on my account."

A slow song came on; he took her hand and guided her to the dance floor. They both were in their own little world. "Violet, you are so beautiful; inside and out. I feel lucky to have you in my life. I have something for you, but I'll wait until after you've opened everyone else's presents."

Violet looked up and batted her eyes. "You could give me a little hint on what it is."

"Let's just say, it's something that you don't already have and you'll be surprised to get."

Violet looked puzzled. "That could be a number of things. Give me another one."

He wrapped his arms back around her. "No. You have to wait like a good little girl."

"Yes, Big Poppa."

The night was slowly coming to an end. People gathered in the room where the gifts were being kept. The girls each took turns opening their gifts. Rose opened up her gifts first. The first gift happened to be from Violet. Violet had found an antique cherry wood musical jewelry box with a matching miniature ring box. Rose's eyes looked watery as she thanked her. Rose thanked everyone as she unwrapped the other gifts.

Violet was handed her gifts to open. Rose's assistant wrote down the names of each person so they could later send out thank you cards. When Violet got to the final gift, she looked up at Rose. Although it didn't have a card, the wrapping paper gave it away, because as kids, their parents would always wrap their gifts in floral paper with their namesakes. She slowly unwrapped the gift. Inside was a sterling silver photo album trimmed in violets. She opened it to pictures of herself and Rose. She looked up at her sister with tears of joy. They embraced and all you could hear were "ooh" and "ahh" from the people in the room.

They both thanked everyone for coming as everyone went back to mingling. Violet spotted some members of the board and she shook each one's hand. "Thank you all for coming. Under the circumstances, I wasn't sure I would see you guys here."

The chairman spoke as if he were the spokesman for them all. "We wouldn't have missed celebrating with you. We're still family."

Violet smiled and acted as if she agreed. She was about to walk out to the patio, when she heard the doorbell ring. No one else was around, so she answered it. It was a courier from one of the mail services and she was surprised he asked for her specifically by name. She signed the receipt and closed the door. She took the gift with her as she walked outside to the patio where Rose, Janice, Marcus, and Terrence were waiting.

Rose looked down at the gift in her hand. "What's that?"

"Someone sent a courier here with one of my gifts. I'll open it in a minute. I wanted to tell you again how much I've enjoyed this birthday."

Rose hugged her again. Tonight they could not seem to get enough hugs. "You are the best sister and, no offense Carmen, best friend a woman could ask for."

Carmen looked at the exchange. "No offense taken. I'm glad to witness this."

Everyone else nodded in agreement.

Marcus pulled Violet to the side. "Dear. It's time. I know you've waited all night for this, so I'll be right back."

"Okay. While you're gone, I'll go ahead and open up this last gift."

Janice came over to see what she had. "Girl, hurry up. You've gotten some nice gifts tonight. Remember what you don't want, you can send my way."

Violet laughed and carefully opened the gift.

"I tell you. We're going to be here until your next birthday before you get that open."

Violet continued to open it and after she briefly viewed the contents of the box, she fainted.

Chapter 36
ROSE

Rose heard Janice yell, "Somebody help me. She's fainted. Somebody help!"

Rose rushed over to where Violet had fainted. Her assistant brought out a wet cloth and they placed it on her forehead. Marcus was back by then and swooped her up in his arms. Rose followed him and Janice inside. She yelled, "Take her up to my bedroom."

Marcus placed her on the bed as Rose waited for the paramedics to come. "Janice, what was she doing before she fainted? Was it something she was drinking?"

Janice recalled the night's events. "She was fine until she opened her gift. We were laughing, but after she opened the gift, a blank expression went across her face and the next thing I know she was falling to the ground."

"Can you go get the gift? Maybe someone sent something poisonous. I hear the paramedics now."

While Janice was retrieving the gift from the area where Violet fainted, Rose met the paramedics at the door and guided them to where Violet was located.

"I'll move out of your way. I'll be right over here if you need anything. Please tell me she'll be okay."

The paramedics examined her and were able to wake her. She didn't say anything when she first woke up. They looked her over thoroughly and found all of her vital signs in order. They diagnosed her systems as stress related. They asked her a couple of questions and confirmed that she would be fine. It was determined she needed rest. During the whole ordeal, Marcus and Rose both were on the sidelines watching.

The lead paramedic pulled Rose to the side and delivered a message from Violet. "She asked to be left alone and she's also ready to go home."

Rose responded, "I'll make sure she gets home safe and sound."

The lead paramedic continued to say, "She's asked that someone named Janice take her. Can you call her and make sure she does?"

"Janice is downstairs." Rose glanced in Violet's direction. "You said she was okay, so why does she look like she's still out of it?"

"She's just exhausted. She should take it easy for the next couple of days."

Rose signaled for her assistant to show the paramedics out. "Ask Janice to come upstairs please."

Her assistant responded, "Yes, Rose."

The paramedics left and the only people still in the room were Violet, who was lying in Rose's bed; Marcus, who sat on the edge of the bed looking down at Violet; and Rose, who stood worrying with her arms wrapped around herself.

Rose whispered, "Marcus, she should stay here for the night. I'll make sure she gets home in the morning. I'll tell Janice she can stay overnight too if she wishes."

"I'm not leaving her like this."

Rose still talking low, so she wouldn't disturb Violet, said,

"Marcus, under the circumstances, I think you should go ahead and leave now."

They both were startled when Violet spoke up. "Yes, I think it's best that you leave."

Marcus moved closer and tried to hold her hand. "Baby, you had us both so worried. We were trying not to disturb you."

Violet let out a fake laugh. "I'm sure you were."

Marcus, with a confused look on his face, responded, "If you wish I'll leave, but I'll be back in the morning to see you home."

Rose added, "I can go find you something to sleep in and you can stay here in my bed. Don't move."

Violet tried to sit up. "Rose, that won't be necessary. I'll be sleeping in my own bed tonight."

Rose went near her. "The paramedics said you needed to take it easy and not get yourself upset. Just stay the night and we can get you home in the morning."

Violet laughed again.

Rose was really concerned now. "Violet, what is wrong with you? How much did you have to drink?"

Violet got up out of the bed and started looking for something. "All I want to know is where are my shoes?"

Marcus volunteered a response. "They are over in the corner. Let me get them for you."

She responded, "No. I think you've done enough."

Rose walked up to her and tried to calm her down. "Violet, you're acting strange. I don't know what has gotten into you. Just sit down. You don't need any shoes. You're not going anywhere tonight."

Marcus chimed in and said, "Yes, baby. It must be the champagne talking. Just sit down and relax."

Violet stood in front of Rose. She took her finger and shook it back and forth in Rose's face. Her words came out slurred as if she was drunk from too much champagne. "You know I'm the luckiest woman in the world. I have two people who care so much about me, that they would do anything to keep me happy."

Rose took her hand. "Baby, you are exhausted. Come sit down by me. Marcus, go downstairs and get us some tea please."

Violet yelled, "Marcus, when you go downstairs don't bother to come back up."

Rose was getting upset. "What is your problem, girl? We're only trying to help."

Violet reached over and slapped her and Rose didn't retaliate, because she was shocked. The next words out of her mouth were, "What the hell?"

Marcus turned around too, because he heard the sound of the slap.

Janice had walked in the moment Violet slapped Rose. Janice handed something to Rose. "This will explain everything."

Rose only glanced at what Janice handed her. It was a tabloid with a picture that showed her and Marcus arguing at the hotel in Mexico with a caption: *Hot and Spicy: Another Thorn in Sister's Side—Reported Sighting of Hollywood Actress Rose Purdue in lover's quarrel with twin sister's boyfriend—professional basketball player Marcus Jameson.*

Rose rubbed her left cheek, which still stung from the effects of Violet's slap. She looked directly into Violet's eyes and said, "I can explain."

Chapter 37
VIOLET

Violet spoke in a calm voice. "Explain what? The two people I've trusted have betrayed me. You of all people." She shook her head in disgust.

Rose tried to explain. "It's not what you think. Let me tell you the whole story."

Marcus put his two cents in. "Violet, we bumped into each other. The picture is all distorted."

"Deny to the end. Why? Who am I? Bet you both had some good laughs at my expense. What was it Rose? You stole my husband and you couldn't stand for me to be happy with another man. Is that what it was?"

Rose was wiping tears away by now. "No. You have it all wrong. Please, let me explain."

Violet bent down and retrieved her shoes. "It's in your best interest to stay clear of me. I am two seconds away from knocking you the hell out."

Marcus tried to explain himself, but Rose stepped in and started cussing Marcus out. "I told you, you were trash. Get the hell out of my house. You've done enough damage for one night."

Marcus looked over at Violet and started walking in her direction. Violet held up her hand. He stopped in midstep. "Violet. I'll let you calm down and I'll call you in a few days." He laid something on the bed. "This is your birthday present. I love you."

As he walked out, she grabbed the box and threw it. It hit him on the back of the head. "You don't know what love is. Take your gift and leave me the hell alone. Do not bother to call me at all. I never want to hear from you again."

He continued out the door, rubbing the back of his head.

Janice was trying to calm her down. "Come on, Violet. I've had Terrence load your things in the car and we can go ahead and leave."

"I'll be ready in a minute. I have a few more things I need to say to my darling sister."

"You sure you're all right?"

"I'm fine. Give us some privacy please."

Janice left and closed the door behind her. Rose's personal assistant stood by the door. Violet looked up at her. "You can leave as well. I promise not to kill her, but when I finish saying what I have to say, she's going to wish she was dead."

Rose gave her a reassuring nod, so she left and closed the door behind her.

Violet felt Rose's eyes on her and Rose started to talk, but Violet interrupted her. "For once you're going to listen to me."

"But, Violet, you don't know the whole story."

Curious as to what lie she had this time, she gave her a chance to explain herself. "Okay. What is your story?" Rose by now was standing near her, when Violet said, "If I were you, I would keep your distance right now."

Rose backed up out of swinging distance and told her the real version of what actually took place in Mexico. "There was no lover's quarrel. He was there with another woman and I was confronting him about it."

Violet's face was expressionless and her eyes pierced straight through Rose. "Are you through?"

"Yes. It's the truth and that's all I have to say about it."

Violet laughed. "Well we know how your truths are. They get a little distorted every now and then."

"I know this must have been a shock, but you'll realize I am telling you the truth. I wanted to tell you, but I didn't know how to."

"What I realize my dear sister is this, I realize that once again you have made me look like a fool. You have put on an award-winning performance. I fell for it, and boy did I fall. I thought you were getting over your selfishness and that for once you actually cared about me."

"I do care, that's why I didn't know how to tell you about Marcus's affair."

Violet looked out the window and watched as the remaining guests and caterers left. "Of course you couldn't tell me about his affair, because it was with you. Answer this, why? Why do you want everything I have? You have the world at your beck and call. You are the prima donna. You are every man's fantasy, but yet, every time I get a piece of happiness, you want it too."

"Violet, it's not like that. I want you to be happy. I'll do whatever I can to make you happy and you know that. You're just upset now. Tomorrow you'll realize that you're mistaken."

"What I was mistaken on, was ever trusting you and letting you back into my life after the stunt you pulled with David. I should have known you couldn't be trusted."

Rose's tone sounded desperate. "I don't know what else to say. I've changed. I am no longer that woman. Please see my side. I'm begging you."

Violet turned around from the window and clapped her hands three times. "Bravo. Another award-winning performance. You're begging me for forgiveness. Now I have seen it all. I can't believe that Queen Rose is begging me for anything."

"I know you're upset, but please think about what I've said. I'll have Janice take you home if you like, but you are welcome to stay here."

"I would rather be homeless living on the streets, before I stay one night under your roof after what you did to me."

Rose kept her distance, but continued to explain herself. "I'm sorry. I know I should have told you as soon as I found out. He threatened to tell you that I made a pass at him, that's the only reason why I didn't."

"You're going way out. Don't blame him. You were in control of the situation and you decided to stab me in the back. You did it and as usual, you're trying to push the blame on someone else."

Someone knocked on the door. Rose yelled out, "Give us a few more minutes."

Whoever was at the door sounded as if they were walking away.

Violet ran her hands through her hair. "Oh, I'm through here. There is one last thing I need to say before I leave, though. Don't call me for anything. If you're sick, I don't want to hear about it."

Rose, teary eyed, said, "What about Momma? What are you going to tell Momma?"

Violet stood in disbelief. "Oh, what do you want me to tell her? You want me to tell her how my dear loving sister tried to take my man once again? Do you want me to tell her how the months of rebuilding a relationship with you was in vain, because you are still the same egotistical, selfish, conniving wench that you've always been, and that after all of these years I'm still putting up with your mess?"

"Violet. Please don't. Let's talk to her together."

"I don't owe you anything. Right now I don't want to talk to anyone. I just need to get away."

"Let me pay for you a trip somewhere. You just name it and I'll have my assistant set it up."

Violet yelled, "You are something else. You always think your money is the answer to everything. Well it's not. Your money can't erase the pain of betrayal in my heart. The pain of not having the kind of sister that I can depend on; the pain I feel because I have to break Momma's heart, because I cannot and will not allow you into my personal circle anymore."

"It doesn't have to be like that. Just think about what I said. I'm telling you the truth."

"Rose, you have been acting so long, you wouldn't know the truth if it reached out and bit you. If we run into each other, whether it is at Momma's or out in public, please stay out of my way. Don't send any reporters near me, or else they will get another exclusive. I am no longer your punching bag. I will no longer let you walk over me and use me the way that you have. I thought we had reached an understanding, but it's clear we hadn't or else you wouldn't have done what you did."

Rose reached out to Violet, but she continued to walk out the door. Violet turned around with a sad, defeated look on her face. "One more thing."

"Yes."

"Happy birthday. Thank you for making it one that I will never forget." Violet slammed the door, walked down the stairs and continued out the front door, where Janice and Terrence stood waiting for her.

Janice wrapped her arm around her and walked her toward the limousine. "Are you going to be okay?"

Violet closed her eyes and reopened them as if she was trying to clear her vision. "I will be."

Chapter 38
ROSE

Rose ran after her and stood at her front door as she watched them pull off in the limousine. She closed the door and headed straight to the alcohol. She was walking through her dining room to reach the kitchen, when she saw Lance sitting at the table. "What are you still doing here?"

"Janice told me what happened and I figured you could use some TLC."

Rose felt completely drained. "Look, Lance. This has been a long difficult night for me. I don't have the energy to fight with you right now."

Lance went to her and held his arms out for her to embrace. "I'm not here for you to fight with. Let me love you for this one night. I know we have a past, but I want to be there for you. Let me help erase the pain even if it's just for a brief moment."

Rose needed to feel loved, so she allowed him to embrace her. "I'll probably regret this in the morning, but oh, well."

Lance found a bottle of champagne and two glasses, and walked with her to her bedroom. He ran her some bath water and he proceeded to wash her body with a soft blue sponge.

She leaned back and lost herself with each touch. He dried her off, picked her up, and placed her on the bed. He took the bottle of champagne and poured some in each glass. When she looked up, she saw the desire in his eyes. He continued to pour champagne, but not in a glass; he poured the remainder of the champagne over her body. He started at her left breast and sucked on it and then took his tongue and kissed and licked every drop of champagne from her body. He took his right hand and used his fingers to play with her center.

As she moaned, he licked between her breasts, and continued until he got to her belly button. "Lance."

He teased her navel with his tongue. "You like that, baby?"

"Ooh, Lance."

He then placed circular kisses between her thighs and she released all of the frustration from the previous hours. His mouth was drowned with her moistness. He then placed a condom on his erect manhood, and entered her slowly. Her body responded by arching and she matched each thrust with her own. They both reached a climactic peak as he yelled out, "Roseeeeee."

Rose watched Lance as he slept. She drank both of the glasses that were on her nightstand. The sexual release was great; however, it only compounded the emptiness she now felt in her soul. She lay back down and attempted to sleep. She replayed everything in her head, ending with the confrontation that occurred. She fell asleep, but had nightmare after nightmare.

Rose dreamed that she was at home relaxing on her patio, when her phone began to ring. She picked up the phone, but no one was there. She continued to relax on her lawn chair and the next thing she knew, she felt something slimy on her. She tried to look, but her sunglasses were so dark that she couldn't see what was touching her. Whoever it was, had slimy, sweaty hands. As her dream progressed, she was able to take the sunglasses off and she could see that it was Marcus caressing her body.

She yelled for him to stop touching her. Out of nowhere, Violet walked out of the house and saw them in a compromising position. Violet screamed at them both and Rose tried to explain to her about Marcus and his slimy, sweaty hands. Violet didn't want to hear it and raised a gun and she was about to shoot when the gun jammed, so Violet aimed again and placed her index finger on the trigger.

Rose woke up frightened and to Lance's roaming hands.

Chapter 39
VIOLET

If anyone would have told me I would be dealing with this type of betrayal not just once, but twice in my lifetime, I would have told them they were out of their mind. I've heard of backstabbing friends, but sisters. This is like some of the stuff you would see on those late-night talk shows.

My phone keeps ringing off the hook. I just let my answering machine pick up, because I don't feel like being bothered with anyone right now. It's been, what, about a week since I found out about Rose and Marcus. I know you can't believe everything you read in the tabloids, but I have to look at my sister's track record and she has proven to be untrustworthy.

Marcus is a different story. It goes to show you. You can't judge a book by its cover. He seemed so sincere and to top it off, he knew about what happened between David and me, and he still went there. I guess it must be true about men and their fascinations with twins.

If he calls me one more time or sends me one more bouquet of flowers, I'm going to scream. I've been redirecting the flowers to the nursing home and the hospital near Cren-

shaw. The flowers haven't brightened up my day, but maybe they can brighten up someone else's. He's another one that thinks money can buy anything. He and Rose make a good couple. Now they can do their dirt in the open. I guess I should listen to the messages. So in case Momma or Janice call, they will have room to leave a message. Bad news travels fast, since it seems everyone is calling me to see if I'm okay.

Violet listened to her messages. Although she knew who left most of the messages, she found some paper and pen to write with just in case it was somebody important.

"Violet, it's me. Please baby. You can't avoid me forever. I know I made a mistake about not telling you about my trip to Mexico. That picture was innocent. Come on, baby. You know I wouldn't have an affair with your sister."

"Lies, lies, and more lies. You were supposed to be spending time with your parents, but you couldn't even remember the lie you told me. You could have at least said, I decided to take my parents on a trip to Mexico for the weekend." She continued to listen to her messages.

"This is your momma. Baby, I know you're hurting. Call me, so we can talk. I've talked to Rose and she's reassured me that she didn't do it this time. Listen to her, baby. She sounds like she's telling the truth."

"Momma, Momma. You keep falling for it. Can't you see, she's such a good actress, that she can make you believe the sky is green when she puts her heart into it?"

The next message played. "I wanted to let you know I'm here for you when you're ready to talk and the center is missing you, girl. Hang on in there. They are wrapping up the investigation and Mr. Carlton is about to go down." Violet laughed because Janice was so animated with her voice.

She received several more messages from Marcus and then the last one was from Rose. "Sweetie, I know you're hurting, but I'm here for you. I know by now you've thought about it and realized what I told you is factual. You don't need him, and he's not worth your tears."

"You're right about that. He is not worth my tears and neither are you. I could get over losing him, but after all we've done to get our lives together, you betrayed me again. I feel like a dagger is stuck in my heart."

She erased the messages on the answering machine. She decided to go pull weeds out of her garden. Normally, working in her garden would relax her, but nothing she had done this week could release the strain she felt on her shoulders and neck. Her head was pounding from an intense migraine and she knew she couldn't go on feeling like she had the weight of the world on her shoulders for much longer. She needed to figure out some way for her to get past the pain and move on.

After she worked in the garden, she cleaned up, ate a light dinner, and tried to relax by watching a couple of classic comedy movies.

Maybe I need a change of scenery. I could always move, but where would I go? I don't think I should stay here, because this whole town is full of Rose, and I need to keep my distance from her for a while. I don't want to go back down south to Louisiana. I know Momma's there, but it's probably best I start over new somewhere where I don't know anyone.

That night before retiring for bed, with her heart and mind heavily laden, she knelt down and prayed. "Our Father, I know I'm supposed to forgive, so I can also be forgiven, but how can I? Right now I can't, so what should I do? Lord, please give me a forgiving spirit. Have mercy on me. I know I can't understand why those I care about choose to hurt me. I humble myself before you. Please direct me in the path you would like for me to go. Work through me, so that I can forgive others, as you have forgiven me so many times. Amen."

She turned off the lamp on the nightstand near her bed and fell asleep. She was able to sleep peacefully for the first time since the night of her birthday.

Chapter 40
ROSE

"Carmen, I don't care what you have to do or who you have to threaten, but I need to know how that photo got in the tabloids."

"Calm down. I told you I was working on it. I tried to warn you a few weeks before."

Rose paced back and forth in front of her bedroom window. "You mentioned something about some pictures, but you didn't tell me it was a picture of Marcus and I arguing. If I would have known that, I could have told Violet everything and all of this could have been avoided."

Carmen tried to sound comforting. "I know, dear. You're quite innocent in all of this and once again the tabloids have blown things out of proportion."

"I hate it when you try to talk to me in your grandmother voice."

"Dear, you better be glad you are in distress, or else our conversation would be terminated. I told you I would find out what I can. In the meantime, you need to take a chill pill and work on Rose."

"Now you trying to judge me. Where did that come from?"

Carmen cleared her throat. "All I am saying is, although you didn't commit this crime, you need to examine yourself and see why your sister would believe a tabloid story over her own flesh and blood."

"I thought we were past all of that, but apparently not. Look, I need to go take care of some things. Just do your job and call me back when you have some news for me."

"Wait, I think I know where they got the story. Cindy just brought me a note about someone being on hold in reference to it."

"Well what are you waiting for, talk to them and call me back. Better yet. I'll hold."

While she waited on Carmen to return to the line, she placed the phone on speaker and got dressed. There were some things she needed to take care of before going to rehearsal. With all of the things going on with her sister, she had neglected rehearsing for her first concert. She had called Violet every day, but she wouldn't answer her phone, nor had she returned any of her many messages.

How could I allow anything to interfere with my career? I have left her countless messages. If she wants to pout, she can. When she realizes that this time she was wrong, she'll be calling. In the meantime, I need to get my act together, so I can give the world the Rose they've come to know and love.

Carmen came back on the line and called out her name a couple of times. "Rose. Are you there?"

"Yes. I was thinking about getting to rehearsal this time."

"Yes. Please do that. Your concert is coming up soon and don't forget you have an audition tomorrow. I shouldn't have to remind you, but if you get the role, you will be up there with the other big-name actresses."

"I know. Now back to the reason why you had me on hold for fifteen minutes."

"Are you sitting?"

Sounding agitated, Rose said, "Just get to the point."

"Someone close to you sold a story to the tabloid and exaggerated things."

"What do you mean someone close to me? Besides Violet, you and my personal assistant are the only two close to me."

"Eliminate two and who do you have?"

While she was talking to Carmen, her assistant knocked on the door. Rose didn't answer, so she turned the knob and walked on in. Rose cut Carmen off. "I need to call you back. . . ." Rose took the phone off speaker.

Carmen tried not to sound worried. "Why? Is Tina there now?"

"Yes and I need to take care of them."

"Don't do anything. Why am I telling you that? Just don't get into any trouble. I'm on my way now."

Rose hung up and her assistant started to speak. "Rose, I wanted to confirm your appointments for the day. I tried calling you, but you weren't answering your phone, so I came on up."

Rose walked up to her and grabbed her by both arms and began to shake her. "You Trick. I trusted you. I've paid you royally and you betrayed me by talking to some tabloid and on top of that you fed them a bunch of lies."

Her assistant was able to get free from her hands and stepped back shocked from the rage coming from Rose. She started to stutter. "I didn't do any such thing. I don't know what you're talking about. Who told you that?"

"Don't worry about it. I want to know, what did I do to you? I have opened up my home to you and not only do I pay you a nice salary, but I give you fringe benefits all of the time."

Her assistant turned around and walked toward the door.

"Maybe the stress of losing your sister is causing you to be confused. I don't know what you're talking about."

She was almost at the door when Rose grabbed her by the shoulder and pulled her around. "Look here. I don't have time to play games. You have five minutes to get your stuff and get the hell out of my house. You will be hearing from my attorney."

Her assistant then let out a hideous laugh. "Queen Rose has spoken, so I guess I better bow down or get stepped on."

"What the hell?"

"You heard me. I didn't bite my tongue."

"You are five minutes away from me kicking your no-tan behind."

Her assistant kept laughing. "I never meant for you to find out this way. Actually, I never meant for you to find out."

Rose pointed in the direction of the door. "You need to get the hell out now."

As she began walking out, she said, "Poor Rose. Now she has no one to control. No wonder you don't have a man. Your own sister won't have anything to do with you."

Rose snapped, grabbed her by her long blond hair, and they started tumbling on the floor. They were still fighting when Carmen entered the house. The noise and screams were loud enough to be heard downstairs.

When Carmen opened the door, she saw them both on the floor with arms swinging and hair being pulled. She had to interfere and separate the two. She told the assistant to leave. "If you know what's best, you'll get your things and leave while you can. I can't promise you I can control her for more than five minutes."

Rose did her best to get past Carmen. "Let me go. I have some unfinished business with her."

Carmen took a strong hold on her arm and led her to a chair in her room. "No, what you need to do is calm yourself down. She will get what's coming to her. Trust me. You don't want to give the tabloids anything else to report on, do you?"

"Screw the tabloids. I don't care about them or that tramp that just walked out of here. Can you believe this? I let her into my private life and she does this?"

Carmen had a look of pity on her face. "What you need to do now is relax. What is the name of your masseure?"

"Ramone."

"I'll call Ramone over and have him give you a massage. You need to relax and don't forget about your rehearsal this evening."

She got up and gave Carmen a hug. "Thank you for putting up with my temper tantrums, and not leaving me. You are the greatest."

Carmen pulled out her cell phone and made a couple of calls in search of a new assistant for her. She also made sure Rose's passwords were changed to her voicemail and e-mail. "Rose, don't forget to change your alarm security code. I would hate for her to try to come back."

Rose walked Carmen out. "I promise to do everything you told me. Thanks again."

Rose went back upstairs to prepare for her full hour massage. She meditated over the events of the past few weeks and tried to find some balance in her life. She decided she wouldn't let anyone, including her sister, get to her anymore. It hurt too much. Lance had been stopping by, but she couldn't let him or any other man distract her. It was clear to her that no one could be trusted and she had to do what was best for Rose at all times.

After her massage, she dressed and headed over to the dance studio to rehearse. Everyone was amazed at how quickly she picked up on her routines and rehearsal went smoothly. She stayed after everyone else left. She looked in the mirror and even though she had declared earlier her independence from the world, she didn't like the reflection in the mirror. She gathered her things, turned off the lights, and headed home.

II

TO LIVE IS TO LOVE, TO LOVE IS TO FORGIVE

(Ten Years Later)

Chapter 41
VIOLET

Violet woke up and looked out her window at the beautiful mountain view. Ever since she moved to San Jose ten years ago, she had developed a morning ritual that she'd followed almost every day. She would shower or take a long bath, depending on which day of the week it was, then she would spend the morning meditating. This morning, she had a meeting with a developer. She had finally received the financing she needed to build her dream place. It would be a house used for wayward teenagers. She knew that these kids sometimes just needed a safe haven and someone there to listen. She had received many awards for some of her past efforts; because of that, she was able to get grants to help complete her latest project. The huge donor insisted she use one of his developers and because of his huge contribution, she saw no reason not to.

She looked in the mirror to make sure everything was in place and gave herself a thumbs up because the suit accented her best features. Although she was not one to harp on looks, she knew first impressions mattered. She always tried to look her best when attending meetings. She grabbed her briefcase along with her suggestions and copies so that she would have an extra set to give the developer. She was walking out the door, when her phone rang. She rushed back to grab it, just in case it was someone calling to reschedule. "Hello."

"Oh, baby. I'm glad I caught you. I haven't heard from you in a while. Just wanted to make sure you were fine."

Violet smiled. "Momma, I'm doing great. I am actually on my way to a meeting. You know the project I was telling you about. I have the financial backing I needed, and it's becoming a reality."

"I'm so proud of you. You go to your meeting and call me back later. I love you."

"Love you too."

The call put a smile on her face and she left for her meeting. She felt a sense of confidence as she walked into the office building. She had to ask the security guard in the lobby for directions to the developer's office. Apparently they were new in the San Jose area, and didn't have their names on the official directory yet. The elevator stopped on the top floor and she was immediately impressed by the décor of the office. She signed in with the company's receptionist and waited patiently for someone to come get her.

A young man who looked to be fresh out of college greeted her and led her into the corner office. While they were walking, he introduced himself and gave her an overview of what the day's meeting would be about. When he opened the door for her to walk in, there were several other people in the office sitting around an oval table in plush, black leather chairs. A tall African-American male was standing up by the wall talking on the telephone. She walked to her seat and as she sat, the man on the phone ended his conversation and turned around. She looked up and their eyes locked.

She tried to keep her composure throughout the meeting. The sight of the man made her lose her concentration at first;

however, when she was asked to give her presentation, she blocked him out and thought only of the children. Everyone there was impressed with how thorough her presentation was. They began to feel the same passion she had and vowed to make the project a success. They committed to erecting the building as quickly as humanly possible, so that she could fulfill her quest.

The man stood and volunteered to walk her out, so the others gathered their things and left the conference room, closing the door behind them. She tried to ignore the fact that they were now alone.

She gathered her presentation and unplugged her laptop. The man didn't say anything until he saw she was through gathering her things.

"You still look beautiful and I'm not talking about physically either; you have this special glow."

She pretended to not hear him and started walking toward the door.

"Violet, let's not do this. We'll be working closely for the next few months. Can we attempt to be friends?"

Violet, not wanting to cause a scene, and not sure of how she would feel after seeing him after all of these years, swallowed and then turned to him. "David, you're right; however, don't expect anything but cordial conversation."

As promised, David walked her out and looked as if he wanted to hug her, but instead extended a hand out to her. "Thank you. I think you will be satisfied with how things turn out."

She shook his hand and went to her car. After she knew she was safe and out of hearing distance from their office, she let out a scream. A woman driving next to her, looked over at her as if she had lost her mind.

Why me? I must be destined for this. Out of all of the developers in California, it had to be David. Why didn't I figure it out by the name? He must have changed the name of his company or maybe he's working for someone else now. Either way, I can't believe my luck. What's surprising me, is that I didn't want to throw anything at him. I was only uncomfortable, because of our past and it made things awkward. Wait until I tell Janice.

Chapter 42
ROSE

"That's a wrap," the director yelled, as the movie Rose had been shooting for the past six months came to an end.

Rose rushed to her trailer so she could gather her things and pack. She wanted to catch the next flight back to LA. If she were lucky, she would make it back in time to go by Roscoe's Chicken and Waffles. She enjoyed her stay in Canada, but there was nothing like some chicken and waffles for breakfast, lunch, or dinner.

When she reached the airport a few people recognized her so she gave a few autographs.

Over the past ten years, her movies had given her international fame and although she had only recorded two albums, they both went platinum and she could still rock the house. With her beautiful songbird voice, she received requests to perform and sing on soundtracks quite frequently. She had a meeting with a new young producer later on in the week, so she could finish the title song for the movie she just filmed.

She slept the entire flight back to LA and was thrilled Carmen had a car waiting for her, because she hated to wait around in airports. She wore a hat to cover her long curly hair and some shades, hoping she could get her bags before being recognized. She almost made it out the door to where her driver was supposed to be waiting, when she heard her name being called. Instead of ignoring what she heard, she automatically turned around. Flashes of bright lights greeted her. It was a photographer from one of the tabloids.

At that point, the driver saw the commotion and figured out she needed his assistance. He went up to her, identified himself, and swiftly grabbed her bags, while protecting her and guiding her to the waiting limousine. With everything that had happened, she had forgotten all about going to Roscoe's Chicken and Waffles. When he dropped her off at home, she thanked him and gave him a nice big tip.

Since it was late, she decided to take a long bath. She sighed with relief, because she missed being in her own tub. After she soaked for a while, she went directly to bed. She woke up the next morning to the ringing of her cell phone. She scrambled to locate it; she hadn't unpacked anything when she'd arrived home the night before. By the time she found her phone at the bottom of her purse, the caller had hung up. The number showed unavailable, and when the phone rang at her home, she figured it was the same person.

"This better be good. It's eight o'clock in the morning and some of us are trying to sleep."

"And hello to you too."

"Oh, sorry Carmen. I thought it was some telemarketer, or worse, a reporter." She tried to wipe the sleep from her eyes.

"I heard about the incident at the airport from the limousine company this morning. I wanted to make sure nothing else happened."

"I'm fine. You know I'm an expert now when dealing with photographers."

Carmen laughed. "I wouldn't go that far. A few are still trying to sue you for kicking them in the nuts."

"How am I supposed to know that they aren't trying to attack me? It was all done in self-defense." Rose was fully awake by now.

"Sure. You better hope the judge is a female, because a male judge won't take too lightly to hurting of the balls."

Rose laughed until her side hurt. "I haven't laughed this hard in a long time. I don't mind you waking me up now."

They continued with their light conversation and Carmen reminded her of her interview and photo shoot with a popular fashion magazine. "Don't be late."

"I won't. I'm getting better on the time now."

They hung up and Rose began her day. The first thing on her itinerary to do was to contact her hairdresser. She was in need of an emergency perm. After making her hair appointment, she called and made appointments for her feet and hands. Everyone showed up in record time. While sitting under the dryer, she meditated. Her mind was full of thoughts of her mother and sister and her career.

Sometimes no matter how hard she tried to mask her feelings, the pain from the emptiness inside surfaced. She poured herself into her craft and even though she didn't have too many trusted friends, she was well respected in Hollywood. She learned her parts well and was accommodating to other actors that she worked with. She was a director's dream and you either loved her or hated her. Either way, she demanded respect and most of the time got it.

Later during the day, she went to the photo shoot Carmen had reminded her about. When she got to the location, she was thrilled to see that the magazine editor was Lisa, the same woman who interviewed her years before when she was trying to repair her reputation from her sister's infamous interview. She reached out to shake her hand. "Hi. It's good to see you again."

"Yes. It sure is. I've followed your career over the years and I must say you have developed into a fine actress."

"Thank you. That means a lot to me."

She was escorted to what looked like a photographer's

studio and she was informed that after the photo shoot, they would meet up again for the interview. She felt comfortable with the photographer, so the shoot didn't take long. She was asked to change into several different outfits. They had a hair stylist on the premises, and for one shot, her hair was pinned up. Her curls were tight, so when the shoot was over and she let her hair down, she still had the fresh look she had walked in with.

The interview went smoothly. Rose tried to answer all of the questions.

"Although you haven't, as of yet, earned the prestigious award for your acting, do you feel as if the movie you just shot is the one, and do you feel the award selection is bias?"

Rose tried to answer the questions carefully, so she wouldn't piss anyone off. "I think there is so much talent out there to choose from, that it's very difficult to pick one person to get one award. I'm sure my time is near and the movie I just finished is definitely one that probably won't go overlooked."

Lisa was tapping the table with her pen. "How is your family doing?"

Without blinking an eye Rose responded, "As far as I know everyone is doing fine."

"Well that's good."

Rose tried not to show any nervousness. Lisa continued with her questions.

"I would like to give you the opportunity to clear up some other personal matters. You know our readers love to know what's going on behind the scenes."

Rose laughed. "I know. I have no problems sharing some things."

Lisa took a sip of coffee. "It's been reported that Lance and you are an item again."

"Lance and I are associates and because of things I would rather not discuss here, we could never be a couple again."

"His ex-wife has told reporters the reason why they recently got divorced was because he was still in love with you, and he spent more time running behind you than taking care of his husbandly duties."

"Now that might be true, but rest assured I did not encourage him to leave his wife. He did it because he felt it was best for everyone involved."

"Let me make sure I have this straight. You are still associates, but you never gave him a reason to leave his wife?"

Rose nodded her head in agreement. "You are correct."

Lisa asked a few more questions about her favorite designer and ended the interview. "Thank you again, Rose, for your time."

"Anytime." She gathered her purse and keys and Lisa walked her out to the area near the magazine's main lobby.

Rose placed her shades on, walked out to her car, and got on the highway. It was a beautiful sunny day, not that much wind, just pleasant. Ignoring the fact that she had just gotten her hair done, she let the top down on her convertible and drove on to her next destination, her beachfront home.

Chapter 43
VIOLET

Violet looked at the flight time and hoped she heard Janice right about the airlines and the time. The message she left was garbled. She was about to call Terrence and ask him, when she saw her friend waving her hat in her direction.

They greeted each other with a hug. They hadn't seen each other in months. Janice usually came to visit her, because she didn't like going to LA. Janice was now happily married to Terrence after dating him for two years. They didn't have any kids, but it never seemed to bother the happy couple.

"How's my brother-in-law?"

"He's fine. He told me to tell you hi and that he is counting on you to keep me out of trouble."

"I'm in social work, but I'm no miracle worker." Violet laughed.

"Ha. Ha."

After they picked up her bags, they decided to go to a popular soul food restaurant in the area before heading home. "We could get the food to go, if you like."

"No. I don't get out much without the company of my

husband and you've spoken highly of the restaurant, so I want to enjoy the ambiance."

They made it to the crowded restaurant, but didn't have to wait long. Once they got seated, they resumed their conversation. Although they communicated regularly through e-mail and by phone, it wasn't the same as being face to face; so they took this time to get caught up with what was going on with each other.

In between eating her hot wings, Violet asked, "Does it bother Terrence that you haven't had any kids yet?"

"No. If it does, I'm unaware of it. We both decided to let things take their course. We've even talked about adoption."

"Janice, that would be good. There are plenty of kids out there who need good, loving parents and you both are good role models."

"Thank you for saying that. For a while, Terrence thought you didn't like him, because he was friends with Marcus."

"I hope you set him straight. There's a big difference between the two. To think you couldn't stand him when you guys first met, and I was all goo-goo eyes over his trifling friend."

Janice wiped her mouth with her napkin. "I know, he almost missed out on this."

They laughed. "I'm glad to see that you're happy and he's been nothing but good for you, ever since you've met."

"I know; he's definitely a jewel. I don't know if you care or not, but Marcus hasn't had any good luck since you dumped him. He has so many paternity suits out on him. The way things look most of those women will get his pension; that is if he even makes it to retirement. I know he's struggling financially because of all of the back child support and lawyer fees."

"Really? It's that bad? Well, every dog has its day as they say."

They toasted to that as they waited for their dessert. They

both ordered peach cobbler topped with vanilla ice cream. Janice wasted no time getting straight to the point.

"How are things going with you working with David so closely?"

"I was wondering when you were going to get around to it. It's actually better than I thought it would be." Violet continued to sip on her daiquiri.

"You know I was shocked when you told me he was the developer. I could imagine how you felt."

"Let's just say, I had butterflies. As I was telling you on the phone, I no longer felt any anger toward him. It was just an awkward feeling."

Janice looked at her as if she didn't believe her. "Anything else you want to tell me?"

"There isn't anything to tell. We meet at least a few times a week. Normally there are other people around. I'm supposed to meet him next week to give them the approval on the final draft. The house will be built with the special requirements that are needed and I will no longer have to deal with David."

Janice looked at her with her mouth turned up. "Sounds like you're trying to convince yourself, more than you're trying to convince me."

"Whatever."

Janice laughed at her and almost spit her drink out and pointed toward the door. Violet turned to see what caused the mishap and noticed David walking in with a beautiful redhead.

"Don't look now, but Mr. Whatever is walking this way."

Violet didn't look in his direction again. "Act like we're in deep conversation and maybe he won't see us or will walk on by."

It was too late, because David spotted her and along with his companion walked directly to their table. "Hi, Violet, and who do we have here?" He leaned down to hug Janice. "How are you, stranger?"

Janice stood up and gave him a hug. "I'm doing lovely and yourself?"

He released a hearty laugh. "Great, now that I'm in the company of all of these beautiful women."

Violet noticed the interchange, but still remained quiet. David's companion began to clear her throat. "Oh, I'm sorry. Ladies, this is Cherokee. Cherokee, this beautiful lady to your left is Violet—I don't know if you remember her. And the lady that I hugged is her best friend Janice."

Cherokee gave Violet a tight hug. "I've missed you Aunt Violet."

"Cherokee, you've grown into a beautiful young lady."

Cherokee blushed. "Thanks." She turned toward David. "Uncle D, excuse me for a minute. I need to powder my nose. I'll meet you at our table."

He responded, "Okay, Sweetheart."

Janice blurted out, "Uncle D?"

"Yes. That's my brother's daughter. She flew in last night and I promised to show her a night out on the town. I feel like an old man, with her around."

Violet cracked a joke. "Hate to tell you, but you are getting up there in age. I'll send the waitress over shortly with some Geritol."

David enjoyed her playfulness. "Oh, I got your old man. Well ladies, it's been a pleasure. Violet I'll see you next week, and Janice I'll see you when I see you."

Janice lowered her voice before saying, "Now see that wasn't too bad."

They finished their desserts and went to Violet's house. They were both exhausted from their long day, but ended up talking until the wee hours of the morning.

Violet said sleepily, "I don't know about you, but I need to get some shut-eye. Everything you'll need to freshen up with is in the bathroom down the hall. I'll see you in the morning."

They gave each other a hug and called it a night.

Chapter 44
ROSE

"Lance, wake up."

Lance turned over and placed his arm around her and mumbled, "What time is it?"

"It's time for you to get your butt up and get out of here. I have a full day today."

"Today is Sunday. Can't you chill and relax for a minute?"

"I have things to do. You need to get your behind up now."

He yawned. "I can stay here while you run your errands."

Rose got up and yanked the cover off of him, exposing his naked body. "No, you can't. When I leave, everyone else leaves."

"You drive a hard bargain. You better be glad I'm crazy about you."

She clapped her hands. "Whoopee. Lucky me. Now get your tail up and get dressed. You're holding me up."

While he showered in her bathroom, she used the shower in the bathroom down the hall. She found him fully dressed when she returned. In a seductive voice, he said, "You need to stop walking around in your underwear. You have me on hard now."

"Lance, when aren't you on hard?"

He walked up to her playfully and whispered in her ear, "It's your fault. You're just so beautiful."

She kissed him and continued to get dressed. "I'll walk downstairs with you."

She was glad to be back in the States. She enjoyed traveling, but there was no place like home. Although Shreveport, Louisiana, was her hometown, she had long ago adapted to LA as her home. It had been a couple of years since she visited with her mother, so she made a mental note to make a special trip to the Bayou state.

She drove up the coast and found her favorite beach spot. Lance assumed she had other things to do, but she just wanted to get out of the house to spend the day alone and relax. She took out her blanket, her big umbrella, and a novel by Francis Ray, one of her favorite romance writers. She discovered some time ago that this was the quietest spot along the beachfront. Most people who came to the area specifically came to relax. Families or rowdy teenagers usually ventured to another part of the beach.

She stayed there for the entire day. She was so relaxed, that if her stomach hadn't growled, she would have forgotten she hadn't eaten anything the entire day. She decided to go by and get an order of Chinese food. She got home and continued her day of leisure out on her patio.

She noticed that her message light was blinking, but she ignored it and made a mental note to check her messages later.

She ate her food and relaxed with another romance novel. A light bulb went off in her head. The book she read while on the beach would make the perfect movie. She could see herself playing the heroine role. She usually did suspense and comedy films, but now she wanted to venture off into other areas and doing a romantic movie that was not a romantic comedy would be exciting. She would pitch the book she just read to a couple of producers to see what their take on it would be. If not, she would get with the author and attempt to finance the project herself. She fell asleep under the starlit night with the novel over her chest.

The next morning she felt rejuvenated. She cooked an omelet and afterward checked her messages. She had several messages from Lance and then one from her mom. She decided to take a long hot bath first and then she would start returning phone calls.

She lathered her body with rose petal fragrance lotions and her favorite French floral scented perfume. She dressed casually in a white pair of Capri pants and white cotton top. She found a pair of white slip-on sandals, grabbed her cordless phone and a glass of lemonade and headed to her patio to make some phone calls.

The first call she made was to her mom. "Hi."

"Rose, dear. How have you been? Your Momma is getting up in age, so you might want to call and check up on me more often."

Rose crossed her legs. "Mom, you're just as healthy as I am." She uncrossed her legs and sounded concerned. "Is there something you're not telling?"

Her mom coughed. "I'm fine. I just have a little cold."

"Momma, are you sure? I can get you the best medical attention if you need me to. I wanted to surprise you, but I'll be down to see you in a couple of weeks. I need to wrap up some loose ends here, but if you need me sooner, I'm only a plane ride away."

"No, baby. I'm fine. I'm taking the medicine the doctor gave me and I'm feeling better already."

"Are you taking your insulin shots?"

"My sugar is fine. When exactly are you coming to visit?"

"It'll be in a few weeks. I'll call you a day or two before I come."

"Good. I'm not going to keep you long, because I know you're a busy lady."

"You make me sound like I don't have time for my own Momma," she said as she drank the last drop of her lemonade.

Her mom coughed again. "No dear, that's not what I'm implying. Just hurry up and come see me okay. I better get off here now. Love you."

"Love you too." She hung the phone up and wondered if her mom had been telling her everything.

She immediately found her palm pilot and checked her next available date. She called the airline and made reservations. She let out a sigh of frustration, because under normal circumstances, she would have had an assistant take care of things like this, but she could never find one that she truly trusted. She handled the major things through Carmen and her office, and everything else she personally took care of herself.

She was always happy to talk with her mom, but it also left a bout of sadness. When Violet first stopped talking to her, she assumed that in time she would come around, so she poured herself into acting and singing. As months went by, they were not making any progress. When her mom told her that Violet had moved to another city, it broke her heart and spirit. She knew it was a very slim chance of them reconciling. She only knew what was going on with Violet if her mom volunteered the information. She cherished the two times of year that she would hear from her sister and those were during her birthday and Christmas. She never heard her voice, but would get a beautiful card in the mail acknowledging those two days. Other than that, she had given up hope.

* * *

*My dear sister, the one time I told you the truth, caused a
rip between us that's lasted for more years than I care to
count. I hope that one day you'll be able to forgive me.*

Rose wiped tears from her eyes with her hand. "What is
wrong with me? I can't let this get me down." She reached
for the phone and made the rest of her calls.

Chapter 45
VIOLET

Janice and Violet ended up rushing to the airport. They both overslept and didn't count on Monday traffic being as horrendous as it turned out to be. "Janice, call me when you get there."

Janice gave her a quick tight hug. "I will and don't forget about what I said about Rose. Just think about it."

"You won't stop, will you?"

"Not as long as I'm your friend; you can count on it."

They hugged again and Janice went to catch her flight.

Violet had some free time, so she decided to do something she hadn't done in a while and that was shopping. She pulled up to the nearest mall and ended up buying herself four new outfits and a couple of sexy lingerie items. Although she didn't really date, she liked to feel sexy and satin or lace lingerie made her feel that way. As she was walking out the door to her car with all of her bags, David's niece opened the door for her.

"Violet."

"Cherokee."

"Nice seeing you again; my uncle has only nice things to say about you."

"Nice seeing you too. I hope you enjoy your stay here."

"Maybe we can get together for lunch or dinner before I leave."

"Let's do that."

She didn't really mean to make plans with David's niece. She remembered as a little girl, Cherokee always looked up to her. She had a time trying to open her car door, but managed to do so without dropping a bag.

Once she reached home, she was in the mood to cook some baked chicken, so she put it in the oven and then tackled the unpacking of her shopping bags. As she was unpacking, her phone interrupted her. She almost tripped over a bag trying to answer the phone, but avoided falling by an inch.

"This better be someone important," she yelled. "Hello."

"Hi, my flower." The sweet sounds of her mother's voice came from the other end.

"Mom. Whew. I was trying to avoid tripping on something I had on the floor."

"You okay?"

"Yes. How are you? I just talked to you a few days ago. Is that cold better?"

"Yes," she said as she cleared her throat. "The medicine the doctor gave me is working fine. I feel fine, but this nasty cough is lingering."

Violet didn't like the fact that she had been sick for almost two weeks. "Just make sure you do what the doctor tells you."

"I am. I wanted to see if my baby could come see me sometime soon."

"I can be there tomorrow if you'd like."

Her mom hurriedly said, "No, baby. You don't have to rush. How about coming down in two weeks? If you can, try to come for an entire week."

"Sure, Mom. I'll make my reservations today."

"Good. I will see you soon. Now take care."

"No, you take care of yourself. Love you."

When they hung up, Violet felt as if her mom was trying to set her up for something. She shook the feeling off and continued unpacking the shopping bags. She was putting the lingerie in one of her dresser drawers, when she stopped and held one up and admired it in the mirror.

Now I don't know why I'm looking to see how it's going to look. It's not like I have anyone to impress anyway. They'll only be under my regular clothes.

Violet finished putting the clothes away. She decided to make a green salad to go along with her baked chicken. By the time she finished making the salad, the chicken was ready. She said her grace and savored the well-seasoned chicken. The lettuce and tomatoes she used for the salad came from the local market, but tasted as if they could have come from her mother's garden. She ate until she was stuffed.

She went to her den and grabbed one of her favorite romance author's new books off the bookshelf. This author was able to capture the essence of romance and captivate the reader from page one. She also liked the added element of suspense. Since she didn't have romance in her own life, reading about it gave her a sense of satisfaction. She read as much as she could before falling asleep. The next morning she was awakened by an ache and crook in her neck. "I must stop doing that. I always fall asleep on the couch."

After her shower, she sprayed on some lilac smelling perfume that she had been wearing for over ten years. She went to her closet and took out her favorite lilac suit. Instead of wearing her hair pinned up as she normally did, she decided to wear it down. She used the curling iron to give her the flair she needed. She found her lilac pumps and some accessories and although she didn't wear much make-up, she put on a color of lipstick that complemented her outfit.

She headed to David's office. She was stuck in traffic; however, fortunately she had given herself enough time to get from one side of San Jose to the other. Otherwise, she would be late. She exited and took the side roads to her destination. She barely made it to her meeting in time. She rushed to get on the elevator and whoever was on it, held it open for her, before it could close all of the way.

"Thanks." She looked up into David's gorgeous eyes.

"You are quite welcome," he responded with a twinkle in his eyes.

She tried to ignore the feeling of attraction that seemed to linger for him. When she was in LA, he hounded her to get back with him. Here it was years later, and since they'd come in contact again with each other in San Jose, he had yet to make a pass. She could feel his eyes roaming over her body. She began to fidget with her purse as if she were looking for something. The elevator stopped on the top floor. He held the elevator door for her again.

She looked up and saw desire in his eyes. "Thank you again."

David looked as if he was going to say something else, but one of his business associates came up and interrupted. "We have a problem on line one. I was trying to reach you on your cell phone and since you didn't answer, I figured you were in the elevator on your way up."

David responded to his associate. "Excuse us for a moment." He then turned and addressed Violet. "Today's meeting will be in my office. Helen will show you the way. I'll be there as soon as I can. In the meantime, help yourself to some danish and coffee."

Violet followed Helen to David's office. She took a danish off the tray and made herself a cup of coffee with two packages of sugar substitute. She admired David's office and noticed a picture of a little girl on his desk that looked as if she was either three or four years old. He didn't have any other personal photos on his desk. She made a mental note to ask him about the little girl. She was daydreaming when David entered the room. She didn't know how long he had been standing observing her, but when she felt his eyes on her, she acknowledged him and walked around his desk and sat on the other side. For a moment neither said a word.

Chapter 46
ROSE

Rose spent the next few days doing last minute promotions for another movie that was going to be released in a month. She and her costar Trey Dash, one of Hollywood's sexiest black male actors, were hitting all of the hot spots together. The rumor mill around town stated that they were romantically involved. Trey, who chose to drop his last name, was every woman's fantasy. Not only did he have a body built solid like a rock, he was handsome, down to earth, and had charisma for days. He could make an old woman give up her pension with his golden-boy smile.

They were coming out of a posh Beverly Hills restaurant, when Rose bumped right into Lance as he and his friends were entering. "Excuse me."

Lance was able to recognize her although she tried to hide behind a pair of shades and cover her hair with a scarf. "Rose. What are you doing here?"

Rose motioned for Trey to continue walking. "I was having lunch with Trey."

Lance told his friends to go on without him. "I thought you were busy, otherwise, we could have had lunch together."

Rose took her shades off, so that he could see her eyes. "Lance, I don't feel like getting into this right now. This is business. Deal with it or not. Your choice." She placed her shades back on and twisted off in the direction of where Trey had just pulled up in his silver convertible Jaguar. Rose looked in the side mirror and saw that Lance was still standing there, looking at them as they drove off.

Trey sounded curious when he said, "Everything all right back there?"

"Yes. You know how some of you men can be jealous for no reason. Besides, it's not like he and I are in a committed relationship."

"I can understand how he feels. If my girlfriend was as fine as you and was seen out with someone else, I would be a little jealous too."

Rose pushed her shades up over her forehead. "Trey. Let's get this straight. In the world of romance, I am a free agent. No one has papers on me. Lance is just something to do to pass the time."

Trey started flirting with her. "So you're telling me that what I've heard about you two isn't true, and if another man wanted to take you out, you would go?"

"What I'm saying is this. I can go out with whomever, whenever, and do whatever I please."

He flashed his pearly white teeth. "Oh, really now?"

She pushed her shades back down over her eyes and leaned back in her seat. "It also depends on who the man is."

He turned the radio on and they rode the rest of the way to her place in silence. When they reached her house, she invited him in. At first he declined, but then took her up on the offer.

Before leaving to go to the bar, Rose asked, "Would you like something to drink?"

"If you have some Heineken that will work for me."

She winked. "I'll see what I can do."

She walked out of the kitchen and handed him the bottle of Heineken and then poured herself a glass of chardonnay. As they walked back toward the living room area, Trey commented, "You know this is the first time I've been in your house. We've worked with each other on several pictures, but this is the first time I've seen your castle."

She took a sip of her wine. "You've been invited, but I guess you were previously occupied." She continued to drink her wine.

"I would have remembered getting any type of invitation from you," he said as he flirted. "But anyway, I really like your African-American art collection. How long did it take you to collect everything and who is your dealer?"

"Thanks. I've been collecting pieces here and there over the years from different places."

She stopped and turned on her stereo, where the smooth grooves of some ol' school artists were playing. Trey moved with the beat. "Good choice of music too."

"Thank you. Glad you approve."

They sat, talked, and flirted with their eyes and hand gestures. A slow jam came on, and Trey extended his hand out to her.

"May I have this dance?"

She graciously took his hand as he pulled her closer to him. They were the same height with her heels on, so she estimated his height to be about six-feet-one. "You're a good dancer."

He leaned down and placed a kiss on her neck. "It takes two to tango."

"Yes it does," she said as she rubbed his bald head and he placed more kisses on her neck.

They continued to sway to the beat of the slow music. He stopped kissing her on the neck and she could see the passion radiating from his eyes. She guided him to the couch and they continued to kiss while undressing each other. He looked down into her eyes and asked, "Are you sure?"

She responded by kissing his chest and he moaned with pleasure. She pulled him down on top of her and they kissed passionately until her moans begged for him to enter her. Their bodies united and it were as if two freight trains collided as she felt the explosion erupting from her. They were on the couch with him on top of her for what may have been only a few minutes, but seemed like hours. Both were exhausted from the intense lovemaking.

His cell phone rang and brought them out of their daze. Rose asked, "Aren't you going to answer it?"

"Whoever it is can leave a message," Trey said in between kisses. "I'm so drained right now, I don't want to move."

Rose squirmed, which caused him to move from on top of her. She fumbled for her underwear and clothes. "I just realized the time. I don't mean to rush you, but I forgot I had another appointment."

He stood up and kissed her passionately. "No problem, sweet smelling Rose. This won't be the last time. You have all of my numbers. Call me when you finish your next appointment."

She promised to do that and walked Trey to the door. As soon as the door closed, she let out a sigh of relief.

Now, that's some love in the afternoon for you. Trey was magnificent. I didn't think anyone could beat Lance. He didn't even do the extras and I was hot like fire. I had to hurry up and get him out of my house. I don't have an appointment, but I wasn't about to spend all evening or night with him. He seemed like he was all into me too. Let me take a bath and chill, because I can't have feelings for anyone, especially another actor.

As Rose soaked in the tub, she closed her eyes and remembered how Trey felt inside of her. The next thing she knew, she was feeling hotter than a firecracker. She hurried up and finished bathing.

"Ooh. I better stop. Maybe a walk along the beach will help cool me off," she said out loud as she put on a pink and green short set.

She took her daily walk and the breeze coming from the deep blue ocean water was very soothing. When she got back to her house, she walked around to the front and noticed Lance's car parked in her driveway.

Before she could move or say anything, he got out of the car. "Girl, I have been calling you all evening. Where have you been?"

"First of all, you don't come at me like that," Rose said with one hand on her hip. "Second, apparently I was busy, since I haven't returned your call."

Lance looked as if he were about to blow a fuse. "Why do you continue to treat me this way? I only try to show you love and respect. I don't know how much more of this abuse I can take."

She unlocked her front door, and they both entered. Before walking farther into the house, she turned around to face him. "It's like this. I have not made you any promises. I am me. Take it or leave it. I told you from day two, since day one is when I caught you with that brunette, that if you still wanted to be in my company, it would be by my rules."

Lance tried to take her hand. "But baby, I have apologized for that incident. Besides, that was over ten years ago."

"Once a dog, always a dog. Bow-wow."

Lance began to laugh.

"What are you laughing at?"

"I'm laughing at you, because the whole issue doesn't have anything to do with that. You care, but you don't want me to know you care. So your way of keeping me at arm's length is putting up this façade of this hard-core Rose."

Rose threw her hand up in the air. "Please, I don't have time for this. I have an early interview with the *Early Today*

Show and they're located on the East Coast, so that means I need to be at the affiliate station's studio around four in the morning."

Lance gave her a hug and a kiss on the cheek before he exited. "We're still cool, my lady. Get some shut-eye and I'll talk to you tomorrow."

She locked the door behind him and went straight to bed.

Chapter 47
VIOLET

Violet didn't know how she managed to get through her meeting with David. Every time she looked up, he was gazing at her with a look of desire in his eyes. She squirmed a few times while sitting there. She thought they were going to be in a one-on-one meeting, but was relieved when the young man who was fresh out of college also appeared there.

Cherokee called while they were ending their meeting and David told his niece that Violet was also there. David handed the phone to Violet and without thinking, Violet accepted a dinner invitation with her. She handed the phone back to David and after he hung up, he confirmed with her the time and location for dinner. She felt like she had been set up, because now she was having dinner with both David and his niece.

That night after getting dressed, she looked at herself for the second time in the mirror to make sure the outfit she had on wasn't too provocative, but yet, she wanted to feel sexy.

She put on her lilac perfume, grabbed her purse and keys, and headed toward the restaurant.

After she valet parked, a hostess greeted her. She was there before David and his niece, so she ordered a glass of chardonnay to tide her over while she waited. She was finishing up her drink when they arrived. She spoke as they sat down. "I was beginning to think I had the wrong restaurant."

David answered, "No. We were running late because a certain party," his eyes darted in Cherokee's direction, "had to change her dress not once but twice."

"I told him I never know who I might meet while out, so I wanted to look my best," Cherokee said as she placed the napkin in her lap.

The waitress came over and took their drink orders. They also ordered appetizers. The waitress said before she left the table, "I'll be back to take your dinner orders in a few."

David gave a confirmation nod. "Where are my manners? Violet, you are looking lovely as always."

Violet smiled. "Thank you. You're not looking too bad yourself."

Cherokee watched the interchange and a big smile swept across her face. "You know I think I need to go to the ladies room."

Violet, not wanting to be left alone with David, also made an excuse. "Wait, I'll come with you."

When they got in the ladies room, Cherokee went into one stall. Violet went into one of the other stalls so that it looked as if she really did have to go to the restroom. She heard what sounded like Cherokee washing her hands. She left the stall and washed her hands and noticed that Cherokee hadn't taken her eyes off of her.

Cherokee continued to stare. "I think you're trying to deny your attraction to my uncle."

Violet was surprised by her boldness. "There is nothing going on between us."

"That's what your mouth says."

Since they had a private moment, Violet thought now was a good time to tell Cherokee where she stood when it came to her uncle. "I don't know how much he has told you; however, because of our past, it would be difficult for us to have any type of romantic relationship."

"I'm glad we're talking. Yes, he's told me some things. As a woman, I know how it must have made you feel. I know from what he's said, my uncle regrets everything. He's vowed to never marry again, because of what he did to you."

"Be that as it may, that's his choice. I don't have anything to do with it. My life is going great and I don't need the extra headache."

"I understand. But please notice the man you see today. From the looks of things, you've gotten past the drama, so maybe there's a small chance."

Violet saw a little of Rose in Cherokee, because when Rose got hold of an idea, she wouldn't let up. "Not a one."

As they were walking back to the table Cherokee whispered, "That's what your mouth says."

David stood up when they walked up to the table. "I thought I would have to send a search party for you two."

Cherokee reached down and kissed him on the cheek. "Now you know when two beautiful women go to the restroom together, they have to talk." She looked over at Violet and winked her right eye.

The waitress noticed their return and came over to take their order. They continued to talk and Violet listened to Cherokee as she recanted her college days and how she was looking forward to her new job in Boston. Although Cherokee monopolized most of the conversation, David would jump in every now and then with a little humor.

When the waitress placed the check on the table, Violet pulled out her credit card to pay for her meal and David put his hand up. "Don't insult me like that."

She put her credit card back and as they were waiting for the valet attendant to bring their cars, Cherokee and she exchanged numbers and they gave each other a hug. David stood by watching the exchange. Violet's car was brought around first. He walked her to her car and reached down to kiss her on the cheek. "Be safe."

When she got home, she rubbed her face in the same spot where David kissed her.

That night she slept peacefully and woke up refreshed. She went to her home office and turned on the laptop. She needed to finish a couple of proposals. She was so engrossed in her work that when the phone rang, it startled her.

She answered and heard an erratic voice on the line. She didn't have time to say hello, before the caller blurted out, "This is David. It's Cherokee. She didn't come home last night and I was calling to see if she was over there."

"Calm down. No. I haven't heard from her. Where did she go when I left y'all?"

"She went to a club in Oakland that someone told her about and I warned her about going to Oakland with people she didn't really know."

"I'll try to reach her on the cell number she gave me and if I hear from her, I'll let you know."

"My brother is going to kill me. I was supposed to be watching over her while she was in California."

Violet, in a reassuring tone, said, "Cherokee is a grown woman and she's probably fine. Don't worry yourself."

David sighed. "Easier said than done. If you hear from her, call me. Let me give you my home phone and cell phone numbers."

She wrote the numbers down and then ended the call. She looked in her purse and found the number she was given last night. Cherokee answered on the third ring. Violet let out a sigh of relief. "Cherokee."

"Yes. Who is this?"

"This is Violet. Are you okay?"

"Yes. I'm fine. Why wouldn't I be?"

Violet sat back in front of her laptop. "Your uncle just called me and he was worried to death about you."

"I keep forgetting that they don't see me as grown. I'm twenty-six years old and they need to just face the fact that I've grown up."

Violet laughed because she remembered being at that age, although it seemed like many moons ago. "Well Ms. Lady, be that as it may; you are staying with David. You need to respect and inform him when you're going to be out late or overnight, so that he won't be calling me or anyone else panicking."

"Yes, ma'am."

"Oh, not the ma'am. I know I'm old now."

"Can you do me a favor?"

"What's that?" Violet asked as she glanced at the computer screen.

"Can you call my uncle back for me and tell him that you talked to me? Also tell him I'm okay. Explain to him that I'm a grown woman and we talked and now I have an understanding. So that way, when I see him tonight, he won't be so angry."

"I really don't want to get in the middle of things. This is between you and him."

Cherokee begged. "Please. I wouldn't ask you, if I didn't think it would help."

"Okay. I will call him, but promise me you won't do this again. If you can't reach him, you can always call me."

"Thanks, Auntie Violet."

"Whatever. Now get your butt home before he sends out the National Guard looking for you."

Violet didn't know why she felt so compelled to help out a young lady who was virtually a stranger, although her ex-niece. They seemed to click from day one. She picked up the phone and called the last person she thought she would be speaking to with a civil tongue—David.

Chapter 48
ROSE

Rose and Trey had been seeing each other almost every day since they first slept together. The media only speculated about their relationship, but no one could confirm anything. Lance never stopped pursuing Rose and was getting more demanding of her time. Rose didn't want to commit to him, but she did like having Lance around since he was good for her ego. Fortunately for her, he was in New York producing someone's CD and she would be on her way to Louisiana by the time he returned.

She packed her luggage for her trip and forwarded her private line to her cell phone. All other calls would be picked up by voice mail and she would return them later. She called her mom who was apparently not home, so she left a message confirming her arrival time. She waited for the car to pick her up. For some reason she had this annoying feeling that she was forgetting something. The driver came to the door and took her bags to the limousine. She locked the front door and made a mental note to call Carmen, as she followed the driver to the limo.

She almost missed her flight because she had to spend

extra time in the security area because of the long lines. Once on the plane, she felt more relaxed.

While sitting in first class, one of the flight attendants came by her seat, leaned down, and whispered, "Ms. Purdue, we're not supposed to do this, but can I have your autograph for my little girl? She has your posters everywhere. She thinks she's a little Rose."

Rose took the pad and asked, "Her name?"

"Amber. Thank you. Thank you."

Rose handed the pad to the flight attendant and then reclined in her seat. She slept the majority of the trip to the Shreveport, Louisiana Regional Airport. Rose was still asleep when she felt a tap on her shoulder. As she stretched, the flight attendant informed her, "Ma'am. We're about to descend, so we need all of the passengers to let their seats up and fasten their seatbelts."

Once they landed, she went to locate her bags. Her mother and aunt greeted her. "Come let me look at you," her mom said. "You ain't no bigger than a pole." Her mom gave her a tight squeeze.

People were noticing the exchange and some began pointing because they recognized Rose.

Rose turned around to face her aunt. "Hi, Aunt Mae." Aunt Mae was one of her mom's older sisters.

"Hi, yourself. You forgot all about your people." She hugged and kissed her on the cheek.

"Come on," Rose said as she looped one arm between her mom's arm and the other between her aunt's arm. "The attendant will follow us to the car with my bags."

Her aunt looked at her bags. "Chile, you must be moving back to Shreveport with all of those bags."

They told her about what was going on in the neighborhood as they rode to her mom's house. They mentioned how the crime rate had increased with the so-called gangs in the city. They also mentioned how the economy was better in

Shreveport than in most places, because the five riverboat casinos offered the community jobs and had visitors from all over the country spending millions of dollars on the riverboats and in the surrounding area.

She observed the area as they got closer to her old neighborhood. They lived on the outskirts of the city. Houses were built in areas that were once nothing but open fields. Her mom still lived in the same house Rose grew up in, a two-story brownish red brick home with a huge front and backyard and surrounded by plenty of colorful flowers. Maybe because of all of the land, the yard had seemed like a forest to her as a little girl growing up. Because of her parents' landscaping business they were always experimenting with new plants or flowers, so they needed extra land for horticulture. The other houses were either one- or two-story, but didn't have much land surrounding them.

She couldn't wait to get out of the car. As soon as the car stopped, she hopped out and inhaled the fresh air. "I sure have missed this place."

Both her mom and aunt had a funny look on their faces as they listened to her. Her mom reached down for one of her bags and said, "Let me help you with some of this."

"No. I got it. These are too heavy for you."

"I may be old, but I still have my strength," her mom exclaimed, while reaching down to grab the small carry-on bag.

There was a sense of peace when Rose walked through the door. She felt like a teenager who returned home from her first semester in college. When she walked through her old bedroom door, she saw her favorite stuffed teddy bear on the bed, it was still pink, but a little faded. A wave of emotions took over. She had to keep her feelings in check, because she didn't want to scare her mom or aunt. The room was still as she remembered it. The paint still looked fresh. It was a pretty pink. The pink floral curtains matched the pink floral comforter on the twin bed. Her dresser was white and some of the photos she had cut out of magazines were still taped to the mirror. A smile was plastered on her face.

Once her mom and aunt left her alone to freshen up, she regretted the fact that it had taken her so long to visit. Things just weren't the same at home, without her dad being around.

How could I have stayed away so long? I've had some good times here. The only thing that's missing is Dad. I wonder if he would still be proud to have me as his daughter.

Rose sat on the bed and fluffed up her goose feather-stuffed pillow and declared, "Too many memories."

When she walked downstairs, the aroma of fried chicken and cake greeted her. It smelled like a pound cake, which was her favorite dessert. Her mom made pound cake with glazed icing dripping down the sides.

She overheard her mom and aunt talking when she approached the kitchen door. Aunt Mae was speaking low, but she was able to understand some of what she said. "Pearle, I told you she would be the one to give you trouble. I don't blame Violet. I wouldn't want to deal with her either."

"Rose is special. I don't think she realizes some of the things she does or why she does them. She has a good heart, but she just goes about doing things the wrong way."

"I'll say. I told you she was envious of Violet, but you and Louis would not listen to me. Now those girls are grown and acting like children. I tell you. I'm glad Louis is not around to see this."

Her mom was the first to realize that she was standing there. "Oh, dear. I thought you would be taking a nap. Sit down, I will be through fixing everything here shortly."

Rose acted as if she hadn't heard anything and took a seat. "I wasn't sleepy. I slept on the plane and the excitement of being back home has me wide awake."

Aunt Mae stood up and picked up her purse. "I'm about to go to the house. Your cousins want to know when would be a best time to stop by. I told them to give you at least a day to get settled in."

"Thanks, Aunt Mae. I'll make sure I see everyone before I leave."

Her mom wiped her hands on her floral, ruffled, worn apron. "Dear, by chance do you know how long you're staying with me this time?"

"I've cleared my schedule for a week. So you're stuck with me for at least a week."

Her Aunt Mae held her hands up in the air and walked out the kitchen door.

Rose spoke, "Not to be disrespectful, but what is her problem?"

"Rose. Shh. That's your aunt and she's still your elder."

"I don't think Aunt Mae ever liked me. She always seemed to be more partial to Violet," Rose explained as she took a banana off the table and ate it.

Her mom, in a disagreeing voice, replied, "None of us had favorites. We tried to treat both of you girls the same."

Rose ate the rest of her banana in silence. While her mom finished putting the final touches on dinner, the doorbell chimed and then there was a knock on the door. Rose looked up at her mom and asked, "Were you expecting anyone?"

"Yes. Please get the door for me."

Chapter 49
VIOLET

I can't wait to see Momma. Coming home once a year is just not enough. I love the outdoors. I love the smell of all the fresh flowers. Even the cab ride over wasn't as much as I thought it was going to be. The cost of living here is sure better than most places, especially California. She must be in the kitchen. I think I'll walk around to the back.

She walked up to the kitchen door and knocked. She turned the knob and her mom was opening the door at the same time. She placed her bags down and hugged her. "Hi, Mom."

"Hey, baby. I'm so glad you could come."

As they were hugging, she heard another voice. "Mom, I went to the door, but when I opened it, no one was there."

Violet turned around toward the sound of the voice and Rose entered the room at the same time and their eyes locked. They both had a look of shock on their faces. Their mom acted as if she were the happiest woman on earth. "Both of my babies are here."

Rose was the first twin to speak. "Hi, Violet. It's good to see you."

Violet didn't want to make a scene in front of her mom, so she simply ignored Rose. "Hi. Mom, I think I'm going to go unpack my things and I'll be back."

"That can wait," her mom said in a displeased voice. "I just finished dinner. Go put your bags up and then come back down. Rose, help your sister with her bags."

Rose reached out to grab one of her bags, and Violet put her hand up. "That won't be necessary."

Rose insisted, "Nonsense, I got it." Rose took one of the bags and waltzed up the stairs.

Violet looked over at her mom and before walking out the door said, "We need to talk. What is she doing here?"

Her mom shrugged her shoulders as if she had no clue to what was going on.

Violet questioned herself out loud. "What have I walked into?"

She headed to her old room and Rose was placing Violet's bag on the bed. "You really do look great, Violet."

"Thanks. Thanks for bringing my bag up."

"You're quite welcome."

They both stood there in silence until their mom yelled for them to come back downstairs to eat. "Feels like old times, huh?"

Violet managed a small laugh at her comment.

Over dinner, their mom tried to pull each one of them into a conversation by asking specific questions about the different things she knew was going on in their lives. "Violet, how is your project coming along?"

Violet left out the fact that the developer was David, especially since Rose was there. "They should be through building it in two months and I've already started the application screening. That is what takes up most of my days. The second phase is to do the interviewing. I have a couple of people on staff and we'll go from there."

Her mom reached out and squeezed her hand. "I'm so proud of you, baby."

Violet blushed. "Thanks, Mom."

"I'm going to retire early tonight. I got up early anticipating your visit. Can you girls clean up for me?"

They both stood up to help her out of her seat. "I'm fine. Just take care of the dishes, okay?"

They responded in unison. "Yes, Mom."

Violet looked over at Rose. "You want to wash or dry?"

"I'll dry."

"It figures," Violet said under her breath.

Rose didn't say anything to her smart response.

As Rose was drying the last dish, she said, "You know. We can't go the whole weekend not saying anything to each other. I don't know about you, but this is not going to work."

Violet wiped her hands and threw down the towel. "I came to see Momma. I had no idea you were going to be here or else I would have come another time."

Rose kindly stated, "Apparently we were the only two who didn't know, so I suggest we try to make the best of it."

"First of all, you don't tell me what to do. I'm not one of your flunkies. I'll do whatever it takes to cause the least amount of stress for Momma."

"Violet," Rose said as she put up the dishes, "I don't want to argue with you. All I'm saying is, we could at least try to get along for a weekend."

Violet got ready to leave the room. "Sure. But I'll be here all week."

As she was walking out, she heard Rose blurt out, "So will I."

Violet went by her mom's room and knocked. "Are you still awake?"

She heard a faint yes and walked in. Her mom was sitting up in bed reading her Bible. "You girls through with the kitchen?"

She walked over and sat on the foot of the bed. "Yes. I had a question."

Her mom placed her Bible on the nightstand by the bed and took off her reading glasses. "I already know what you want to talk about. I'm sorry about tricking you girls, but I couldn't see any other way to get you in the same place."

"Momma, I told you that I can't allow Rose back into my life. She has hurt me one too many times."

"You need to get over it. It has been ten years since you've guys have had any face-to-face contact. I know about the birthday and Christmas cards, so don't even try to mention that."

Violet began to feel like a little girl. "But, Momma."

"But Momma nothing. When I'm gone, the only thing you girls will have is each other. You need to stop this child-ishness and go make up with your sister."

Violet didn't understand why she was the one being scolded, since she wasn't the reason for the mess. "It's not my fault. I've tried and each time I forgive her, she hurts me again."

Her Mom reached on her nightstand and picked up her Bible and held it up. "You see this? This is why you should forgive her and make things right."

She held her head down. "I just can't. I can't put myself through it again. Why do I always have to be the one to make things right?"

"I will drop it for now, but I do want you to sleep on this. Ask yourself how many times have you sinned and gone to the Father for forgiveness? How many times has He forgiven you for your transgressions? How can we expect Our Father in Heaven to forgive us, when we have not shown forgive-ness towards one another?"

Violet hugged her mom good night and walked out of the room feeling like the weight of the world was on her shoulders. When she passed by Rose's old room, she paused for a moment, but kept on walking. She changed into her satin red oriental-print nightgown, got underneath a pretty floral comforter, and went to sleep.

Chapter 50
ROSE

Rose woke up the next morning to the smell of freshly brewed coffee. She rushed to the bathroom to wash her face. Afterwards, she dashed downstairs because her mom's coffee always went quickly. When she got to the kitchen, she saw Violet sitting at the table with the morning paper. Rose loudly said, "Good morning."

Rose tried to ignore the fact that she didn't get a response, so she poured herself some coffee and saw that breakfast was on the stove. She grabbed a biscuit, took a bite of it, and fixed herself a plate of scrambled eggs and sausage. She then sat across from Violet, and with a mouth full of food asked, "Where's Momma?"

Violet looked up for the first time. "Excuse me?"

"I asked where is Mom?" Rose stated while wiping her mouth with a napkin.

"Oh, she and Aunt Mae went to visit some people they know in the nursing home off Mansfield Road."

Rose continued to eat the rest of her breakfast. The house phone rang and neither one of them acted as if they wanted to answer it. Rose placed the dishes in the sink and grabbed the phone. "I guess I'll get it. Hello."

"Rosemary's Baby, what's up? Heard you were in the 'Port City.'"

Rose started laughing. "What's going on, Audrey? You know you was always my favorite cousin."

"Whatever. You went Hollywood on us and forgot all about me."

Rose leaned on the counter. "No, I didn't. You never return my calls and you're sounding just like Aunt Mae."

"Well this ain't my momma, it's me and I called to see what you were getting into today."

Rose looked over and noticed that Violet had left the room. "Nothing. You want to go shopping?"

"Only if you're buying," Audrey responded.

"Well come on. I'll be ready in thirty minutes."

"When have you ever been ready in thirty minutes? I'll be over in an hour."

They hung up and Rose went to find Violet to ask her if she wanted to go shopping. "There you are. That was Audrey on the phone. She's on her way over so we can go shopping. Do you want to tag along?"

Violet continued to brush her hair. "I'll pass, besides three is a crowd."

"Why you have to be like that? It's my treat. Let me do something for you."

Violet walked past her and stated, "You've done enough. Thank you."

As she was taking her shower, Rose tried to keep her temper in control.

I know I haven't been the best sister, but who's perfect? I've bent over backward to make Violet feel comfortable; I've been cordial, but Ms. Can't Do No Wrong acts like she got a stick up her butt. Well, I'm about to have me some fun and enjoy my time with my momma. She can trip, but she'll be tripping by herself.

Rose and Audrey spent the entire day shopping. They hit the mall on St. Vincent Avenue and since they only had a limited amount of stores, they went over to Bossier and shopped there. "Is Freeman's still open?" Rose asked.

Audrey replied, "Girl yes, but my mom is having something at her house for you two, so you might want to save your appetite. You know how we do in the South. If you don't eat or pick over our food, we get awfully offended."

"Yes. Your mom is from the old school and she'll front you out in a minute."

"Girl, ain't nothing changed, but the year."

Audrey brought Rose back to her mom's place. As Rose attempted to ring the doorbell, her mom had already opened the door. "You need to take one of my spare keys. What if Violet or I wouldn't have been here? You would have been stuck outside."

Rose kissed her on the cheek. "I have something for you."

"I told you about buying me things. I don't need anything but what God's green earth can provide."

She took out a box and handed it to her. "Just look at it as a belated or early birthday present. Let me put these away and then I'll be ready to go over to Aunt Mae's with you."

Chapter 51
VIOLET

Violet noticed the attention everyone showered on Rose. She tried to ignore the fact that hardly anyone was interested about her being home. Most of her relatives had stopped by to see supposedly both of them, but Rose as usual, was center stage. She grabbed a cold drink and exited the door that led to the back porch.

She stretched and was not aware that someone else was outside, until he came around and identified himself. "I heard you were here, but I had to come see for myself."

Violet couldn't decipher who was talking so she assumed it was someone to see her sister. "She's inside if you want to see her, but stand in line. She has an audience."

He walked under the moonlight. "I'm looking at the right sister."

She stared and when he tilted his head forward, she recognized him. He was several inches taller than she remembered, but it was the same cute, freckled-nose little boy who broke her heart so many years ago. His cocoa-brown complexion and well-chiseled body was enough to excite any hot-blooded woman. He was standing tall at six-two, dressed in all black, with his black denim jeans, and black button-down shirt. To top it off, he had on some black steel toe boots and a black Stetson cowboy hat. Violet jumped off the porch and ran up to him. "Pierre, I can't believe this."

They hugged and he swung her around. "If I would have known I was going to get this type of reaction, I would have tried to track you down years ago."

"Why didn't you? You know I'm a single lady now."

Pierre took her hand and they walked through the back-yard. "I kind of heard about that. You're looking fly as usual."

She leaned her head back and grinned. "Compliments like that might get you somewhere."

He said admiringly, "My, my, my. Little Violet has grown up. The last time I saw you, you had just graduated from college and was about to marry some busta."

"Come on. If you wouldn't have abandoned me, I would have saved myself for you."

"Please. Your daddy wasn't going to let you marry me. He wouldn't even let you accept my phone calls."

"Phone calls?"

"Yes, when I left for the service, I tried to call you and you were conveniently always out, so I assumed you had moved on without me."

Violet was stunned, because she was heartbroken when she hadn't heard from him. He had claimed to understand why she wanted to remain a virgin until marriage. She assumed he didn't want her anymore and had found him someone more experienced. "I'm learning something new tonight."

They continued to walk until they stood in front of her uncle's big black Dodge Ram truck. He let the back of the truck down and they sat and talked for a while. He continued holding her hand and said, "I guess we had some communication problems."

"Ain't that the truth?"

They continued to talk and catch up with one another.

"Well, here we are now."

"Yes," Violet said. "So why don't you catch me up on what's been going on with you. Seems like you've gotten the 4-1-1 on me already."

Pierre looked out into the night while he went over his life. "I'm now divorced and I try to see my two kids, Jalen, who's ten, and Justice, who's eight, every chance I get. Lately, because of work, it's only been every other weekend as stated in the custody papers."

She sat there and admired him as he talked. She wanted to reach out and feel his cocoa-brown skin that looked as smooth as it was in high school. His hazel eyes still sparkled when he laughed.

One of her cousins yelled out, "Violet, where are you?"

Violet yelled back, "I'm right here."

Her cousin went on to say, "Everyone was wondering where you were."

"Just tell them I'm enjoying the night air. I'll be back in shortly."

They heard the screen door shut and as Pierre stood up, he said, "Ms. Lady, looks like I've taken up enough of your time." He hesitated before saying, "I'll let you get back to your family." He walked her back to the porch. "I would like to take you out at least once while you're here, if you don't mind."

She smiled and in a flirty tone responded, "Maybe. Call me at my mom's and we'll see what happens."

He tipped his hat. "I'll do that. Good night."

She went back into the house and from the way things looked, everyone had split up and were in different parts of the house. The older people were in one room, while the younger adults and kids were in another. She found her mother and sat down on the floor beside her.

Her mother leaned down and whispered, "Why don't you go mingle with some of your cousins?"

"Actually, I'm really tired, so if you don't mind, I'll see if I can catch a ride back home."

Her mom looked at the time and decided to leave as well. "Go see if Rose is ready to leave. If she isn't, then tell her she'll need to catch a ride with someone else."

She uncrossed her legs and got up to go find Rose. Everyone in the room was joking and laughing. She stopped and talked to some of her cousins and then made her way near Rose. "Momma said she's ready to go, but if you would like to stay, just have someone drop you off."

Rose responded, "Audrey and several of us are going to the riverboat casinos. Do you want to come?"

"I don't think so," Violet stated. "I don't really gamble."

Audrey walked over and wrapped her arms around her shoulders. "Come on. Besides, we haven't hung out in ages. You don't have to gamble; you can just watch us. It'll be fun."

Violet shook her head no. "Maybe next time."

"Please," Audrey begged.

Violet started to feel guilty for being antisocial. "Okay. I'll go this time."

They all grabbed their keys and purses and headed for the door. Violet went to inform her mom that she had a change of plans. Her mom was thrilled she had decided to hang out with her cousins and sister. Her mom hugged her and said, "Don't worry about coming in late. I'll keep the porch light on for you girls."

Before leaving, she made sure she went and personally told her aunts and uncles good-bye and then she headed out the door, hoping that she was riding in a separate car from Rose.

Chapter 52
ROSE

Rose said her good-byes as well and waited for everyone to get outside.

I'm surprised that Violet's coming. Actually, I didn't expect her to say yes, even after Audrey asked her. I guess, she decided not to be so antisocial after all. I'm only taking a thousand dollars with me, or else I will end up at the casino all night. I should have worn something more casual. Oh well, I never know who I'll run into.

Rose and Violet rode in Audrey's burgundy Ford Taurus. Rose sat in the front with Audrey and Violet sat in the back seat next to two of their other cousins.

Audrey lowered the music. "Violet, I heard a blast from your past showed up tonight."

Rose turned her head slightly so she wouldn't miss any of the conversation. Violet responded, "Yes. He heard I was here and came over."

Audrey acted as if she wanted to say something, but stopped and then went on to say, "He's divorced and doing quite nicely for himself."

"And fine as I don't know what, too," one of their other cousins chimed in.

Rose remained quiet, but the others continued talking about how fine and sexy Pierre looked.

When the three carloads of relatives got to the casino, the parking lot was full. Rose paid for all of them to valet park so they wouldn't have to worry about walking a mile to get from and to their cars.

Before separating in the casino, they all synchronized their watches and vowed to meet back in the same spot within two hours. When they went through the security entrance to the casino section, the agent asked to see Rose's license and looked at her twice. He acted excited to see her. "Ma'am, do you think I could get your autograph?"

Rose, not wanting to hold up the line behind her, told him, "I'll do it on my way out." He accepted her response and she waited on the side while her sister and cousins were carded.

One of the cousins blurted out, "They must be carding everyone."

"Either that or they're blind. I look every bit of thirty," Audrey seriously stated.

Everyone turned and looked at Audrey. Rose said what she assumed everybody was thinking. "Thirty. If you're just thirty, then that makes us all a day shy of twenty-one."

Audrey laughed. "I remember my twenties."

They laughed and all went separate ways. Some went in the direction of the slot machines, while others went toward the roulette and poker tables. Rose stood there and tried to decide if she wanted to play blackjack or roulette. She decided on blackjack. She won a couple hands of blackjack and then decided to go play the slot machines.

Word had gotten out that she was in the casino. People

were beginning to stare no matter where she went. While she stood in line to cash in her chips and get change for the slot machines, the manager on duty walked over to her and asked, "Ms. Purdue, are you enjoying your time here?"

Rose turned around hoping not to cause a scene. "Yes, thanks. There is no need for special treatment."

He extended his hands out. "If by chance the attention becomes overwhelming, please don't hesitate to use our security."

Rose shook his hand and the line had moved, so she was now in front of the cashier. After getting her change, she walked over to the slot machines, but they were all full on that side of the casino, so she walked around to the other side and found a vacant seat. She sat down and while she retrieved her coins from her bucket so she could play, she saw Violet out of the corner of her left eye sitting two seats down.

As soon as the seat next to her became vacant, Rose got up and went to it. She plopped down with her bucket of coins. "Hi, Violet."

Violet looked up. "Hi."

"How are the slots playing?" she asked her. "I've been playing the tables most of the night."

Violet continued to pull the lever while talking. "They're okay. I just started playing. I was watching some of the others at the tables and got bored, so I decided to play the slot machines."

Rose placed a quarter in the machine and won twenty dollars on her first pull. "I think I might stay at this one." She then turned her attention back to Violet. "It can get boring after a minute. Especially when you're not playing or if you're losing."

Violet didn't say anything else to her, so Rose continued to play the slots in silence. Audrey walked up behind them. "There you two are. We're ready to blow this joint and head over to another one."

Everyone cashed in their coins or chips. They piled into the cars and started off to another casino located across the river. Before Audrey made it to the other casino, Rose balled over in pain. "Ladies, I don't mean to ruin your night, but I think I need to go to a hospital."

Audrey slowed the car down. "What's wrong?"

"My side is killing me and this excruciating pain won't let up."

Audrey called someone from her cell phone and informed them of their change of plans and then she drove in the direction of the hospital. They were closest to the hospital near Line Avenue, so she headed there. When they pulled up, one of the male cousins carried her in. Violet had remained quiet. Rose could see that Violet had picked up her purse with all of her identification.

Rose tried to tell the nurse her symptoms through the pain. At first the admitting nurse wanted to direct them to the state hospital, but as soon as she recognized who Rose was, she changed her tune. Rose was soon admitted to the hospital. They ran several tests. Rose felt completely exhausted. She couldn't remember who was there with her, because the pain medication they had injected began to take effect.

The pain medicine had allowed her to sleep throughout the night. The next morning when she woke up, she noticed her mom, Aunt Mae, and Violet surrounding her. She tried to shake off the drowsiness. "Hey there. Why is everyone looking so gloomy? I'm okay now."

Her mom held her hand. "Of course you are. You had us worried for a minute."

Aunt Mae came closer to the bed and stated, "The doctor is making his rounds now, so he'll be by any minute."

Rose watched as Violet turned the page of her newspaper. Before she could say anything, the door opened, and as if on cue the doctor and a nurse walked in. "How's our patient this morning?"

Rose tried to sit up. "Better than when I came in last night, that's for sure."

He started probing and then continued to say, "I've looked over your tests and you no longer have a fever, so we're going to release you today, but I need to inform you of some things."

"What?" Rose asked, as her family gathered around to listen.

"You have a bladder infection. Fortunately we caught it in time and once treated, you'll be all right. I would suggest that you drink more water and lay off the alcohol and soda." He handed her a couple of prescriptions. "I also suggest that you call your personal physician for follow-up care."

"Thank you, doctor."

"Just get well, that's all the thanks I need." He shook her hand and then he and the nurse exited the room.

Rose was released from the hospital and once she made it to her mom's house, she headed straight to her bedroom. The doctor insisted that she get plenty of rest and she intended to do so, at least for the next few days.

Chapter 53
VIOLET

I didn't plan on spending part of my vacation catering to the Drama Queen. Mom has to go down to south Louisiana with Aunt Mae today to check on another relative, so now I'm stuck with making sure Rose is comfortable. She was asleep when I checked on her a few minutes ago. I don't see why Mom always has to be the good Samaritan in the family. She should have let her brother go check on their cousin's well being.

Violet cooked a hearty breakfast. She placed some grits, scrambled eggs, and two slices of bacon and a slice of toast on a plate and then put it on a tray. She also made sure she included a pitcher of ice water. She carried the tray upstairs. She knocked on the door before entering Rose's room. She heard Rose say something, and assumed she said come in, so she opened the door and placed the tray on a little table their mom had set up in the room.

"I brought you a little something, since you're supposed to keep your strength up."

"Thanks," Rose said. "You can leave it there. I need to get up so I can at least wash my face and hands."

Violet couldn't remember seeing Rose in a helpless position. She went to help her up. "Let me help you."

Rose leaned on her while getting up out of the bed. "Wow. I didn't realize this medicine would keep me in the bed like this. I had different plans for my mini-vacation."

"I know what you mean," Violet said as she helped her up. "Me too."

Rose was able to walk to the bathroom and Violet waited to make sure she was okay. When she returned, Violet sat the table closer to the bed and left Rose alone so she could eat her breakfast in peace. The doorbell was ringing as she walked down the stairs. She looked out of the peephole and after recognizing who was on the other end she opened the door. "I should have known you weren't going to call."

Pierre gave her a hug. "Why should I call when I can just stop by?"

They walked into the living room and each took a seat on the couch. Violet asked, "What brings you over this way?"

"I was driving by and was going to call, and opted for stopping by instead. Hoping your mom didn't throw me out before I had a chance to see you again."

She laughed. "My mom is not here and she wouldn't have done that."

"Sure. I think your whole family conspired against me."

"Yes, we took it upon ourselves to cause you grief," Violet said sarcastically.

"I'm sorry," he said as he took her hand in his. "What got you in a foul mood?"

Violet, not having anyone else to talk to, and it was too early to call Janice back in California, responded, "Nothing. It's just that Rose got sick and now she has to be on bed rest for a few days and I got stuck taking care of her while my mom goes to see about another sick relative."

"Calm down, baby. Come here and lean on my shoulder."

She leaned on him and she felt as if the strain from being at home had lifted and released itself, just from Pierre surrounding her with his arms. "I'm sorry. I know you didn't come over to hear about my issues."

He brushed her hair slightly with his hand. "I came to see you and to find out if I still stood a chance after all of these years."

Violet looked at him with a bewildered look. "Pierre, our lives have taken different paths. We can't go back to the way we were. I didn't even know what being a woman was about back then. I'll be celebrating my fortieth birthday this year."

He took her hand in his again and looked into her eyes. "You are as beautiful today as you were twenty-something years ago. I don't expect to pick up where we left off, because I too have matured. I want the opportunity to see you again."

She held her hand up in protest. "Don't. We both know that relationships seem to be destined to doom, particularly a long-distance one. Besides, I'm working on a project that will keep me busy for at least the next few years."

He took her hand and kissed the outside of her hand. "I'm not going to give up on you. It'll be an adjustment, but it can work. I'll let it drop for now, because I know you have a lot going on."

She sighed with relief. "Thank you."

He looked down at his watch and as he stood up, he said, "I must leave for the office now, but think about it."

She walked him to the door. When they reached the door, he leaned down and kissed her passionately. She tried to suppress a moan, but failed. They kissed for what seemed like hours, but was only a few seconds. She pulled away. "You better get going."

"I will, only if you promise to see me again before you leave."

She pushed him out the door. "I promise. Now go."

He left and he waved at her as he backed from the driveway. She waved back and then closed the door. When she turned around, Rose was standing at the head of the stairway. Violet asked, "How long have you been there?"

"Long enough to see the long, and I do mean long, heated kiss."

Violet smiled for the first time at something her sister had said since they had been at their mom's. "Don't read more into it than what it was. It was just a kiss."

"That's what they all say. I was coming to ask you to bring me some more water. I've been guzzling down water all morning." Rose handed her the pitcher.

"I'll bring some more up in a minute."

As she walked away to get the water, she stopped for a second and placed her index finger over her lips, because she could still feel the effects from his kiss. She filled the pitcher with water and then headed upstairs to Rose's room.

Chapter 54
ROSE

Although I came here to see Mom, I'm glad she left when she did, so that Violet could be here to help take care of me. I was actually feeling better the day Mom returned from south Louisiana, but didn't want to pass on the chance of having Violet wait on me hand and foot. Today will be the day I let them know that I'm 100 percent better and treat them both to a nice dinner out. Now, where did I put those earrings? I hope I didn't leave them at home, because they would go perfect with this outfit.

Rose ran into Violet as she was leaving her room. "Good morning, Flower."

Violet smiled. "Hello yourself. What are you doing out of bed?"

"I'm feeling a whole lot better and I'm tired of being cooped up in that room."

"You better take it easy or Mom will have you strapped to the bed."

"I know. I want to at least come downstairs and maybe return some phone calls."

Violet let Rose walk down the stairs first. Rose could feel Violet softening up to her, but she wasn't going to get her hopes up too high, because she was tired of getting rejected. When she entered the kitchen, she could see that her mother had cooked a big southern-style breakfast. She couldn't wait to eat, so she immediately took her place at the kitchen table.

In a jubilant voice, her mom said, "Now Rose, I could've brought you your breakfast."

"I'm fine," she said as she grabbed her favorite fruit, a banana. "I won't do too much, I promise. By the way, I'm treating you both to a very nice dinner, so don't make any plans for this evening."

Her mom placed a plate full of grits, sausage, and scrambled eggs on the table. "Child, I ain't got nothing to wear to no fancy dinner."

"Momma, you can just wear a dress. How about the black one with the floral scarf? That'll be perfect."

Violet walked in and joined them at the table. Their mom said grace. "Thank you Lord for Your healing power. Thank you for allowing the love to flow through this family. Please strengthen us and never let us sway from Your word. Bless this food we're about to eat and protect us on this day's journey. Amen."

"Amen," Rose and Violet said in unison.

After everyone ate, Violet volunteered to clean up the kitchen. Rose returned a couple of phone calls. She called some of her relatives back who had called to check up on her over the past few days. She hadn't checked her personal messages since she had been in Louisiana, so she dialed up her voice mail. Her voice mailbox was full, so she began listening to the messages and wrote down names and numbers of people she needed to call.

Violet was finishing the dishes as Rose finished checking

her last message. She spoke out loud, "I tell you, some people act like they can't get along without me."

Violet looked up from wiping off the counters. "Trouble in paradise?"

"Nothing that Carmen can't handle. What are your plans for the day?"

"I'm meeting Pierre for lunch and then I'll go visit with some people." She folded up the dish towel. "I'll meet you guys back here for dinner."

Rose picked up her glass and drank the rest of her orange juice. "So what's up with you and Pierre? Any more kisses?"

"Now you know talking about men is a sore subject between the two of us. We've been doing fine this week, let's not spoil it."

Rose went to the sink and washed her glass. "I'm sorry. I was just trying to find out what was going on with my only sister. I shouldn't have to always hear about it from another source you know."

"You made the bed that you now lie in," Violet said with some attitude.

Rose turned around and looked at Violet. "I've also attempted to show that there's no more thorns, so please give us another chance." She didn't wait around to hear Violet's response; she turned and walked out of the room.

Rose went into the living room to return the rest of her calls. The first person she called was Carmen. "Hi, it's me."

"Dear, where have you been? I've been calling you and you failed to leave me your mom's number."

"Sorry. I thought I did. I've been relaxing with my family," Rose responded nonchalantly. "Just so that you won't hear about this elsewhere, I was in the hospital a couple of days ago."

"Too late."

"What do you mean too late?" she asked, as she used the remote to mute the sound of the television. She tried to get comfortable, so she crossed her legs up under herself.

Carmen explained, "The reason why I was calling is because one of the nurses leaked to a local Shreveport reporter that you were admitted there and the article he wrote appeared in the Shreveport paper's front section and it got picked up on the wire."

Rose sounded agitated. "As far as I know, no one has called me to find out what happened."

Carmen got silent for a moment. "It stated in the article that you were not available for comment."

"Hold on, Carmen." She screamed for Violet. "Violet, can you pass me today's paper?"

Violet walked in with the paper and had an attitude written all over her face. "I'll appreciate it if you wouldn't yell the next time." She dropped it by her and then left out of the room.

"Why didn't you tell me Violet was there?" Carmen questioned. "Is your mom okay?"

As she looked at the paper, she halfway responded, "Yes. She's fine. I'll tell you about that later. Okay. I see it here. At least he kept to the facts, unlike some reporters I know."

Carmen finally asked, "What exactly is wrong with you?"

"I have a bladder infection. The doctor gave me some antibiotics and pain medicine and I'm feeling 100 percent better."

Carmen sighed and said, "Good to know. Now I know what to tell the press hounds. Did you ever think the price of success would be this?"

"No," Rose said as she lay the paper down. "I've gotten used to it. Anything else I should know about?"

"Nothing, just the usual."

They continued to talk until Rose's cell phone call waiting beeped. "Carmen, let me get this call. I'll call you right before I leave here, so you can have a car waiting for me."

She didn't wait for a response and clicked over to her other line. "Lance, I was just about to call you."

Sounding upset, he blasted into the phone. "Why did I

have to read about you being hospitalized in the paper? I've left you messages. Did you even think that I would be worried out of my mind?"

Rose un-muted the television and let Lance ramble on with his complaints. Without being interrupted she said, "If you're through I'll answer your questions. Yes, I'm fine. No I didn't call, because I was on bed rest. Yes, I'll be home next week as planned. No, I'm not obligated to let you or anyone else know my every move."

"Baby, you don't know how bad I wish you would let me into your heart and give us another chance."

Rose laughed at his comment. "Lance, you're talking to me now. I know all about the other women." She stopped laughing and continued to say, "I don't care about that anymore because you are just something to do to pass the time. You are fun to hang out with and you're definitely a good lay."

Lance sounded angry. "I'm tired of the way you treat me. I break my neck to make sure I keep you happy. Not once do you show me any type of appreciation. Since you want to go there, I want you to know you've been put on notice. I will no longer be your lap dog."

Rose tried to hold in a giggle and said in a condescending voice, "Whatever you say. Whatever makes you happy."

Lance sounded like he was steaming mad. "I'm going now before I say something we both will regret." He hung up on her.

Rose stared at the phone for a moment in disbelief. "He'll be calling back." She went through her list of numbers saved on her phone and found Trey's number, her favorite costar, on and off the screen.

Trey picked up on about the fifth ring. She chimed, "I was about to hang up."

Sounding as if he was in bed, he said, "Rose, baby. Can I call you back?"

"No, you may not," Rose responded. Not one to be put off, she said, "I'll talk to you, when I talk to you. Bye."

Her mom was walking by and apparently heard the frustration in her voice and checked to see if she was doing all right. She reassured her that she was fine. She then returned to making phone calls. She spent the remainder of the afternoon laying on the couch and watching soap operas.

Chapter 55
VIOLET

Violet didn't know what to expect from her lunch date with Pierre. She told him she would meet him at Pete Harris Café, a popular seafood restaurant located near downtown Shreveport. It wasn't in the best of neighborhoods, but had the best shrimp etoufee and stuffed crabs north of New Orleans. As she was waiting for him to arrive, she reminisced about their last encounter.

I wonder if he was really my soul mate and our timing was just off, or am I trying to think of ways to distract myself from my recent attraction to David. Either way, neither one is worth pursuing. On one hand, I have a man who I thought broke my heart, who is now divorced with kids and has a successful career. Then there's David who betrayed me with my own sister; yet, I seem to be able to now be in his company without wanting to kill him. Why can't I meet a man without all of these extra additives?

* * *

Violet was going back and forth about the two men in her head, when Pierre walked up to the table and took a seat. "Sorry, I'm late, but I had a client who insisted that I be the one to work on his account."

"No problem," Violet said. "It gave me a chance to look over the menu."

She knew he was probably thinking she meant food, but if only he knew she was talking about men.

They chatted in between bites and both realized they still had a lot in common. They were able to easily communicate with one another and had a very pleasant lunch. He walked her to the car she had borrowed from her mom. Neither acted as if they were ready to part ways. He asked her, "Can we meet for dinner tonight?"

"I would, but I promised my sister and mom that I would have dinner with them."

"How about coming over to my place tonight for a nightcap after your dinner?"

She thought about it and declined, but made a counter-offer. "Under the circumstances, I don't think it's wise, but can you come over to Mom's? Let's say around eight o'clock. We should be back by then. Besides, she baked a peach cobbler that will knock your socks off."

He teased her. "You don't have to tempt me with the cobbler. I would have come just to see you." He bent down and kissed her before she could protest.

Violet spent the rest of the day visiting with some of her relatives. The day went by quickly and before she realized it, it was time for her to go home for dinner. She rushed to get ready so she wouldn't hear her mom complain about being tardy.

Violet met Rose downstairs and was only ten minutes late. To her surprise, their mom was not there. She asked

Rose, "Have you checked on Mom? She's usually the one that's hounding us about timeliness."

"I know. She was in the bathroom and she should be coming out any minute."

At that moment, their mom walked up. "Ladies. I see you both look like beautiful blooming flowers."

They turned around and Violet spoke out first. "Mom, why aren't you dressed? Aren't you the one always getting on us about tardiness?"

"My arthritis is acting up and this medicine I took has made me extremely sleepy. You girls go ahead and go. This old lady just needs some shut-eye."

Violet took her hand and walked with her to the sofa. "Mom, we can prepare something or order something."

"No." She protested. "I wouldn't hear of it. Rose wanted to treat us both. She'll have to make up by taking me to lunch before she leaves."

Rose hugged her and reached over to kiss her on the cheek as if she understood what their mom was trying to do. "You have a rain check. Come on, Violet. I'll even let you drive."

Violet looked over at her mom. "You're sure you're going to be all right?"

"Yes. Now you two go, before you're late for your reservation."

They left and Violet drove. They rode in silence. When they reached the popular seafood restaurant, there was a line. Since they had a reservation, they could be seated right away. As they waited for their meal to be served, Rose tried to strike up a conversation. "Do you miss living here?"

Violet took a sip of her water. "Sometimes. It's a nice place to grow up, but I also like the ocean."

Rose's eyes sparkled. "So do I. The ocean keeps me centered sometimes. I think I'll take a month cruise to different parts of the world when I get another big break in between projects."

The waiter brought over their food and they continued to talk in between bites. Violet had been observing Rose over the last few days and noticed that something about her had changed. Rose was still a little bossy, but she didn't let Violet's attitude dissuade her from being cordial to Violet, at least most of the time. The old Rose would have caused drama and would have made sure their mom was put in a position where she would have to choose sides.

As they were eating their dinner, Violet was thinking about some of the things her mom had said that first night she was there. She questioned herself about how she felt about Rose now, seeing that she had indeed changed. She prayed silently that she would be able to forgive her before it was too late.

Violet snapped back into the moment. Rose was talking to her and she only heard Rose's last statement. "A penny for your thoughts."

"I was enjoying this great food," Violet responded. "You know I like the seafood out in Cali, but the seasoning can't touch this."

Rose wiped her mouth with her napkin and took another bite of some garlic bread. "I know. This bread is the bomb. The fish is so good, it's falling off the bone. Not that imitation stuff either."

Violet swallowed her stuffed shrimp. "I know. This is the real deal. I think I've gained about five pounds this week."

"I probably would have too, if I hadn't gotten sick."

"Are you taking your medicine like you're supposed to?" Violet asked. "The first couple of days, Mom and I had to administer it to you, but you know how you are with medicine."

Rose picked up her glass of wine. "Yes, I am."

Violet tried not to sound like a mother hen, but said anyway, "You really shouldn't be drinking any alcohol while taking those medications."

Rose put the glass down without taking another sip. "You're

right. I'm so used to having a glass of wine with my dinner, that it's become a habit."

Violet grinned. "You know that's one of the few times you've just done what I suggested without putting up a fight."

Rose smiled back and winked. "I just didn't want to make a public scene."

They were offered dessert and they both declined, remembering the peach cobbler that was waiting on them at their mom's house. While driving back home, Violet decided to talk about Pierre. She wanted to see how Rose would respond.

"Pierre is coming over tonight. He'll probably be pulling up when we get there, if he hasn't already made it there. Do you want to hang out with us?"

"No," Rose said. "You go ahead and have fun with your man."

"He's not my man."

"From the way he kissed you the other day, he has already staked his claim."

Violet got a hot flash from remembering both of the times he had kissed her. "He is a great kisser. I have to hand that to him."

"I say go for it. You deserve some happiness and he puts some pep in your step. Do what you have to do."

Violet could sense that Rose was actually sincere.

As they pulled up, Pierre was pulling up at the same time. She looked over at Rose and said, "I'll see you inside later."

"You won't see me," Rose responded. "I'm grabbing my cobbler and I'll be upstairs. Stop by when he leaves."

Rose waved hello to Pierre and then she went into the house.

Chapter 56
ROSE

Rose hurriedly fixed her cobbler, so she could be out of Violet and Pierre's way when they came into the kitchen. She went to check on her mom. She knocked before entering her room. "I wanted to see how you were doing."

Her mom placed her Bible down on the top cover beside her. "Doing better. I took a nap and woke up when I heard the door open."

She pulled a chair up near her mom's bed. In between eating her cobbler she said, "You know if I could make cobbler just as good as you, I would be another Mrs. Smith."

"What are you talking about?" her mom jokingly said. "Mrs. Smith ain't got nothing on me."

They both laughed. "Dinner was nice. I wish you would have come."

Her mom took her reading glasses off and placed them on her nightstand. "How did it go?"

"How did what go?" Rose asked as she continued to eat.

"Is Violet talking to you now?"

"She's been talking the whole time we've been here, but

just not the way I would like her to," Rose responded while licking her lips. "Tonight was actually quite decent. We even had a few laughs."

"That's good to hear. As I was telling her, you girls need to find out a way to work out your differences, because I'm not going to be around forever. You only have each other."

Rose finished the last bite of her cobbler and placed the bowl on the nightstand. "You say that as if you're thinking about dying tomorrow."

"I didn't say that, because only God knows our appointed time. I just want you two to be close like me and my sisters are. Some of my sisters have passed on to the other side, but I still have the memories to reflect back on. Don't look back on your life and wonder what if things had been different. You'll be forty this year and it's about time you started acting like it."

Rose hung her head down in shame. "Momma, I've tried everything to make up for my past."

"Have you gone to the Father and asked Him to forgive you my child?"

"No."

"He's who you need to make it right with first and then maybe, just maybe, everything else will work itself out." Her mom patted her hand.

"I know, but I've done so many things that I'm too ashamed to even talk about. What the world sees is an act and I could care less about them, but my own sister can't stand to be in a room with me for more than five minutes. That hurts me deep to the core."

Her mom reached up to hug her. "Dear, I know you haven't always done the right thing, but Violet will come around. You can't erase hurt overnight, only the Father can."

"You know that Pierre dude is in the kitchen with her right now. I hope he is sincere, because I would hate to kick his butt."

"Now, now. I think you've interfered enough in her relationships, don't you?"

"Momma, I know I'll never live down what I did with David, but Marcus was a sneaky character and I should still be whooping his butt for what he did to her—to us."

"I can rest a little easier now that you girls are at least civil to each other. What's going on in your personal life? I always hear the entertainment shows talk about Lance. I thought you guys were through, and who's this new cat they're linking you with? I know he's an actor and is fine as I don't know what. What's his name?"

"Momma. I have never heard you talk like this and his name is Trey. We're just friends."

"I see. Well if I were twenty years younger, I would give you a run for your money."

They laughed and Rose told her about Lance and Trey, leaving out how they both were great in the bed. "So that's all that's going on with me. It's so hard to trust men; that's why I hardly ever date."

Her mom commented, "As far as looks go, they're both lookers, but you can't always judge a book by its cover. Lance seems to have been around for the long haul; if you give him some positive encouragement instead of treating him like he's crap, he probably would keep his pants zipped."

Rose placed her hand over her mouth. "Momma."

"I read the papers and I watch television. I keep up with what's going on in Hollywood. I have to, because my own daughter keeps me in the dark. Anyway, Lance has potential, because he acts like he really loves you." She paused and then continued to say, "Now, Trey seems too much into himself. He's good to have on the arm and to show off, but I wouldn't think about getting attached to him."

Rose shook her head. "You are full of surprises tonight. I'll take all you've said under consideration. For the record, I don't plan on settling down with either one of those jokers."

They continued to talk for a very long time and Rose noticed that she had been in there for a couple of hours. Her mom started to doze off on her. That was her sign it was time for her to go upstairs. When she got upstairs, she looked for her cell phone and checked her voice messages. She normally had the phone glued to her ear, but since coming back home, she had kept it turned off. She noticed she had quite a few messages, and was checking them when she heard a knock on the door.

"Come in."

"Hi. You asked me to stop by after Pierre left."

Rose hung the phone up and smiled. "I just wanted to be nosy and see what time you actually came upstairs."

Violet gave her an 'Oh no you didn't look' and responded, "I'm going to bed."

"Alone?"

Violet managed to smile. "Yes. Alone."

"It was your choice I'm sure, because I'm sure he tried."

"I really don't feel like talking about it, but thank you for being concerned."

Rose not wanting to push the issue spoke out, "Get some rest and I'll see you in the morning."

"You too. Good night." Violet closed her door.

That night before going to bed, Rose did something she hadn't done in years and that was say prayers before laying her head down to sleep. She believed in God and all His power; however she didn't pray on a regular basis.

Father, God. I humble myself before you. I know that I am one of the biggest sinners. Please forgive me for all I've done and said over the years. Especially the hurt and pain I've caused my family, namely my sister, who has always been sweet and forgiving. Help me make decisions in my life that will help others, not hinder them or cause them any harm. I also want to ask you to watch over and protect my mom and sister. They mean so much to me and I ask you to cradle me in your arms and comfort me and last, but not least, Lord if it's your will, please soften Violet's heart, so we can become not only friends, but be as close as two sister's in Christ could ever be. Amen.

Chapter 57
VIOLET

Violet woke up tired, but she knew she had been sleeping for at least eight hours. She got out of the bed and stretched. Her head was hurting slightly, which was the first sign of a migraine, so she looked for her medicine in her purse. She ended up pouring out everything on the bed. She found the medicine and placed everything back in her purse, except for her cell phone. She would check messages and return calls as soon as she could get her migraine under control.

When she got downstairs to the kitchen, no one was there. She saw that her mom had left her some breakfast and a note. She got a glass of water and took her medicine. The note stated that her mom and Rose went shopping. It also mentioned that she was sleeping so peacefully, that they didn't want to wake her up. She warmed her breakfast and then got the morning paper. She always liked to keep up with what was going on locally, so she went to the local section first, before reading the other sections.

The medicine began to take effect. After she read the paper, she took a long hot bath. She was deeply medicated and had actually dozed off when the ringing of her cell phone that was on the bathroom counter, woke her up. She got out of the tub and tried to catch it before it went to voice mail. "Hello."

"Hi. I was hoping to catch you. Did I catch you at a bad time?" the caller asked.

"I am in the middle of something. Give me about fifteen minutes and I'll call you back."

She hung up with David and then dried herself off. She decided to put on her canary yellow Capri pants with a matching striped shirt. She lay across the bed and called him back. "Hi. It's me."

David placed her on hold for a few seconds and then came back to the line. "Sorry about that, but as soon as I hung up with you, a client called."

"No problem. Is everything going okay with the building?"

"Yes. Everything is fine. We're on schedule and it should be complete in no time."

She was happy about that. "How's your niece?"

"Cherokee is fine. She's leaving soon. I'm going to miss her."

"She's a sweetheart and you guys should be very proud. She has a strong mind and she's very determined to succeed."

"You're right and I shouldn't worry about her. Allegra loves her."

Violet was curious as to who Allegra was. She didn't say anything; she remained silent.

"Violet, are you still there?"

"Yes. I was wondering, who is Allegra?"

"Oh, I'm sorry. We do need to catch up, don't we? She's my daughter and the light of my world."

It all came back to her; she was the little girl she saw in the picture on his desk. "I didn't realize you had any kids."

"She's four years old, but her mother and I don't really get along. If I had my way, I would have her all of the time."

"So you did remarry?"

"No. I have never remarried. Allegra's mom and I were friends. We became sexually involved out of loneliness. Neither one of us were with the people we wanted to be with, so we decided to try our hand at a relationship. It was short lived, because the man that she was head over heels for all of a sudden wanted her back. She left me and a few months later I found out she was pregnant. No one knew who the father of the child was until after she was born and blood tests were done."

Violet sat up in bed with David's revelation. "Wow. Now that's some drama for you. She's a cutie pie. I saw the picture on your desk. You always said you wanted a little girl."

David sounded disappointed when he said, "I wouldn't mind having some more kids."

"Good luck on your quest. I don't mean to rush off the phone, but I hear someone at the door."

After she hung up with David, she went downstairs and saw that her mom and Rose had been grocery shopping. "Let me help you guys with those bags."

"Sleeping Beauty is awake."

Violet rolled her eyes at her sister. "Don't start. Sleeping Beauty is now WIDE awake."

Her mom and Rose laughed at her. After unpacking the groceries, they all went into the living room to rest. Her mom was the first to break the silence. "Ladies, I'm going to miss y'all when you leave."

Rose squeezed her mom's hand. "I'm only a phone call away."

"Yes. Me too. Why don't you come stay a few weeks with me? May do you some good to get away."

Rose jumped in and said, "That sounds like a good idea. Then you guys can drive down to LA and maybe spend a little time there as well."

"I don't know. I don't care for flying too much these days."

"It's not that bad." Violet volunteered and said, "If you like I can fly out here and we can fly back together."

Rose chimed in, "Come on, Mom. Violet and I would love to have you."

Violet looked over at her sister, for once they were in agreement. "Yes, Mom. Listen to Rose."

"I'll think about it."

Since this was their last night together, her mom fixed a meal fit for a king and his entire palace. She baked a ham and turkey. She also made stuffed dressing and potato salad. She baked an apple pie, peach cobbler, and a pound cake. Everything was homemade, except for the dinner rolls. She invited over family and friends for the good-bye celebration. Violet was on her way to the kitchen for a second serving of food, when Pierre walked through the front door.

"I heard there was a party going on and I wanted to give one of the guest of honors a farewell gift."

Violet smiled and attempted to hug him. "I would hug you, but as you can tell my hands are full."

He smiled back. "I wish my hands were full of something."

"Whatever. I'm headed to the kitchen so if you want something to eat, I suggest you follow me. It's going fast."

He followed Violet to the kitchen and as she prepared their plates, he went behind her and placed his arms around her and kissed her on the neck. "You know I've imagined you in my kitchen and I won't tell you the details, but let's just say, there was heat, but not coming from the stove."

"Oh really now." She put the plate down and turned around. "In your fantasy, were the kisses like this?" She kissed him with so much passion, he acted like he was floored.

"I'm sorry," Rose said, interrupting them. "I only came in to get a piece of pound cake."

Violet smoothed out her skirt and Pierre wiped the lipstick from his mouth. "No, we apologize. We were only getting something to eat."

Rose looked at them both, but she didn't say anything else. She cut herself a piece of cake and left them alone.

Violet jokingly asked, "Did we get interrupted in your fantasy?"

"No, and I'm glad we did get interrupted, because I would hate for your mom to walk in and see that I've strad-dled her daughter right here on her kitchen floor."

Violet laughed. "It wouldn't have gotten that far."

He took both of their plates. As they headed to the living room, he whispered in her ear, "That's what you think."

After dinner, she said her good-byes to her relatives and walked Pierre out to his car. "Thank you for making my stay here enjoyable."

"Promise me you'll keep in contact and think about all of the things that I said. I think it can work. If push comes to shove, I can even pack up and head out west."

"I wouldn't want you to do that."

He opened up the back door to his car and pulled out a gift bag. "I would do anything for you. I let you go one time without a fight. I won't let you slip through my hands twice. Here's a little something. You can open it now or later."

She took the gift out of the pretty floral gift bag. It was a box, but it had another velvet box in the inside. She opened it and found a 24-karat gold charm bracelet with diamond pendants and the biggest one was that of a heart. "This is beautiful. Thank you." She reached up and gave him a kiss.

"You're quite welcome. Each pendant means something. I wanted to leave you something to think about."

"Trust me. You have left a lot on my mind. I'll call you when I get back to San Jose. I promise."

They hugged once again and he kissed her, making her feel like a dog in heat.

Chapter 58
ROSE

I should be happy about going back to my world, but a part of me wishes I could stay here and live with Momma for the rest of my life. I have thrived on attention, but this week of down-home living has spoiled me. Well, I'm all packed up and ready to go.

Rose headed downstairs with her bags. After discussing their flight plans last night, Violet and she discovered they were scheduled to leave on the same flight, with Violet continuing her flight to San Jose from LA.

Their mom was crying. Rose knew this was going to be hard for her, because they all hadn't been under the same roof at the same time since her early twenties and before her dad had died.

"Momma, are you going to be okay? I'm only a plane flight away."

They hugged and their mom wiped away some stray tears. "I know, but I'm going to miss my babies."

Violet walked in from outside. "Momma are you crying? Don't. You're going to make me cry."

Violet walked over and gave their mother a hug too. Rose felt like telling Audrey to go ahead without her.

Rose mentioned before she forgot, "Momma. I left you something on the kitchen counter."

"You ladies take care of yourselves. I will be all right," their mom said as she wiped the tears from her eyes.

They hugged and kissed their mom several times before walking to the car. As the car pulled out of the driveway, their mom stood in the doorway waving.

"I'm going to miss her."

Violet wiped a tear from her eye. "So am I."

They rode the rest of the way in silence, except for Audrey's occasional comment. Audrey was unable to wait at the airport so they hugged and said their good-byes. While they were waiting around to board their flight, Pierre showed up at the gate. "Hi ladies. I was hoping I caught you before you left."

Violet responded with a smile on her face. "I wasn't expecting you."

Rose left and gave them some privacy. She went to the bookstore located across from the terminal and purchased a couple of magazines for the flight home. Afterward, she found a corner, sat there and thumbed through a fashion magazine. She felt as if someone was staring at her. When she looked up, there were a couple of teenage boys pointing and giggling. She waved at them and continued to go through the magazine. The announcer called her and Violet's flight number for boarding. She looked around for Violet and saw her embraced in Pierre's arms.

For someone who doesn't have feelings for someone, I always seem to find them in heated embraces. I better go separate them, before the child misses her flight. I would hate to explain this to Mom. Then again, it would serve her right. I'm usually the one in the hot seat.

Rose walked over to them and cleared her throat. They both looked up with a look of guilt on their faces. "Seems like I'm always interrupting, but they're waiting for us to board. See you, Pierre."

They said their good-byes and they both walked up the ramp to the plane. After they got situated in first class, they remained quiet and seemed to be in their own little worlds. The steward offered drinks, but they both declined. Rose stated, "I think this medicine has me scared to drink anything but water."

Violet sounded understanding and said, "I feel you. I probably need to cut back on my wine intake as well."

Rose leaned down closer to her, so no one else could hear. "So that scene back there, does it mean you've made a decision?"

"Why, Rose? I see you just won't let up will you?"

"I think it's cute. You deserve to be happy and he's put a smile on your face. Look at you. You're glowing. I haven't seen you like this since, well I won't go there."

Violet nodded her head. "Please don't. Let's just say that I will see what happens."

They continued to fly in silence until they started feeling turbulence. Rose grabbed Violet's hand. "I'm sorry, you would think as much as I travel I would be used to this, but I'm not."

Violet gave her a reassuring hand tug. "I know what you mean. It'll be okay. No need to panic."

The flight attendant announced over the intercom, "Please put on your seatbelts. We are hitting some air pockets and will have to go around them. The storm is widespread, so be patient, don't panic, but for the next ten minutes or so we will be feeling a lot of bumps."

Rose held her stomach as if she was going to puke. "I don't know if my stomach is going to be able to take this."

Violet coached her. "Breathe slowly and deeply."

"I can't. I can't."

"You can and you will. Hold my hand and watch me." Violet demonstrated how she was supposed to do it and Rose imitated her. She became calm and soon the nausea disappeared.

"Thank you."

Violet winked at her. "That's what sisters are for, right?"

Rose smiled. "Yes, and you've been the best sister a girl could ask for. Even when I wasn't good to you, you always showed me love. For the longest time, I knew no matter what others said or did, I could always count on my older sister by two minutes to love me unconditionally."

Violet, looking teary eyed, glanced away and remained quiet.

"You don't have to say anything. I know I've hurt you, but I've prayed you would find it in your heart to forgive me one day. Although I got sick, this past week has been one of the best I've had in years. I wouldn't change it for the world."

Violet turned around and looked at her. "Neither would I."

Although they rode the rest of the trip in silence, Violet held her hand and squeezed it whenever Rose jumped from the turbulence.

Chapter 59

VIOLET

This trip has been very interesting. I didn't expect to run into Rose or Pierre. Rose has shown plenty of remorse and seems to have matured. Pierre is full of regrets and seems to have grown up to be a wonderful man. Only time will tell.

Violet closed her eyes and when she woke up, they were landing in LA. The flight attendant announced that only people whose final destination was LA should exit. All others were asked to stay on board. Violet unbuckled so that she could let Rose out. She reached in the overhead bin and helped Rose with her carry-on.

"Rose, I want to say I had a nice time this past week and regardless of what we've been through, I do love you."

Tears streamed down Rose's face as they hugged each other. Rose responded, "I love you too. Keep in touch. I'll call you or you call me."

People behind them were clearing their throats and a couple had no problem verbalizing their annoyance. Rose smiled at her, wiped the tears from her face, put her shades on, and walked up the aisle. "I can get a hint. I better go, before I get trampled." Rose turned around and blew a kiss in Violet's direction before exiting the plane.

People were still complaining about the holdup when Violet sat back down, but she ignored them and looked out the window. She continued to gaze out the window as they boarded new passengers.

"Is this seat taken?" a familiar voice asked.

When she looked up, it was into David's face.

"Welcome back to Cali," he said as he took a seat.

"Thanks. I didn't expect to run into anyone I knew."

He put on his seatbelt. "This is the weekend I had with my daughter. Normally she comes up, but I had promised her a trip to the Zoo."

"How sweet." They talked the entire flight and before they knew it, they were landing in San Jose.

She grabbed her carry-on bag and David insisted on carrying it for her. One of the flight attendants acted as if she had an attitude, because David didn't return any of her advances and spent the entire flight engrossed in conversation with Violet.

David offered her a ride home and since she didn't feel like waiting on a smelly cab, she accepted. After he placed her bags in her living room, she invited him to stay for dinner. "My mom packed some things and since you were so kind to give me a ride home, let me show you some southern hospitality."

She could see the gleam in David's eyes. "I would be honored. Is there somewhere I can freshen up? I need to wash my hands and relieve myself after that ride."

She used her right hand and pointed. "There's a bathroom to the right."

She decided to unpack later and went and warmed the food. David walked back into the dining room just when she was getting ready to set the table. He offered to help. "I can do that."

She returned with the food and as they ate, she laughed at his recanting of Cherokee's adventures. "I remember when I was young and carefree. Those were the days."

"Yes, and I enjoyed all of our adventures," David slipped and said.

She smiled. Earlier she had come to a conclusion on what she needed to do about her situation. She took the opportunity to clear things up with David. Before they were always in a business setting, but tonight they were in the comfort of her home. "David, I think we should talk. Let me clear the table and I'll meet you back in the living room."

When she walked back into the living room, she saw him admiring her newest collection of Egyptian artifacts. He commented, "These are nice. I see you're still a collector."

"Yes, and I may donate some of my items to the Egyptian museum here in San Jose. If you haven't made it by to see their exhibits, I would suggest that you do so."

"I will." He walked over and sat down on the couch. "Now what did you want to talk about?"

She sat on the chair facing in his direction, so that she could keep her distance. "I don't know where to begin. I guess, I'll just come out and say it. We've been dancing around this thing, since we've come back in contact with each other."

David in a seductive voice said, "You mean the attraction that seems to still be there between the two of us?"

She crossed her legs. "Yes, that's exactly what I'm talking about."

He moved in a little closer to her. "What about it?"

She uncrossed her legs and looked him straight in the eyes. "I know I'm still attracted to you. Let's face it, you're a handsome man; however, that's all it is."

David's smile faded. "So you're saying you don't feel anything else but a physical attraction?"

"Correct. I forgave you years ago; however, I also know that a relationship with you is doomed to fail, because there will always be that little doubt about your trustworthiness in the back of my mind."

He cleared his throat. "I see. So you'll turn down any advances I make toward you?"

"Basically, David. Please don't even try. I don't want to sound cold, but this is my life and I don't see you being a part of it in that capacity. I will admit, I did entertain the thought of it before my trip, but I can't subject myself to being involved with you personally again."

David started begging. "Violet. Baby. I was trying to take it easy. I'm sorry, maybe I was rushing you too fast. I thought maybe us working on this project together would bring us back together."

Violet tried to remain calm, because it was hard for her to make the decision. She responded, "A part of me wants to jump back into your arms and allow you back into my life, but the other part is telling me to let it rest. I loved you then and will always love you; however, I am not in love with you and quite honestly I don't think I ever could be in love with you again."

David got up and headed to the door. Violet gave him a good-bye kiss. He poured out his heart before leaving. "Violet, you are a precious flower and any man that gets you is lucky to have you in his presence. I wish I could be the man to put a smile on your face, but you're probably right. Our time together has passed, and I will go to my grave regretting the fact that I caused you so much unnecessary pain."

"Thank you, David. I think we needed to talk, so we both could move on."

He leaned down and placed a kiss on her cheek and then gave her a compassionate hug before saying, "Good-bye."

She closed the door behind him and wiped the tears from her eyes. She then went to unpack and was now ready to move forward with her life.

Chapter 60
ROSE

"Carmen, can you please tell them I will be there as soon as I can. I'm stuck in traffic and I can't run everyone off the road just to get to their stupid photo shoot."

Carmen, in her normal calming voice, said, "I swear you're going to give yourself a heart attack, girl. Calm down. Just get there when you can. They will be there. I want you to relax. What I need to know from you is how many tickets you need for next week's movie premiere?"

Rose got off at her exit. There was a long line to turn at the light, so she tapped her left foot as she waited for her turn. "I don't really have anyone else I want to invite. Well, on second thought give me ten. What I don't use, I'll give back and you can give them to somebody in your office."

"I'll do that. Get back with the names."

"I will. Well I've finally made it, so let me go. Talk to you later."

Since being back in Los Angeles, Rose had spent days promoting her soon-to-be released movie. She was also taking photo shots for her next movie that was due soon. She had managed to dodge Lance and the only time she spoke with Trey was during their promotional setups. This photo shoot would wrap up her commitment for the movie and she could then relax before taking on another project. She was even thinking about doing another music CD.

After the photo shoot, she saw Trey waiting in the lobby. Before she could pretend not to see him, he came up to her and blurted out, "Why have you been avoiding me?"

Rose put her shades on and threw her scarf over her left shoulder. "I haven't been avoiding you. I've seen you almost every day since I got back."

He ran in front of her and opened the door for her. "You know what I mean. I've missed you. I need you."

Rose gave out a hearty laugh. "Trey baby. You're so cute when you're like this; however I have things to do, people to see, so I'll call you later okay." She brushed him to the side with her hand and continued to walk toward her car.

He yelled behind her, "I'll be waiting."

She responded out of earshot, "Don't hold your breath though."

She drove home.

I can't believe some men. That's why I'm the way I am. If you don't fit into my agenda, then keep on keeping on. Trey thinks I'm stupid. He doesn't call me until he hears that I'm back in town. When I called him from Louisiana he had some skank in his bed and forgot all about returning my call.

Look at Lance sitting outside of my house. If I could trust him, he would be a good man, because he spoils me. But I don't trust him out of my sight.

Lance walked up to her car and opened her door. "Baby, I couldn't wait another day to see you."

He leaned down and hugged her. In her fake happy voice,

she said, "Nice to see you too, but you should have called first."

Lance followed her inside. "I have called you all week, but you've been too busy to talk with me."

She sat on her sofa and started going through her mail. "I had to make up for being gone." Tuning him out, because he wasn't saying anything she wanted to hear, she asked, "By the way, are you going to be in town next Tuesday? That's when my movie premiere is and I need an escort."

"Is all I am to you is an escort?" Lance asked sounding frustrated. "Look at me."

Rose continued to go through her mail.

Lance sounded really upset by now. "Rose, look at me."

The sound of authority in his voice caused Rose to stop what she was doing and she gave him her undivided attention. "What?"

"I need to know you feel something. Why are you the ice princess? Why can't you allow yourself to feel?"

Rose took her time responding, so they sat in silence until she did. "Apparently I feel something since I've let you hang around me all these years; however, you hurt me and I don't want to take the chance of you hurting me again."

"Baby, that was years ago. I can't even remember her name now, that's how unimportant she was to me."

Rose moved from where she was and looked out the patio door. She kept her back toward Lance and spoke. "That's just it. I thought we had something special and then I found you with that woman. I know about the other women too, but you're off the hook for those, because we don't have a real commitment."

He went behind her and gave her a hug. "Baby, if you just say the word, I promise I will leave all those other women alone. I don't really date anyone besides you, and you keep pushing me further and further away. A man needs to feel like he's needed and loved too. That's all I'm saying."

Rose let out years of frustration and years of hurt and started sobbing. She turned around and Lance cradled her in his arms. He led her to the couch and she leaned into his chest. He ran his hands through her hair and held her until she gathered her composure. She glanced up and asked, "So where do we go from here?"

Lance moved off the couch, got on one knee and then took something out of his pocket. "I didn't plan on doing it like this, but there is no better time than the present. Rose Purdue will you take me, Lance King, as your husband. I promise to love you unconditionally and be faithful to the end."

Rose wiped the tears of joy from her eyes. He opened the box and placed a four-karat ring on her finger. "Lance. I don't know what to say. I want to say yes."

He kissed the palm of her hand. "Then what's stopping you?"

"Nothing," she said as she looked at him and then at the ring. "Yes. Yes, I'll marry you."

He took her in his arms and that night, for the first time in a long time, Rose felt as if she had a chance at real love and happiness.

Chapter 61

VIOLET

Violet was under her covers. "I hate to end this conversation, but you're about to hear me snore in a minute."

"What makes it different than the other two or three nights?" Pierre laughed.

"Pierre, I will get you back for that comment. I don't snore."

"Says who? If you ask Alexander Graham Bell, he'll tell you that you do." They both laughed and said their good-byes.

Pierre is something else. He has kept his word about communicating with me every day. If he doesn't call me, he's sending me an e-mail. We have even set up instant messaging, so when we're both on the computer we can chat. He offered to send me a two-way pager, but I told him that was too much and he should just call.

After David and I had our little talk, I felt like a new woman. I guess all of those times that he wanted me to meet with him to talk, I should have. I would've been able to move on much earlier. It's been done and now I'm open to receive and, most importantly, give love again. I've met some nice guys over the years, but they never stood a chance. Pierre is a sweetheart, but I'm going to take it slow with him. If he's all that he seems to be, then we'll be together; otherwise, I'll move on without him. I'm so sleepy so let me get me some sleep.

She slept peacefully and the next morning she went to meet the builders at the site so she could see their progress. She was impressed and made notes on her notepad of some ideas on what she would need for decorating as she passed through and reviewed the final phase. She saw David as she was leaving and waved. He waved back and she continued on to her car.

When she got back home, she had several messages on her answering machine. Several were from Rose and she laughed as she listened to them. "I see you're still using that ancient answering machine, well anyway, I have some good news and just wanted to share it with you. Also, hold on. Well just call me back."

A couple more messages were from solicitors and then another message from Rose. "It's been a few hours since I left that last message, I'll try you again."

She decided to call her new employees first to see how they were coming with the selection process and then she made a call to Rose. She was about to hang up, until Rose answered sounding out of breath. "Hello."

"It's me. I got your messages. Everything okay?"

Panting, Rose said, "Yes. Everything is just lovely. Hold on a minute, let me turn this fan off." She waited. "I'm back. How are you?"

Violet sat in her favorite chair in the living room. "I'm doing great. What's going on with you?"

"First thing's first. I want to invite you and a guest to my movie premiere next week. I know this is short notice, but I'll pay all expenses; just give me the okay."

Violet opened her mouth to decline, but changed her mind and instead said, "I might just take you up on the offer, but the guest I would like to invite may not be available."

"Why don't you call and ask Pierre if he's available and his travel arrangements will be made as well."

"How do you know it's him? I could be talking about a friend here."

"I might be the Queen B but I'm not the Queen of Egypt." They both laughed. "I'll ask him and let you know."

"See, I knew I was right. You go girl. Two snaps."

Violet laughed. "You're so silly."

"I also want to know if you will be my maid of honor."

Violet's mouth dropped wide open. "What, when did this happen and with who?"

Rose told her about Lance and how he proposed and how she felt about him. "I can't think of anyone else I would like to be by my side as I embark on a new chapter of my life."

"Thank you for asking. I'll be your maid of honor and congratulations. Have you told Mom?"

"No. I wanted to tell you first and ask you that. Now that you've confirmed you'll do it, I'll call her. I'm also inviting her, Aunt Mae, cousin Audrey and her man to come out too. Everyone can stay here. I have plenty of room."

"That sounds like a plan. I'll call you back and let you know if you should add Pierre to the list."

She immediately called Pierre after hanging up with Rose. "What are you doing, handsome?"

"Thinking about you."

"Are you sitting down? Rose called to invite us to her movie premiere Tuesday and also told me that she was getting married."

"What? Well that's good news, isn't it?"

"Yes. It threw me for a loop, but I did accept the offer to be her maid of honor."

"I told you things would work out between you two."

Violet twirled her hair with her fingers. "We'll see. Are you available to fly out here for a few days?"

"For you, yes."

They continued to talk for about an hour and then Violet called Rose back to confirm. Rose informed her that everyone else had also accepted. "Sounds like a mini-reunion," Violet said.

"Yes and I'm looking forward to having everyone here. I guess I better check to see what I have, so I can get the house fully stocked."

Violet told her bye and retired to bed early. She only had a few days to find herself a dress.

Who would have thought that I would be happy about going to a Hollywood premiere? Rose baby, we've come a long way.

Chapter 62

ROSE

Lance was giving Rose a massage and she kept dozing off. "Humm. Lance, you're better than my regular masseure."

As he massaged her leg muscles, he said, "I've been meaning to ask you about your masseure. The last time he was here, he looked a little too happy and why'd he have to change his name? He's no more a Frenchman than I am."

Rose laughed. "Ramone is harmless. You have nothing to worry about."

He kissed the back of her ankle. "I know I don't. Can't nobody love you more than me."

She lay there as he aroused her every senses. They ended up making love until the early morning. The next morning, she slid out of bed quietly, trying not to wake him. She took a shower and when she walked out of the bathroom, he was awake. "I didn't mean to wake you. I need to go run some errands, because everybody will be here tonight."

"Is there anything you want me to do?" he asked as he moved the covers.

Rose sat on the edge of the bed while she put on her

stockings and replied, "Yes. Please make sure the gardener and the catering service are set up properly."

"Sure, love."

She reached into her purse and handed him a set of keys. "These are for you. I think it's about time you have your own set."

He pulled her back on the bed. "Thank you, dear."

She tried to pull herself up and playfully hit him, "Lance. Let me up or I'll get all wrinkled."

He tickled her until she gave in to him. She kissed him and left.

She decided on driving her Escalade because she had a lot of places to go and wouldn't have room to fit everything in the convertible. The first stop was to her favorite designer. The Rose Petals line, the line created in her honor, was doing fabulous. After she tried the dress on for the last time, one of the assistants wrapped it up and offered to deliver it, but she took it with her. She was also given the accessories to complement the dress. She wanted to buy Violet a dress, but thought better of it. They were making progress and she didn't want to come off as if she were trying to be controlling.

She got home in time to give the caterer last minute instructions. "Ma'am, we have everything under control. We'll be at your beck and call for the rest of week as agreed for all meals."

"Thank you."

Rose went to find Lance. He confirmed the arrival of the limousine. The driver had been waiting, so that he could take her to the airport to pick up her relatives. Lance nervously said, "I would like to go, if you don't mind. They will be a part of my family, so I might as well meet them now."

She loved the idea, so they rode together. She asked Lance to meet Violet at her gate, since she was the only one besides Rose who knew him. Rose was to go meet her mom and other relatives at another gate. They agreed to meet up at the limousine.

Rose was reading a newspaper left on a chair next to her when she heard her mom say, "There goes my baby."

She stood up and hugged everyone. "I'm so glad you all could come. Let's go get your bags and Mr. Pierre, Violet is going to meet us at the car."

Her mom asked, "Is she here yet?"

"She should be. Lance went to meet her for me and he's going to take her to the car."

Her Aunt Mae tried to keep up with everyone else's walking pace. "How are all of us going to fit in one car?"

"I have rented a limousine to be at your disposal your entire stay here."

Audrey walked next to her and looped her arm with hers. "Thanks for the trip. I told my friends to look for me on the entertainment channel."

Rose laughed. "You're the one who should have pursued a career in show business, Ms. Melodramatic."

After collecting everyone's luggage they headed to the limousine. Lance and Violet spotted them first and Violet hugged everyone and gave Rose a hug. "Thanks Sis for inviting me. You know they thought I was you on the plane and everybody on the plane was asking for an autograph. The flight attendant had to announce on the intercom that I wasn't you."

"I'm so sorry."

"For once, it didn't bother me. The funny part, I had signed a few autographs for some people while I was waiting on my flight, and those same people sneered at me when they found out I wasn't you." Everyone around them laughed.

Lance assisted Rose with getting everyone situated in his or her rooms. Rose pulled Violet to the side. "I have one room left. Do you want your bags to be in the same room as Pierre or do you feel like bunking with me?"

Violet looked at her. "Let's see, which is the lesser of two evils?" Rose's mouth dropped open and Violet laughed. "Just kidding. I'll sleep in your room, because I don't want Momma saying anything, and besides Pierre and I have not gone there yet."

"The way he was looking when he saw you, told me that won't be long."

After everyone got situated, they all met up in the dining room. "Rose, your house is lovely. I really like how you have everything decorated. I must say I'm impressed," her Aunt Mae stated.

"Thank you, Aunt Mae."

After dinner, they all lounged around on the patio and enjoyed the night air. Rose stood back and observed. Lance came up behind her and commented, "Seems like everyone is happy, doesn't it?"

Rose continued to look at the happy setting. "Yes, it really does. Thank you for all of your help today."

"I told you if given half the chance, there's no telling what would become of us. Together we're remarkable and unstoppable." He turned her around and gave her a long sensual kiss.

They stopped kissing when the family started to applaud them. She blushed and turned toward them. "With that encore, ladies and gents, I'm going to bed. Tomorrow is going to be a long, busy day. You're welcome to stay out here all night if you like. Make yourselves at home. *Mi casa es su casa.*"

Her Aunt Mae looked at her mom. "What did she say?"

Her mom responded, "She says, my house is your house. That's Spanish."

"I know it was Spanish. I just didn't understand what she said."

Rose heard their interchange and laughed as she made her way up the stairs.

Chapter 63
VIOLET

"A nickel for your thoughts."

Violet looked over at Pierre. "I thought it was a penny."

"It was, but because of inflation, it's now a nickel."

Violet laughed. "You're something else."

Pierre took her hand, picked up a beach towel off the rack, and they went for a stroll along the beach located behind Rose's home. As they walked and held hands, the waves from the ocean became soothing to her soul. They found a quiet spot and Pierre placed the long towel on the sand and commented, "This is so relaxing. I can see why you like the coast now."

The stars were bright and as she looked into his eyes, she got caught up in the ambiance. "I love it here. In San Jose, I have to drive about twenty or thirty minutes before I get to the coast, but it's well worth the drive."

He embraced her, leaned down and gave her a long tantalizing kiss. She moaned and debated on what to do, because before making the trip, she vowed to let their relationship take its course. She was really feeling him and from the bulge in his pants, he was too.

He was the first to break their embrace. "I think we better stop. I don't know how much more of your sweet kisses I can take without wanting to pleasure you."

She gazed at him, and with her eyes reflecting desire said, "I guess we better head back."

He held her in his arms and they both forgot about their previous protest. "Baby," Pierre said as he moaned. "Come on, before I take you right now."

They brushed the sand off themselves and went back to the house. As she was about to open the door to Rose's room, she turned around and whispered to Pierre, "I think I'm ready."

"Ready for what, baby?" he asked in his sexy voice.

She reached up and kissed him.

He was almost panting. "Whew. Let's take this downstairs to my room before someone walks out and sees us."

She agreed, so they walked hand in hand to his room. Fortunately, everyone else's bedrooms were upstairs, so they would not be heard or disturbed. They made love for the first time and as she lay embraced in his arms, Violet felt as if their souls were entwined and that she had finally met her destiny.

The next morning, when she woke up she realized she didn't have any of her clothes downstairs, so she would have to sneak up to Rose's to change before her mom or aunt saw her. "Baby, I didn't bring a change of clothes, so I need to sneak upstairs."

Pierre, in a husky voice responded, "You're so cute." He placed kisses on her shoulder. "I can't wait to get you to myself again. Last night was better than I could have ever imagined. It just confirms our connection. It was as if our souls connected." They kissed again and Pierre walked her to the door. He whispered, "Hurry back."

When Violet walked in the room, Rose was up and getting dressed. Rose joked, "I take it you enjoyed the ocean view."

Violet tried to ignore her comment. "How are you this morning?"

"I'm fine and from the looks of things you're feeling GREAT."

"I know I was supposed to come upstairs," Violet said as she went through her suitcase. "But I got sidetracked."

Rose bent down to fasten her shoes. "I'll say. I should have told Lance to stay over, so I could have gotten sidetracked."

They both laughed. "Thanks for understanding."

"I'm just glad to see you happy."

Violet wanted to share this with someone and Janice wasn't there, so she blurted out, "Although we only recently reconnected, he does his best to keep a smile on my face."

"If you're happy, I love it."

"You really do mean it, don't you?" Violet asked with a curious look on her face.

"Yes, I do," Rose said. "Now let me go make sure breakfast is ready to be served, so when people start coming downstairs, they don't have to starve." She kissed her on the cheek and left Violet in the room by herself.

Let's see, what did I bring to wear during the day? I know what I'm wearing tonight. I know what I forgot to do last night and she's going to kill me. I didn't call Janice to let her know I made it. I hope she understands I got a little distracted.

When Violet made it downstairs, everyone had eaten. Pierre was out on the patio reading a book. "What are you reading?"

"I found this book of poetry and was wondering which one I should recite to you."

"Did you find one?"

"I sure did, but it'll have to wait for another time." He smiled wickedly. "When we have some privacy."

She smiled and flirted back at him. "Well, I'll be ready in a few. I can't wait for you to meet my friend Janice. She's different, so don't say I didn't warn you."

Rose let Violet borrow her convertible, so they hit the highway and headed to Janice and Terrence's place. When they made it to Janice's place, Violet and Pierre couldn't keep their lips apart. They were kissing when the door opened and acted like teenagers who got caught doing something they weren't supposed to do. Violet asked the person who opened the door, "Is Janice here? I'm her friend Violet."

The guy who opened the door responded, "Violet, you don't remember me?"

Violet looked closer. The man standing in front of them was dressed in a jogging suit that had seen better days. His hair was in dire need of a barber. When she looked him in his eyes, she recognized him. "Marcus. You look so different. What happened? I mean how are you?"

"Can a brotha get a hug?"

She ignored his question. "Marcus, this is Pierre. Pierre, this is Marcus who was a professional ball player." Under her breath she said, "One that played himself out."

They shook hands and as they were talking, Janice and Terrence walked into the front room. "Violetttttttt!"

They hugged and she introduced them to Pierre. "Pierre, this is my best friend and her husband Terrence. Terrence and Marcus are friends."

Pierre extended his hands out to both of them. "Nice to meet you both."

Marcus stood and watched the interaction and then commented, "I was leaving." He continued out the door, but in hearing distance said, "Nice to see you again, Violet."

Violet didn't acknowledge him.

Pierre followed Terrence into the game room, while Violet and Janice played catch-up, as if they didn't talk at least once a week already. "So tell me, is the special glow I see because of what you two have?"

Violet interrupted her. "Shh. You don't have to broadcast it to the world."

"I'm so happy for you. He seems really cool. Not bad, Ms. Thang."

Violet jokingly said with an attitude, "Don't hate." They continued to talk and giggle.

Violet and Pierre spent the first part of the day hanging out with Janice and Terrence. They then parted ways and hung out with Violet's family until it was time for everyone to get ready for the night's events.

Chapter 64
ROSE

"Violet, can you help me zip this dress?"

Violet walked over and zipped Roses's dress. "You look absolutely breathtaking. The floral print and sheerness of that dress makes you look absolutely gorgeous."

"Thank you. I started to have my designer make you one, but I didn't know if you would wear it."

"If it looks half as good as this one, you should have."

Rose freshened up her make-up. "I'll have him ship you one next week. I already know your measurements."

Rose put on her accessories and when Violet returned from the bathroom, she was fully dressed. "Violet, that is a stunning dress. No wonder our parents named you Violet, because purple is definitely your color."

"You think so?"

"Yes. Well the Purdue sisters will be making a grand entrance tonight." They high-fived each other.

"I'll go make sure everybody is ready and we'll be ready whenever you are, Rose," Violet said before exiting.

"Thanks, it means a lot to me that you came," Rose stated as Violet continued out of the door.

Rose felt a slight pain in her side, but it subsided. She grabbed her cocktail purse and headed down the stairs. Everyone remarked at how elegant she looked and they all headed out to the waiting limousines. They piled into two different limousines. Lance, Pierre, Rose, Violet and their mom rode in one limousine, while everyone else rode in the other. Janice and Terrence were also riding with them.

"Thanks, Rose, for inviting Terrence and me to your premiere. That was very generous of you."

"Janice, I think it's about time we get to know each other, since we're going to be sister-in-laws," Rose stated as she held up her engagement ring.

Her mom examined it. "I still can't believe Rosie is getting married. Just a few weeks ago, you detested men, now look at you."

Rose gave her mom a disapproving look. "Momma, that was supposed to be between you and me."

"Child hush. Lance ain't going anywhere. If he was, he would have left you a long time ago." Everyone nodded in agreement.

On the way to the premiere, Rose told them what to expect and warned them about being caught up in the Hollywood hype. She warned them of all of the reporters and photographers and fans. When they pulled up to the theater, the place was packed. "Don't be nervous. Remember cameras will be flashing and reporters will be stopping you to ask you questions. I might have to leave you guys for a while, to do some sideline interviews. Lance knows how it is and he'll stay around y'all to beat off some of the hounds."

Their mom seemed nervous. "Oh, my. I didn't know it was going to be this many people. Are all of these people going to be inside too?"

Violet stepped in and responded, "No, Momma. They're just fans. They're here to see who they can see and what everyone is going to be wearing. You can stick close to us. I'll probably get stopped too, since we look alike."

They all got out of the limousines to flashing cameras. They were finally able to make it inside to their prospective seats. After the movie, everyone in the theater applauded. It was a great drama based on the life of a couple of civil activists. All of the major actors made the characters real. Lance told Rose, "I think this is one of your best roles yet. You played the role with class and style."

"Thank you. Can you make sure they make it to the car? I need to do a couple of interviews and I'll catch up with you later."

He kissed her on the cheek. "I'll see you soon, sweetheart."

She walked around and did a couple of interviews. Rose tried to keep them short, but every major entertainment station was there. She also had to take pictures with Trey because he was one of her costars. They hadn't talked one-on-one since she accepted Lance's engagement.

"Hi, beautiful," Trey said.

As the cameras flashed, she responded, "Hi, yourself. No one really knows this, but I wanted to tell you Lance and I are engaged."

Trey gave her a hug. "Congratulations. I'm happy for you."

She looked surprised. "You are?"

"Yes. Rose, you're special and you deserve someone who can dedicate himself to you. I'm enjoying my bachelorhood and I don't see settling down anywhere in the near future."

Carmen was trying to get Rose's attention as she finished her conversation with Trey. "Trey, thanks for everything. Be good." She blew him a kiss and walked over to where Carmen was standing.

"Rose, you have one more interview and then you can go celebrate with your family."

"I thought I was through."

"You'll want to do this interview. It's for the ANC *Friday Night Edition*."

Rose got excited. "Well, where are they? Let's get this show on the road." She felt a sharp pain in her side and bent over a little.

"Are you okay? We can always reschedule."

"Yes. I'm fine. Just lead the way."

After the interview, she went to the limousine where her family was waiting for her. The driver saw her approach and opened the door for her. "Sorry you guys. Every time I headed towards the car, I got pulled in another direction."

Violet was the first to talk. "We understand. We've been enjoying the glamorous life." They all chuckled.

Janice said, "We've also been enjoying a fully stocked bar filled with snacks. I'm so full, I don't think I can eat anything else."

Lance reached over and grabbed a finger sandwich. "This is just the beginning. We're going to drop Momma at home." Their mom looked up and smiled at him as he continued saying, "Then we're going to Planet Hollywood for dinner. We've made sure Momma and Aunt Mae or anyone else who decided to stay at the house will be taken care of."

Rose was delighted that everybody seemed to be getting along. She looked around at everyone in the car and gave a genuine smile, not the kind she gave the cameras all night long, but a smile of joy and contentment. It was like one big happy family. She looked over at Janice and Terrence, her new extended family.

Planet Hollywood was packed with stars and groupies. They were finally seated and they all tried to eat between people snapping their pictures. "Audrey, are you okay over there, cuz? I know the flashes can be annoying. I've learned to tune them out."

Audrey pulled out her compact mirror and placed some more lipstick on. "Girl, yes. As long as they get my good side, I'm all right."

They all laughed and continued to enjoy the night. By the time they got ready to leave, some of the fans had left. Rose was glad, because she didn't want to have to fight their way out to get back to the limousines. "Janice, you and Terrence can use the other limousine if you like and I'll have someone come pick you up, so you can get your car tomorrow."

Terrence and Janice looked at each other and both said in unison, "Sure. Thanks."

They hugged and as Rose was stepping into her limousine, she fell out in pain. "Somebody help me. My side."

Lance rushed over to see what happened. "Rose baby, what's wrong?"

Violet placed Rose's head on her lap. "It's her side. It's probably her bladder, she was having problems with it when we were in Shreveport." Violet stroked her head. "Rose dear, did you follow up with your doctor?"

In between pains, Rose responded, "No. I didn't have time. Somebody hit me upside the head and put me out of my misery."

Lance told the driver to take them to Cedars-Sinai Hospital. He rubbed Rose's feet while she lay on Violet's lap. Lance and Violet tried to comfort her. The ride over to the hospital was silent except for the wails of pain that came from Rose.

Chapter 65

VIOLET

Violet was pacing the floor as they waited for the doctor or nurse to come out and inform them of Rose's status. Pierre tried to comfort Violet as they waited on the results of the tests. Violet turned to Pierre and Lance and asked, "Should I go ahead and call Momma or wait until we have some concrete news?"

"Why don't I go pick her up, so I can tell her in person? That way she won't be as worried. If you get an update, you can always call me on my cell phone. I'll turn it on as soon as I get outside," Pierre said, while hugging Violet. "Baby, everything will be okay."

Pierre met the limousine driver in the hallway and left to go get their mom. Lance and Violet took turns pacing the floor. After an hour had passed, a doctor walked out and asked for Rose's closest relative. Lance and she both walked over to him and identified themselves as her sister and fiancé. "We discovered some things, but she's going to be fine."

Violet felt relieved. "What's wrong with her? Is it her bladder?"

"Yes. We have it under control though. We want to keep her overnight for observation."

"Did the nurse tell you she had some problems a few weeks ago with her bladder?"

"Yes, and fortunately she got treatment for it; however, something else set off this bout of pain."

Lance and she said in unison, "What?"

The doctor reached out to shake Lance's hand. "Well sir, you're going to be a daddy."

Lance stared in disbelief. "What? Who me? A daddy?"

"Yes. She told me to tell you that, just in case she was knocked out when you came to see her. She wants to see you both, but only one can go in at a time."

"Lance, you go ahead. I'll call Pierre and I'll see her when you're done."

She watched as the doctor led Lance down the hall. She called Pierre and told him the news. "She's pregnant, can you believe it?"

While she waited on Lance to come out, her mom and Pierre showed up.

Violet hugged her mom. "She's going to be okay. Did Pierre tell you everything?"

"Yes."

"Why are you crying? She's going to be fine."

Her mom used her handkerchief to wipe her face. "My baby is having a baby. I'm going to be a grandmother."

Violet put her arms around her mom and walked her to a chair in the waiting room. "Momma, don't cry. It's only going to make me start crying and then they'll kick us both out for flooding the place with tears."

Her mom laughed. Pierre stood to the side and watched the mother and daughter interaction. Her mom held her hand. "I'm so glad you girls are finally working out your differences."

"It's been rough, but I'm trying."

"That's all I can ask for. I love you both."

"I love you too, Momma."

At that moment Lance came out. Violet walked up to him. "How is she doing?"

"She's a little drowsy, but she wants to see both of you."

Violet could see the concern on her mom's face. "Momma, you go in first."

"Are you sure?" her mom turned around and asked. "We can go in together."

"No Momma, I need to go in by myself."

Pierre walked up to Violet with a cold drink and a cup of ice. As she took the drink from him, she said, "Thanks. Thank you for being here."

"I told you I'm in this for the long haul. I don't plan on going anywhere."

"I'm going to hold you to it."

Pierre hugged her and kissed her forehead. "We'll talk more when this is over, but I want you to know that I've decided to relocate to the San Francisco office, which will at least put us in the same state."

"Pierre, when did you decide that?"

"The day I saw you again at your mother's house."

"But how did you know I was going to agree to give us another try?"

"I didn't. I just prayed that you would."

They embraced and remained that way until she saw her mom come out of Rose's room.

"Mom, how is she doing?"

"She's doing better than she looks. They have things hooked up to her, but I was reassured it's to monitor her throughout the night."

"Well let me go." She headed toward Rose's room. As she walked, she couldn't help but remember the last time she saw her dad. It was in a hospital and ever since then she had hated hospitals.

Violet got to the door and peeped her head through the door.

Chapter 66
ROSE

"Violet, I smell your sweet lilac perfume, so come on in sweetie."

"Hi, Rose. You gave us a scare for a minute." Violet stood at the end of her bed.

"Come over here so I can hold your hand. If I could move more, I would give you a huge hug and wouldn't let go." Rose tried to hold back the tears. "You don't know how much this means to me. When the doctor came in earlier and told me that you were out there waiting, I broke down and cried."

Violet held her hand and with teary eyes said, "Rose, maybe you shouldn't talk, because you need to have your strength for you and the baby."

"I'm okay. I need to get something off my chest." Rose sniffed. "The tears I cried, were tears of joy and pain. Tears of joy, because I felt it in my soul that you still loved me. I cried tears of pain, because I was the cause of your pain for so many years. I'm ashamed; yet, you found it in your heart to forgive me time after time. Not only did you give me your love, you've been there for me, when no one else was."

Violet, unable to control her tears, cried and in between tears said, "Rose, you don't know how much I wanted to remain angry with you, but I've finally had to let it go. Mom said something to me that stuck and I had to come to terms with what she said. I asked myself, how could I not forgive my sister, when God has forgiven me over and over?"

The nurse entered and informed them that visitation hours were ending. Their mom, Lance, and Pierre walked in. Lance went and stood on the other side of Rose's bed and said, "Rose, whether you want me to or not, I'm spending the night."

Rose squeezed his hand.

Violet leaned down and hugged Rose before turning to walk out the door behind Pierre and their mom. Before Violet walked out the door, she turned and said, "I love you, Rose."

Rose smiled back and blew her a kiss. "I love you too, Violet."

ROSES ARE THORNS, VIOLETS ARE TRUE

Reading Group Guide

1. Rose and Violet's parents pacified Rose as a child. While growing up, Violet is told by her mom to overlook Rose's actions. Do you think their parents are the root cause of Rose and Violet's issues they now face as adults?

2. Violet has pent up frustration from how Rose has treated her over the years. She gives an uncensored interview with a national publication. Rose feels she should have kept their personal business private. Is there a better way Violet could have handled this or do you agree with how she shattered Rose's image with the public?

3. David loves Violet, but later ends up with Rose. Do you think Violet should have given him a second chance? Why do you think David slept with Rose in the first place?

4. Rose admits to not having many friends. The only friend she can claim is her agent, Carmen. Do you think her selfishness or competitiveness ruins any chance of her having friends? Do you think her not being able to get

along with Violet is another reason why she hasn't been able to cultivate friendships with others?

5. Violet struggles with forgiving Rose and David. On a visit to their mother's house, Violet's mom speaks with her about forgiveness. What was the turning point in Violet's life that allowed her to forgive not only Rose, but also David? How hard is it to forgive others?

6. Rose goes through a transformation when she gets to Louisiana. Can people change after years of being "one way?"

7. The sisters lost years where they were either "barely getting along" or not talking at all. What does this say about "holding grudges?"

www.sheliagoss.com